Tatiana

by

Dorothy M. Jones

Vanessapress
Fairbanks, Alaska

First edition 2001
ISBN: 0-940055-51-1

Elmer E. Rasmuson Library
Cataloging-in-Publication Data:

Jones, Dorothy Miriam, 1923-
Tatiana / by Dorothy Jones. – 1st ed. – Fairbanks :
Vanessapress, c2001.
p. cm.
ISBN 0-940055-51-1
1. Aleut women–Fiction. 2. Women–Alaska–Aleutian
Islands–Fiction. 3. Aleuts–Fiction.
PS3610.O477 T38 2001
Printed in Canada

Design and layout by Sue Mitchell, Inkworks
Cover art by Sara Tabbert, Marmot Press

"Dorothy Jones brings passion and understanding to the struggles of Native Americans held captive in the ways of the Western world. Tatiana is the poignant story of loss and survival, told with tenderness and compassion. The title character is a modern Native American heroine."

—Margaret Mehring, Ph.D.
Documentary filmmaker and
director emerita, Filmic Writing Program,
University of Southern California

"Dorothy Jones writes what she knows about, real tales of survival. Her compassion and honesty toward her characters [has] touched many hearts."

—Tatyana Mamanova
Publisher, *Women and Earth*

Acknowledgments

In addition to my friends in the Aleutians, I received inspiration, support, and criticism from many people: my late husband, Bob Jones, Margaret Mehring, Stewart Stern, Lillian Rubin, Karen Carlisle, Barbara Svarny Carlson, Sue Henry, Lucille Frey, Mariana Foliart, Jane Gelman, Connie Wolfe, Fay Blake, Mort Newman, Norman Chance, Nancy Chance, Ray Hudson, Mollie Anderson, Sarah Schulman, Carla Helfferich, Maeve Doolittle, Gene Mangiardi, Elle Vandevisse, Mary Lee Nicholson, Barbara Nachman, Ann Chandonnet, Sally Hertz, Doug Veltre, and my children—Chuck Jones, Scott Cole, and Lori Larsen.

INTRODUCTION

This book is fiction, but it's inspired by actual events and my personal experiences as a resident and researcher in the Aleutians. For dramatic effect, I have created some of the dialogue, characters, and actions.

Two chapters in slightly different form have appeared as short stories in *Women and Earth:* "Ephreama" (October, 1997), and "Ephreama 2" (March 1999).

DEDICATION

For the Aleut People.

ONE

When I wake in the morning, first thing, I listen to the sea. If I hear the water quietly licking the sand, I know it's a fine day for washing clothes in the creek or fishing and gathering clams and mussels on the beach. But if I hear waves crashing on the shore, I know a storm is here, or coming. That was the sound that greeted me this morning. Too bad. I wanted to catch some sculpin and pogy for my thirty-eighth name day dinner. Well, I was used to storms. There was plenty of inside work to do. We sisterhood women were weaving new grass mats for the church. That's what I decided to do on this early winter morning in the year 1938.

But I didn't feel like getting up yet. Something was nagging at me. I huddled under the covers and felt a longing for Katya, my aacha. Not everyone is lucky enough to have an aacha. It's a special friendship, like when two people have the same birthmark or birthday.

Katya and I were born on the same day, same time, same place, and nursed from the same breast.

My mind drifted back to our twelfth name day, the last one we celebrated in Umaka where we were born. Everyone in the village was there. Of course, there weren't so many people in Umaka, only fifty-two. There weren't many visitors from other places, either. Umaka is located at the end of the Aleutian Islands, hard to get to from other villages, including Akusha, where I live now. It didn't matter. We had everything we needed right there. We dug our houses into the side of a hill, partly underground, like our ancestors. We warmed those barabaras with stone lamps that burned seal oil. We made everything we needed. There was no store except shelves in the second chief's kitchen, loaded twice a year when supply ships arrived.

All the guests brought food to the party, all except Matrona, my godmother. She surprised Katya and me with a gift of spirit dolls, one for each of us. I still dream about my doll. It was woven from rye grass and had black stones for eyes. Matrona told me to hold that doll whenever I did something that might upset my ancestors. Angry ancestors can cast an evil spell, but she said my doll was stuffed with good spirits. Katya's and my spirit dolls were twins, like Katya and me. We weren't really twins, but it had felt like we were since the moment we were born.

Many times Mama told me the story of our birth. It was a wild stormy night. The wind was so strong it threw kelp and debris from the beach and knocked people over. There was one midwife in our town, and sometimes Matrona, my godmother, helped deliver babies. Both she and the midwife were tending Mama when I showed up. It wasn't so lucky that Katya decided to make her appearance at the same time.

Katya's mama, Efgenia, was home alone when her cramps bent her over. She set out for our barabara, knowing Matrona and the midwife were there. Her arms and legs were so cut and bruised when she arrived, Mama figured she must have had to crawl over stones and brush all the way. She had to climb down the entrance ladder to get inside our house, but she missed the last few steps and fell to the floor. At that very moment my head showed between Mama's legs, it is said. And when Matrona went to Efgenia and lifted her skirt, she saw the top of Katya's head.

A great uproar followed, the midwife giving directions to Matrona, Matrona and the midwife issuing instructions to Ekaterina, our neighbor. "Get clean rags and hot water. Bring boxes to put the babies in."

The house started to fill fast. People held Katya and me and pranced around and chanted. But the celebration ended suddenly when Matrona let out a wail. She was at Efgenia's side, feeling her pulse, putting her hand over her mouth to see if there was breath. There was nothing. Efgenia never saw her baby.

The sudden bang of the door in the other room jerked me away from my reveries. The family was stirring. It was time to get moving.

Our house is modern, above ground, not snug like a barabara. Wind rattles the one window in the kitchen and blows in under the door and through cracks in the walls. The house has two rooms, the bedroom where Peter and I sleep, and the kitchen where everyone else sleeps and all the goings-on happen. The house is larger than a barabara, but our bedroom is cramped. There's only a foot of space between the bed and the footlockers on one wall, Peter's stacks of books on another, and fishing gear and nets in the corners. But I'm thankful for a room with a door and a bed off the floor—the others sleep on pallets in the kitchen.

I slipped into my gingham dress—handmade, gathered an armload of weaving grass from under the bed, and went into the kitchen. Paulie, ten years old, his hair standing up in three stiff tufts, sat naked on the pee pot right outside the bedroom door.

Alicia, thirteen, in underpants, a sweater, and boots, ran in from the outhouse. She was slender like her papa but faster of movement. She seemed always to be in a hurry. As she passed Paulie, she reached over and tried to flatten his hair. He pulled away and started making faces at her, opening his eyes wide and pulling the corners of his lips down to his chin. Alicia tried to hide a smile, but it spread across her face anyhow. Her smile reminded me of a crescent moon slowing rising above the mountaintops. I think Paulie liked her grin, too— he went to such lengths to make her laugh. Nicky, my brother, behind me eight years, wearing long johns and jeans, was loading coal into the stove. He had made the stove from an old oil drum. Nicky makes many things. His hands talk more than his mouth.

Nadia, sixteen, in a gingham dress made from the same bolt of material as mine, carried two buckets of rainwater in from the porch. Nadia came to live with us when she was four, after her parents died in the smallpox epidemic in Azian Bay, a village on a nearby island. Funny, all these years and I don't know much about Nadia. She's private, like Nicky. And like Nicky's hands, her wide eyes speak for her. They seem to see behind words.

"Wash up," I said to Paulie as I ladled water into the basin on top of the counter. Paulie had made that scoop from a cockle shell. While he bathed I filled a chai kettle and put it on the stove to heat. Then I started kneading flour, yeast, sugar, gull eggs, and seal oil for alaadix. Fry bread is everyone's favorite in our house. I always make it on name days. That is, if I have flour. After Alicia dressed she plopped down in a chair in front of me, waiting for me to braid her hair. I twisted those soft, long, shining strands, black as a raven. By the time I finished, the bread was ballooning. I punched it down, shaped it into small balls, and dropped the balls into boiling oil in the skillet. All of us stood around watching the alaadix brown and sizzle in the pan.

We didn't talk while we ate; that was our custom. But I wanted someone to mention my name day. Forget about it, I told myself as I watched the children carry their dishes to the counter and get ready to leave for school. "Wear your raincoat," I instructed Paulie before he left. It makes me sad, maybe mad, that children have to wear store raincoats. I used to make kamleikas from sea lion intestines and mukluks from its skin. But the men don't hunt qawax very often since they gave up their skin boats for putt putts. I was picturing those slender skin boats sailing out to sea. I loved watching the men as they climbed into the hatch, lashed the skirts of their hooded kamleikas to their edges, and gently stroked the water with their double-bladed paddles in the rhythm of a slow dance. I started to feel sad, thinking soon people will forget our Aleut baidarkas. I tried to cheer myself by imagining Paulie hunting in the old way when he finished school.

Nicky was pulling his rain clothes on too. He was going to the dock to unload supplies from the ship that had come in the night before. Nadia was packing some smoked fish to take to the Old Man and Little Hunch. They're two of the oldest people in town, both too crippled with arthritis to gather their own food. So they eat at our table or we bring food to their houses, the two little weather-grayed buildings down by Ptarmigan Creek.

After everyone left, I picked up some strands of grass and started to weave. Weaving is my passion. But this day my attention wandered. I got up and went over to the shelf holding a fish Nicky had carved from walrus ivory. I fondled it, put it back, and thought of weaving again. I went to the bedroom to get some grass I'd dyed red. I'd forgotten where I put it. I looked in a footlocker holding odds and ends. Ai-yee, Katya's amber beads were lying on top—the beads I gave her for her wedding gift, the beads she was wearing when I found her. If only Katya was here to wear them on our name day. Katya and I have been aachas from the beginning. As we grew, we did everything together. We were so close it was like we entered each other. I was never sure if an idea started with her or me. Or if something happened to her or me. I needed Katya like a flower needed the sun. Why had she turned away from our life?

A shocking thought came to me—if Katya could reject our way of life, so might others. My own children? No, I would stop them. But I didn't stop Katya. I had to keep the peace. I couldn't fight with my aacha.

Two

The temperature suddenly dropped. Rain turned into sleet, then snow, and a howling gale blew. The storm lasted for three long days and nights. On the fourth, today, the sun parted the clouds and cast a pink glow on the mountains surrounding our island. A good day for fishing. I dressed and went to lift my canvas fishing jacket from a hook near the door, but it wasn't there. Alicia must have worn it to school. I put on a heavy sweater with pockets big enough for line and a knife, picked up a basket and headed for Nellie's house. She's my fishing partner. People call her Fat Nellie because she's round like a ball. She doesn't bounce, though. I joke. I love Nellie.

It is said that Nellie makes the best bird feather parkas in all the Aleutian Islands. She has a passion like I do for my weaving. She was sitting at the table sorting puffin and cormorant skins when I walked in. They were piled everywhere—on the table, counter, chairs, even the floor. I sat down across from her, and without looking up, she smiled a greeting. "My mouth waters for flounder," I said.

Wordlessly, she got up, anchored her dark hair with a turquoise-colored comb, put on a lightweight parka, stuffed bacon rind for bait in the pocket, and set out with me for the dock.

On the way, we met Sylvia South, Nellie's promyshlennik friend. Sylvia and her husband, Ralph, moved to Akusha two months before. He's the new manager of the Northern Seas Company store. Nellie had told me Sylvia was different from other promyshlennik. She visits Nellie just to drink chai and talk, not like other whites who come by with a particular mission—the teachers to deliver messages, the doctor from the Coast Guard vessel to give shots, and bosses to find out why someone didn't show up for work.

Sylvia had a long-legged stride; in moments she was breathing in our faces. She was tall, nearly as high as the door to my house, and lean, the bones showing through her skin like someone who's sick.

"Ah, Nellie, a beautiful day—finally. Will I ever get used to this miserable climate?" Her voice hurt my ears. Maybe she was deaf. She turned feverish eyes to me. "I'm Sylvia South. And you?"

I knew she wasn't deaf because she heard my soft-spoken answer. "Tatiana Pushkin from Umaka."

"Aha, I've heard about you—best basket weaver in town, people say. I'd love to see your work." Before I could say something, Sylvia asked where we were going.

"We're hungry for flounder," Nellie answered.

"Oh, nuts. I was on my way to visit you, Nellie. I'll come again tomorrow." Then Sylvia turned away from the beach toward the main path in town.

"Lordy, Tatty, why did you say you're from Umaka? You haven't lived there since you were twelve years old."

"When I see whites everywhere I look, I think of myself living in Umaka."

Nellie opened her mouth to say something, but she stopped. We were at the dock and we didn't talk when we fished.

I paused to breathe the warm air and gaze at the calm sea. The only sound was water breaking against dock pilings and gulls flapping their wings and screeching as they fought over perches on top of the pilings.

Plenty of flounder were tugging at our lines. We filled our buckets in a short time. We were thinking of going down to the beach to gut them when my line caught on something so heavy it nearly flew out of my hand. Nellie and I probably had the same thought—halibut. It was a big one. I played that line until my arms and shoulders ached. Nellie watched, so intent I wondered if she thought the power of her eyes would keep that fish on the line. Thoughts of a halibut feast kept me going. I pictured the table crowded with guests. And after eating, sitting around the stove listening to the Old Man's tales about his sea adventures. I brought the halibut in. It weighed maybe forty pounds. We carried it and the bucket of flounder to the water for cleaning.

Paulie and Nellie's son, Gavril, were standing near the shore watching my brother, Alexi, mend a broken rib of his baidarka. Alexi, three years older than me, is one of the last men in the village still hunting in a skin boat. Most of the others use skiffs and dingies and a few have dories. "Ah, Nell, I still see us helping Alexi build his first baidarka."

Twenty years had passed and the memory was still sharp as a spearhead. We kids had combed the beaches for driftwood for the boat frame. No trees grow in our country, so we collect what wood the tides wash in. Leonty Sherebin, second chief, was in charge of construction. He coached the younger men. Leonty was blind, but the best carpenter in all the Aleutians. His wife, Parascovia, was a star, too—the best skin sewer in town. She guided the making of the sea lion skin cover for the boat. I was part of the crew that helped her cut, stretch, and sew that qawax skin onto the boat.

A moon, round as a ball, lit the beach the night the boat was finished. Maybe half the people in town joined the celebration. Leonty, his silver hair shining gold in the moonlight, wore a shoulder-length mask with a walrus carved on its face and sang and thumped on his sealskin drum. His beat was slow at first. Then it got faster and more stirring. He chanted and shouted at the top of his lungs, kicking his bowed legs out and leaping in the air over and over until he fell to the ground exhausted. After that Parascovia danced and shook rattles she'd made from the beaks of birds. The rest of us chanted, slower, quieter, like a child's bedtime song. The party ended with Innokenty, first chief, telling stories about his ancestors. We sat in a close circle around him to make sure we didn't miss his soft-spoken words.

The memory set off a deep longing. I tapped Nell's shoulder. "I have a vision, Nell. I see Gavril and Paulie building a baidarka when they're older."

"Why wait for them? Anton could build one right now if he'd just forget about that school."

Anton, sixteen, my oldest child, was the first in our town to go to higher school, the Indian school in Oregon. "Sometimes I want him home, too, hunting with the other men."

Nellie waited for me to go on. She knew I wasn't finished. She knew I felt like a forked twig about his schooling. "Anton's a scholar like his papa. He could be the first Aleut priest in our country. Oh, how that would swell Peter's heart. Mine, too."

Nellie opened her mouth, then quickly closed it. She didn't want to say something that might pain me. A moment later, the low whistle of a ship's horn caught our attention.

We ran to my house to drop off the fish and then hurried back to the pier. I kept my eye fixed on the bay, watching water spit and churn. Soon, the dark gray hull of a boat came into view, its red and green running lights flashing in the distance.

"Maye it's the mail boat," Nellie said in a lively voice. The government ship, *Aurora,* brings mail every month. Nellie watches for that ship like an eagle searches for prey. Letters are her only contact with her daughter, Mavra, who married and moved to New Harbor, a village on a nearby island. I wait for that mail boat, too, because of Anton. But this day, I wished for the fishing boat that carried Peter. He'd been gone a month, traveling with Father Burdofsky to the villages. Once we had priests on nearly every island. But after the Revolution over there, they all returned to Russia, all but Father Burdofsky from New Harbor. Peter's a deacon. It's part of his job to help father baptize, marry, and bury in all the villages.

The ship dropped anchor. Three men stood at the rail waving. I knew two of them were hunters from their chests grown hefty from many years paddling boats at sea. The third man was slender as a blade of grass. That was Peter. He was born with a short leg, so he didn't train for the sea like the others. He stayed home reading and studying. Now he's fluent in Aleut, English, and Russian, and a master at translating, too. He's put our Russian church services, hymns, and psalms into Aleut. I know those three languages, too. But I'm not so good at translation.

Peter and I didn't speak in words his first afternoon home. After we ate he picked up his fiddle and played songs of his own making. A Russian trader from Vladivostok gave that violin to Peter's papa maybe sixty years back. He said it was built by the same master who made instruments for the tsar. When Peter started playing church hymns, Alicia and I joined in on the accordion and guitar. We three created music until it was time for vespers.

The church is our jewel. It has a main building, two side chapels, and above, two gold-trimmed cupolas, one on top of the bell tower. Even though I've seen the inside of that church hundreds of times, it still takes my breath away—the brightly colored stained glass windows, tall candelabra with flickering tapers, and icons in dark frames cracked with age.

Vespers was crowded. Everyone knew Peter was back. I'd been choir leader for the past five years, ever since Peter was made deacon. Before that, he led the choir. Now his first night home I felt a familiar rush of warmth as I led the singing in harmony with Peter's rhythmic chants. A few times I was so caught up in our duets I forgot other people were around. Once, I started singing the service in a round. The corners of Peter's full lips twitched as he tried to hold back a grin.

After vespers Peter and I ran by the sea. That was our habit his first night home. Our town lies on a one-mile stretch of black sandy beach between Akusha Bay to the east and a rim of tall, rugged mountains to the west. The shoreline, curved like a big smile, is lined with houses. Other buildings lie scattered to the foothills, maybe a quarter of a mile. We started at the south end of the beach where the dock, warehouses, supply station, store, and promyshlennik houses are located and ran to the north end marked by the Baptist mission and two-room school house. Winded, we sat down on a log where Icy Creek flows into the sea. I felt playful, so I began chanting psalms like I was deacon. Peter answered in the voice of the choir. We continued that game all the way home.

Peter was tired. He hadn't slept the night before. You'd think he'd be used to the sea, but the rolling and pitching still knotted his stomach. Lying together in bed, the soft, fine hair on his head warming my breast, he started to tell me about his trip, but he stopped after a few words, and I heard the soft, regular whisper of his breathing. I lay awake listening, trying to etch that sound in memory for the day he'd no longer lie beside me. A goofy thought. Peter always returns. I scolded myself and tried to fix my mind on other things. But some will stronger than mine soaked my soul in that fear. I couldn't still the voice that told me that Peter was in danger. I've heard it since the day Peter and I went against our marriage custom.

The memory sprang to the front of my mind. I had just celebrated my seventeenth name day. I hadn't thought about marriage until the elders' council suggested me as wife to Makary, an orphan who lived at the Baptist mission with my aacha, Katya. Nellie filled me in on the details. Her father was on the council and she listened in to meetings held at her house. Makary wanted a wife and Leonty, second chief, suggested me. He pointed out that I was a top basket weaver and seamstress and knew how to make boots and kamleikas from qawax skin. Everyone spoke agreement but Innokenty, first chief. He was silent. So the others looked at him. "I almost object." That was all he said.

After the meeting, Leonty came to me and asked if I wanted to marry Makary. I didn't answer. I didn't know what I wanted to do. I knew only that I had to get away by myself. I walked by Ptarmigan Creek in back of the village listening to the mellow chirping of rosy finches. I watched them dart among the willows looking for food, the same way they scurry after grass and sticks in the spring when they're building nests. Suddenly, swift as the flight of the finches, an answer came to me. I knew I didn't want to build a nest with Makary. He was like my brother. Well, he was like Katya's brother, so he felt like mine, too.

I walked to the end of the creek where it meets the sea. I remember watching three sea otters splashing in the shallow water, then diving. I searched the bay to see where they'd surface. I started to feel quiet inside. I was too young for marriage, I told myself. Then, in the distance, I saw Peter limping toward me, lifting his right shoulder with every drag of his short left leg. When he reached my side, his voice cracked as he spoke. "I heard the news."

"I don't want to marry Makary," I told him. "It feels wrong to think of him as husband."

"Do you want to marry someone else?"

"I haven't thought. It's not time for marriage."

"It's not time for me, either. I'm supposed to go to the seminary next month."

I nodded, knowing that everyone wanted Peter to train as priest. We'd been without a priest for twenty years, since Father Paul left. I had never questioned Peter's seminary plan before. But suddenly the thought lay like a stone in my belly.

A few minutes passed. Then Peter asked me, "Do you want me to forget the seminary?"

I felt like laughing, but I sealed my lips.

Peter kept talking. "Little Wren, sometimes I lie awake in bed dreaming that my grandfather and Father Paul and the elders suggest you for my wife. I smile and see your heart-shaped face and talking eyes and hear the sound of your laugh, like water gurgling over rocks in the creek. But other nights I wake up sweating from a nightmare that they chose a strange woman from another island. Is it wrong to want to pick my wife?"

"The elders know the laws of our ancestors. They know who fits together best."

"Do you want the elders to pick your husband?"

"The elders are the suggestors. I don't want to fight them. But I wish they'd suggest you at my side." I reached up and brushed a lock of hair back from Peter's right eye. It always fell there.

Peter did a little hopping dance. "Hey-dee-dee, hey-dee-dee." And then he said, "We'll ask Innokenty together. We'll tell him we've decided." Innokenty was also Peter's grandfather. He'd raised Peter since he was six after Peter's parents and sister died in the measles epidemic.

"Innokenty is counting on you going to the seminary," I reminded him.

"I'll tell him our son will go. I'll tell him our son will be the first Aleut priest in our country."

Walking back to the village, I remember feeling like singing out, like shrieking to the sun and sea and sky, "Peter and I are going to be together." And then, hearing the long, mournful call of the sparrow with the golden head, I shuddered. Was our marriage wrong? Was it wrong to marry for love? Our ancestors didn't. The word "love" wasn't in our language. I learned about it from American moving pictures and magazines and schoolbooks. Would Mama have thought it wrong?

Innokenty called another council meeting as soon as Peter relayed our decision. Nellie described this one, too. She said the members' eyes grew wide when Innokenty broke the news. There was a long silence and a roomful of grim faces. Then Innokenty told a story that still brings a smile to my lips.

"This is a story told by my grandfather. Hundreds of ravens spent their days scrounging for food on the beach of our village. Then, when the light faded, the birds flew to the mountains, to a protected place under a ledge where they slept. One night a huge snowy owl swooped down under the ledge and snatched a sleeping raven in its claws. Last they saw of that bird. Next night they set up a guard of two ravens. In the dark when the owl showed up, the raven guards chased it away. But while they chased one owl, another stole a sleeping raven and flew off with it. Next night they set up three guards, but three owls showed up and one of them snatched another sleeping raven. Fourth day, at dusk, as they were flying to their mountain retreat, a young raven flew off in the wrong direction. The flock circled around that raven trying to direct it back on course. But somehow that rebellious young raven escaped the circle and flew off again. This time a second young raven joined the first. And the two flew in a different direction from the rest. Just as the flock was about to surround the young rebels, a very old raven instructed the birds to follow those two young ones. And the young ravens led the entire flock to a distant mountain, higher than the one they'd always rested on. No owls came that night or the next or the next. So the ravens had a better place to sleep, so it is told."

I felt calm after Nellie related Innokenty's story, but shattered when she then repeated one Leonty told right after that.

"A long time ago, this young man and woman decided by themselves to marry. They didn't talk it over with parents, godparents, chiefs, elders, shaman, no one. Then they had a child. It died two days later. They had a second child. It had many deformities. It died, too. They had a third child. When it died, the young man and woman asked the shaman why. 'You went against our inheritance and angered our ancestors,' the shaman answered, it is said."

I remember feeling sick to my stomach after hearing that story, thinking our marriage would bring a curse on the village. I felt sure it did several months later when the flu came. Our town had a population then of two hundred—not counting the twenty whites. The flu killed forty-three of our people. Including Mama.

These memories were making knots in my stomach. I pushed them aside and curled up against Peter's back, so close I could feel his warmth in my veins. And there, I slept the night.

THREE

I woke with a start next morning. Peter was groaning. Loud. I reached over and touched his cheek.

"I must have eaten poison. I've got fierce pains in my belly." His voice was hoarse. I never knew Peter sick a day in his life. I trembled. Leonty's warning story sounded in my ears.

"I'll get Anesia and Marie," I said as I hurried into my clothes. Anesia was the last of the old-time healers. She'd been training Marie to replace her for the past sixteen years, ever since Marie moved in with her. I wanted to fly to their house, but I trudged along at the pace of a snail. The path was so slick with ice, I had to walk in the snow beside it. With every step my leg sank halfway to my knee. I yanked it out only to sink the other one. It seemed like I'd never get there. But finally I was in her house. A silent house. Anesia was still asleep.

"Anesia, Peter's very sick." I nearly screamed the words.

Anesia was used to waking up fast. She was getting on, but she leaped out of her bed as quick as

Paulie does. Marie rushed in from the bedroom. They dressed in a hurry. Anesia picked up a bag of herbs and we set out for my house.

Peter was howling with pain, his hands pressed hard against his stomach. Anesia knelt beside his bed. "Where's the pain? Touch the sore spot again. Let me feel it. Tatiana, bring some oil."

I ladled seal oil from a container on the kitchen counter into a cup, carried it to Anesia and watched her gently rub Peter's stomach with it.

"Any better?" she asked him.

Peter moaned. Anesia leaned over and pulled some markasha roots and wild parsley from her sack. She didn't have to tell me what to do with them. I went to the stove and boiled water for herb chai. Peter was still moaning when I returned. I cradled his head in my arm and lifted the cup to his lips.

He couldn't swallow. "It's like a sharp knife stabbing my side," he whispered.

"Get dressed, Peter. We're going to the steam house. I'll burn herbs for a bath," Anesia said.

Slowly, using his elbows, Peter hoisted himself into a sitting position. Then, inch by inch, he shifted his body to the edge of the bed. He grimaced with every motion. And suddenly, clutching his stomach, he fell back on the mattress. Anesia looked bewildered. Maybe she didn't know what else to do. But seconds later, she issued another instruction. "Marie, get some spit from the Old Man." Feeding the saliva of the oldest person in town is a last resort hand-me-down cure. Our Aleut methods used to heal. Nowadays they don't work so well. My knees went weak. I feared they'd buckle. I thought of Miss Parker, Alicia's teacher. She was like a nurse, not trained, but she was in charge of the medicines, so she got plenty of experience.

"I'm going for Miss Parker," I said as I wrapped a shawl around my shoulders.

Someone had thrown sand and pebbles over the main path and I was able to run all the way to the school. People saw me whiz by like a motor boat. They gathered in a cluster and I knew they were speculating. I rushed into the schoolroom. I didn't know how Mrs. Parker would react. This was her first year in Akusha and I'd seen her only two times at the store. She had a large square face with bushy brows and two protruding front teeth that hung over her bottom lip. Her ample body looked like it was stuffed into a tightly laced corset. I noticed she didn't smile or talk to anyone at the store. Would she interrupt her class to help Peter? Would she know what to do? Would she send me away without any response?

I was gasping for breath. "My husband is sick. He has terrible pains in his stomach. Please come."

"I'll be there at the lunch break," Miss Parker answered in a cool voice.

I planted my feet firm on the floor. "His pains are so bad he can't get out of bed."

Miss Parker gripped the edge of her desk while she considered what to do. Her eyes looked soft with concern. But her lips were pressed tight together. "The lunch break is only thirty minutes away."

There was nothing to do but go home. The house was quiet except for the slurping sound of Peter sucking in the Old Man's spit from a spoon Anesia held to his mouth. Marie pressed a hot towel against his stomach.

News travels as fast as the wind in Akusha, and people started to drop in—Nellie, her sister, Anna; Parascovia and Leonty and their daughter, Evdokie, my age. A while later Innokenty came in. Usually he walks with his spine straight. But this day he shuffled into the house, his head bent. His face, lined like weathered wood, had a green hue. And his eyes, usually gentle and grave, held fear. I took his arm and led him to the rocking chair. Then I brewed more chai and sliced fresh bread Nellie had brought. The time dragged until I heard the noon church bell. Soon Miss Parker showed up. I led her to the bedroom. After Anesia described Peter's symptoms, Miss Parker lifted a rubber bag from her satchel. "Fill the enema bag with warm soapy water and bring a bucket for Peter to do his business in," she told me.

I followed her instructions. Then she sent us all from the room. I heard Peter cry out again and again.

A while later—it seemed like a month—Miss Parker called me back into the bedroom.

"Come clean the bucket, Tatiana?"

When I returned from that chore, I saw her give Peter a sodium bromide to ease his pain.

Miss Parker looked scared, too, like she knew nothing else to do. She made a sudden decision. "I'm going to the school to radio the doctor on the Coast Guard cutter. If I'm not back in an hour, Tatiana, give Peter another bromide."

My legs were trembling again. I sat down on the floor right next to Peter's bed. Nellie brought me a chair. The others sat around the table in the kitchen just a few feet away from the bedroom. No one said anything. There was nothing to say. Just wait.

The quiet was broken when the door flew open and Sylvia South rushed in. "I heard about Peter. Can I do anything?"

Nellie shook her head and motioned Sylvia to sit down at the table with the others.

The bromide began to wear off. Peter was groaning again. I held his hand. He doubled his body in two. His tears splashed onto the cover. I gave him another bromide and told him Miss Parker was talking to the Coast Guard doctor.

The door opened again. Miss Parker was back, panting so loud I figured she ran all the way. She spit out her words, like the sound of an outboard motor starting up. "Dr. Gold said your appendix busted,

Peter." She gulped some air and went on. "The Coast Guard is bringing him here right away." She took another breath. "The ship is about two hours out. Dr. Gold said to get ready for immediate surgery."

"Surgery!" My throat closed up.

"Yes, and no time to lose. He said we'd need boiled sheets and rags, all the bandage material we can find, and plenty of Coleman lanterns." We had only two fifteen-watt lightbulbs in our house, and they didn't give much light.

While Miss Parker was still talking, everyone went into action. That didn't surprise me. What did was seeing Sylvia South rush out with the others and return soon with an armload of sheets.

Peter relaxed after Miss Parker gave him some morphine. In fact, he lay limp as a landed fish. His eyes were glazed and dull and his skin looked whiter than Sylvia's. I talked in a soft voice, trying to soothe him while I kept my ears tuned for the sound of a boat horn.

Finally, I heard it. Nellie did, too. She jumped up and rushed out. Minutes later, she returned. "It's the *Aurora*," she announced in a mournful voice. There was no celebrating the mail boat this day when time was squeezing us like a vise.

Peter started to groan again. I don't know how long I sat by his side before I heard another ship's horn. The Old Man hobbled in. "The doctor's here," he said. In moments, Dr. Gold and his first mate came in. The first mate had a bulky build and a ruddy complexion, but Dr. Gold's skin was the color of a gull and he was as thin as a pipe cleaner. He looked like he was the one in need of care.

He shooed everyone from Peter's room except his first mate, Anesia, and me. Then he opened his bag and took out two long, sharp knives. I felt faint and started to leave. "Stay. I may need you." Dr. Gold said.

I nodded, but I was afraid I'd pass out. I called on Mama's spirit. Then I straightened my shoulders and slipped on the rubber gloves and face mask Dr. Gold handed me. He held an evil-smelling towel over Peter's mouth until Peter started to breathe deeply. He painted Peter's belly with some red liquid and then cut into him like he was butchering a seal.

I bit hard into my lip, feeling the pain of that knife in myself.

Dr. Gold kept barking instructions to the first mate. "Sharp knife, forceps, small scissors." His voice rose a pitch. "Cotton cloth, there's a lot of blood."

My ankles turned to mush. I fell down to my knees. I reached for Mama's spirit again. I couldn't find it.

Evdokie came into the room. As president of the church sisterhood, she was used to taking charge of things. "I'll take your place." I gave her my rubber gloves and mask and went into the other room.

Innokenty was shaking so hard his teeth clacked. Nellie's sister, Anna, was sitting quietly by his side. Nellie was passing bread and dried fish around. Sylvia was trying to read to the children, but they were too upset to hear. She must have noticed, for she stopped reading and suggested they play a game. Paulie brought over two bone rings with sticks attached. He and Alicia showed her how to play qamtidax. Paulie threw the ring and stick in the air in a way to make the ring fall on the stick. He missed. Then it was Alicia's turn. She caught the ring on her stick. But she showed no interest in taking her prize—tweaking his ear. The children weren't able to fix their interest on games or anything else for that matter.

Neither could I. So many demons were chasing around in my brain I decided to lie down on Alicia's sleeping mat in the corner of the kitchen. Maybe then I could clear my head. I felt the hot angry breath of my ancestors on my neck. It was an omen. Peter was going to die. He wouldn't live to see Anton ordained as priest of our church. He was cursed, the curse our marriage brought, the curse that killed Mama.

After twenty years you'd think the memory of that flu epidemic would have vanished, but it was as real as yesterday's walk on the beach. Near the end of the epidemic, Akusha had become a ghost town. The school and store were closed. No one even went to church. I remember how forlorn I felt one day walking down an empty, silent path. A strong north wind blew debris across yards and pathways. A high tide flooded the beach, right up to Evdokie's back-yard fence. No gulls called. No ravens swooped by in the wind. The sky was as empty as the streets.

Then Mama's sister, Sophie, came out and walked in the direction of Leonty's house. Moments later, Marie and Anesia joined her. Others followed after them. They heard the sounds of Leonty's hammer and saw, and knew another coffin was in the making. Our villagers formed a silent vigil, gathering together in a mute and gloomy shuffle to learn the name of the latest victim.

Mama was the last. I still shudder to think of her suffering. Fever, chills, headache, pain stabbing her eyeballs, and muscle aches all over her body. At the end, she couldn't breathe and blood dripped from the corner of her lips. Aunt Sophie, Alexi, Nicky, and I were by her side when she died. It was so sudden. Her mouth fell open and her jaw locked. Nicky cried out, "Mama, Mama, Mama."

I had put my arms around him, and sucking in my breath so I wouldn't sob, I had said, "She's gone. It's over, it's over."

I hadn't realized I spoke those words out loud. "Yes, it's over," Dr. Gold said, standing beside my chair. His shoulders sagged and his hand trembled.

"Peter? Is he—"

"He would have been dead in another hour if we hadn't operated."

It took a few minutes for his words to sink in. "Is he all right?"

"Looks good. His breathing is regular and his pulse is nearly normal. I'll check on him every few hours until the ship leaves tomorrow. I think he'll be fine."

Nellie laughed with relief. The color came back to Innokenty's face. Alicia and Paulie started to bicker over some bone rings. The crisis was over. I should feel joy. I did. But there was a heaviness in my chest, something nagging at me. What was it? I wanted Anesia, not outsiders, to heal Peter. She was a star healer before promyshlennik brought their diseases to our country. Yet, I told myself, whites didn't bring busted appendix to our islands. We had them before. Maybe our healers had no cure. Thank the Lord, Dr. Gold knew what to do. Still, I had two hearts about Peter's saviors.

FOUR

Peter was recovering. At first, he ate like a sparrow and slept like he was hibernating, but today, a month later, he gobbled half a platter of alaadix before going to church to teach Russian class.

It was Saturday, the morning of my weaving class. I have five students—Nadia, Alicia, Nellie's daughter, Agnes, her niece, Lupia, and Evdokie's oldest child, Akinia. In the warm months, we hiked to the hills and I showed them where to find rye grass, the best grass for weaving. Then I taught them how to collect, dry, sort, and cure the grass. Now, in the cold months, we sat around the table, pulled close to the stove, and they watched me braid the strands into mats, baskets, and other containers.

"What are you making?" Agnes asked as I started to weave. "A basket," I replied. It was for Sylvia South—my way of thanking her for helping Peter.

The girls fastened their eyes on me as I wet my fingers and rubbed water along the blades of grass to make them flexible. Then, using my long, pointed thumbnail, grown long on purpose, I parted the grass, the inner strands for warp and the tough, outer ones for weft. After that I wove the warp strands together for the bottom of the basket.

Good thing it was time to end the class because Nellie blew in waving a letter. I had heard the *Aurora* come in earlier. Nellie and I picked up each other's mail, whoever got to the school first. Teachers run the post office, too.

"Anything from Mavra?" Agnes asked.

Nellie shook her head and handed me the letter—it was from Anton. She then went over to the stove and filled a pot with water for chai. The girls took this as a signal for dismissal. They had planned to take a steam bath after class, anyhow, and out they dashed.

Nellie served chai and sat down across from me waiting to hear Anton's news. His letters were like diaries. Knowing the mail boat comes only once a month, he wrote them over many days.

I held the letter in my hand without opening it. I wasn't sure what I wanted to read. If he wrote that he loved the school and did well, Peter would smile. But if he said he hated it and wanted to come home, I might smile. I was split apart in my feelings about Peter's schooling. I opened the envelope and read the letter to Nellie.

"November 27. Sunday afternoon. I have a story to tell. Remember the adventure books I read in fourth grade about Columbus and La Salle exploring strange seas and lands? I used to dream about being an explorer, too. Well, I had my chance last Saturday. I don't think I'm made for that occupation. For the first time, Mr. Steele gave us passes to go into Salem, me and four other students. We were excited and didn't know where to go first. It was so big, a hundred Akushas could fit into that one city. Would you believe it has eight moving picture theaters and restaurants serving food from different countries? I pictured eating in all those restaurants. It would be like traveling the world. There were separate stores for everything—shoes, hats, toys, tools, even eggs."

Nellie's mouth fell open. "A separate store for eggs!"

I couldn't picture it either. I got up and heated more water.

"Go on," Nellie said.

I refilled our cups and then continued reading.

"But all of that was nothing compared to the music store. I thought I was in heaven—every instrument I knew of and some I didn't. And sheet music and records and Victrolas and radios. And they let you play records in little booths for free. The other guys weren't interested in the music store. They went off. But I couldn't leave there. I forgot about being an explorer. I forgot about my friends. I forgot about everything except that magic store. I listened to a recording of Mama Carter singing gospels, and

Hungarian dances, and a beautiful violin piece played by someone named Milstein. There's more to tell, but I'm tired now.

"November 28. Monday evening. I lost track of time in that music store until an explosion nearly blew me off the ground. It was the loudest roar I've ever heard. We don't have that sound in the Aleutians. It's thunder—clouds crashing into each other. I guess our Aleutian clouds are more polite. Ha ha.

"The thunder was followed by a blizzard, great sheets of rain soaking everything. I decided to find my friends from the school. I ran from shop to shop and restaurant to restaurant. I even got permission to search the movie houses. They were nowhere. It was getting dark and everything began to close up. I thought I knew where the bus to our school stopped, but I couldn't find the place. I asked people on the street, 'Where's the bus to Indian school?' They didn't answer me. They were rushing to get out of the rain. I ducked into a restaurant and asked people there, but no one knew. I bought a cup of coffee and a sweet roll, and before I finished, the manager started turning off the lights. I looked for other stores that were open, but everything was dark except the street lights. I was one scared explorer. The rain soaked my clothes, my hair, my skin. Chrissakes, I thought I'd freeze to death. I ran to the back of a store where there was an eave that sheltered the doorway. I rolled myself into a ball and huddled in that doorway, but still the wet and cold soaked into me. I had to get up every few minutes and jump around to warm myself. I did that most of the night. Then I was too cold to get up anymore. I just lay there, numb in my body and brain, too numb to even care if I died."

I took deep breaths before reading on.

"I think I would have died if a law man hadn't found me at first light. 'What's your name?' he asked me. I couldn't think of it. I couldn't think of my own damn name. When I didn't answer, the law man asked, 'You a student at the Indian school?' I said, 'yes.' And he drove me back to the school.

"My room mate, Tiasook, an Eskimo from up north, just came in with three other students and a deck of cards. I'm learning plenty of card games in this place. To be continued.

"November 29. Tuesday afternoon. Mr. Steele met me at the door to the dormitory this morning. His face was as red as fire. He turned his voice to top volume. 'It will be a cold day in hell before you'll get another pass.' I can't remember all he said, but he kept screaming. At first I was scared. Then I figured, what the hell. I don't care if he sends me home. As a matter of fact, I hoped he'd say those words. But he didn't. Suddenly, he gave me a hard look and left the dorm.

"The rest of that day and that night, too, I kept thinking about coming home. Now comes the bad news. Tiasook told me he heard that the school ran out of money. There wasn't any left to send us home for the summer. I said he must be mistaken because Mr. Steele promised to send us home every summer and possibly every Christmas, too. Tiasook wasn't mistaken. I don't want to stay in this place any longer. I don't think I can stand it. I don't know what I'll do if I can't come home."

My hand was shaking. I put the letter down. I was afraid. I thought about Constantine Churginoff's suicide after three years at the Indian school without a single visit to his home in Azian Bay. The school never told anyone the reason he died. But Azian Bay people knew. His mama explained the death to me once. "He never saw his people, his country for three years. It killed his spirit."

"Anton's spirit is fading, Nell," I said.

She poured more chai. And, we sat together, without words, until the dusky sky turned black.

FIVE

Nellie and I walked along the path beside the beach on the way to Sylvia's house, to deliver the basket I'd made for her. The clouds were low in the sky and a light snow was falling. I paused to watch the magic of weightless flakes dropping gently onto the black sand. I glanced at Nellie. She didn't share my pleasure. Her eyes were hooded as if to cover over something painful. I waited, knowing she'd tell me by and by.

She sighed, a long deep sigh, and then said, "Lordy, lordy." Another sigh. "Sylvia visited yesterday. And now I understand why they moved to our country. They had two children, a boy and girl, twins, same age as Alicia and Agnes—so young, so young. It was the day of their school picnic. Sylvia said the children were so excited, they fussed over their clothes, changing them a couple times, fussed over their sandwiches. Finally, when they were ready, Sylvia drove them to school. She watched them board the bus with twenty-two other students. Lordy! Lordy! Later the phone call came. The bus had gone out of control, spinning around and around in circles until it crashed into a concrete wall. Twelve children, yes, twelve children died."

"Sylvia's, too?" My voice caught in my throat.

She nodded, drew a deep breath and went on. "Sylvia and Ralph lived in Chicago. A big place, thousands of people and cars and buses and cement walls. They had to get out of there, far away, to someplace small, without buses and concrete. Ralph was boss in a grocery store with a funny name—Piggly Wiggly." Nellie laughed. "We should give our store a funny name like that. How about Squishy Fishy?"

Nellie turned her face away and wiped a tear. I loved the way she could laugh and cry at the same time.

"After Ralph learned about the job at our NS store, he and Sylvia studied maps and books about Akusha. Sylvia took anthropology in college. She liked the idea of living in a Native village. So when she and Ralph learned there were no busses or cars here, they decided to come."

I hardly knew Sylvia, but my soul ached for her sorrow. Two children suddenly dead. What would I do? How did Nellie stand it when she lost her son Kiril in a boating accident?

We walked slowly to Sylvia's house. I'd seen it many times, but only from the outside. So after we hung our parkas in Sylvia's closet, I took some time to look around. The walls were covered with a heavy sand-colored paper that had raised brown and rose-colored figures on it. The wood floors were shiny like mirrors—dark brown and smooth as velvet, so different from our rough, wood-planked floors. Patterned rugs—oriental rugs, Sylvia called them—lay in the middle of the floor. I wanted to study those patterns for basket designs, but I couldn't concentrate on them, for Sylvia kept talking. This main room also had a couch and four chairs stuffed like pillows and covered with material like a bedspread. Next to the couch and chairs were small tables. Good tea tables, I thought. But magazines were fanned out on top of them.

"Sit, sit," Sylvia said, pointing to chairs.

I'd never seen chairs spaced so far apart, too far to hear the others sigh or smell their perspiration or see their faces flush.

"I hear Peter's up and around," Sylvia said.

There was concern in her voice but I wished she wouldn't shout. I nodded.

"Is he completely recovered?" she asked.

Suddenly, I smiled. I realized an answer to something. I always wondered why whites spoke in voices so loud it hurt my eardrums. Sometimes I thought it was to frighten our people. It had that effect. Now I knew, they had to shout sitting so far apart.

"Peter's fine; he's even planning a hike to Bolisof."

"I never heard of Bolisof," Sylvia said.

"It's the other village on our island, about eight miles to the north," Nellie explained. "I have relatives there."

"Is Bolisof like Akusha?"

"Not so big. Only eight barabaras in that place. No frame houses, no school, very old-fashioned."

Sylvia leaned forward in her chair. Her voice sounded vibrant. "Oh, Nellie, an ancestral village. Will you take me there?"

It was time to change the subject. I went to the closet, lifted Sylvia's basket from my parka pocket, and put it in her hand.

Sylvia's eyes sparkled. "Peachy keen," she exclaimed. "I've seen Aleut baskets in the Field Museum in Chicago, but I never dreamed I'd own one."

I smiled to see her eyes bright with pleasure. And then, she said, "Now I want a whole collection."

My smile fell. I wanted to leave. But at that moment Ralph walked in, shook the snow from his jacket, and draped it over a hook in the closet. Ralph ran his finger across his fat nose, the color of fireweed, as if he was trying to figure out why we were there. Then Sylvia thrust my basket into his hand. "Tatiana made this for me. Did you ever see such fine work?"

His beady eyes narrowed as he turned it and examined it from every angle. "Say, these would go like wildfire in the store. The ship's crews would love them. They're always looking for souvenirs. Tatiana, you could make a lot of money."

Now, I was sure I wanted to leave. I went to the closet for my parka. Sylvia came after me. "Don't go, Tatiana. Stay for lunch."

Before I had a chance to answer, Nellie accepted the invitation. So, I stayed, too.

Ralph was moving around and talking at the same time. He opened a cupboard and brought out a bottle filled with liquid the color of clotted blood. "I like a glass of burgundy with lunch. Want some?" he asked as he poured wine into a glass that had a stem like a heron's leg.

What is this? I wondered. Is he going to get drunk? Nellie looked uncomfortable, too. We both refused Ralph's offer.

Then Ralph started asking questions, one after the other. "Is your husband a sea hunter?"

"No."

"What does he do, then?"

"This and that."

"What does he do on a regular basis?"

"He's a teacher."

Ralph looked puzzled. "I know the two teachers at the school here. Where does he teach?"

"Around town."

"Oh, not for a living, then."

My skin started to itch. Why didn't Ralph know these things? He'd been living here long enough.

Sylvia looked uneasy, too. I figured she was embarrassed by Ralph's ignorance. She hurried to the table with food and motioned us to sit down in the eating room. Then she set bowls of some thick green stuff in front of us. It looked like muck from the bottom of the marsh. I didn't realize I was staring at it when Sylvia said, "It's split pea soup." I tasted it. I didn't like the feel of it going down my throat. It was like swallowing mud. So I stopped eating it.

"I meant it, about selling your baskets in the store," Ralph said.

"They'd go over big. You'd make some good money."

I didn't answer Ralph. I make baskets for gifts. I don't sell them unless I need money for flour or coal or the church fund.

Sylvia carried a platter of meat to the table. It had a brownish-gray color, like meat gone rotten. When she saw me staring at the food again, she said, "It's tongue, cow's tongue, delicious." I was shocked. I never heard of eating part of an animal's head. After we feast on an animal, we carry the head to the sea to give it a drink of water, our way of giving thanks. And then we drop the head back in the water to attract cod and halibut, our way of promoting good times.

Sylvia was pressing me. "It's good, taste it."

I tried it. I thought I'd choke. So I sat quietly at the table not eating. Nellie stopped eating, too.

In our country it's no matter if someone doesn't feel like eating. So I was surprised to see her look so troubled. "I'm sorry you don't like the food. I wish I had known you were coming; I'd have asked you what you liked."

"Maybe you should have served them raw fish," Ralph said.

Red splotches broke out on Sylvia's neck. "You have no right to say that."

Ralph's nostrils twitched. "This is my house. I'll say what I please."

I wasn't used to a fight with words. I wanted to stop it. "If it wasn't between husband and wife," I said, "I'd say something."

Sylvia laughed. "But Tatiana, you just did say something."

Ralph still looked sullen. But he shut up his mouth.

Nellie and I didn't talk after we left Sylvia's house. Maybe we didn't have words for what just happened. Halfway to my house we passed Little Hunch sitting on her porch.

Nellie and I smiled as we walked toward her. She was the only grown woman in town shorter than me, stooped by the hump in her back. Little Hunch's eyes searched ours. "Chai?" she said in the way of an invitation.

We followed her inside. While the water boiled she brought a plate of raw pogy to the table. Nicky had given it to her earlier that day. Nellie and I still didn't feel like talking, so Little Hunch sat in silence, too. Then, as we got up to leave, she handed both of us a gift, ptarmigan feathers, whiter than new snow on the mountaintops.

Six

Storms come every day now. Today, a mighty gale howled and whistled around our house and drove snow into giant drifts. Nicky and Paulie spent the morning clearing a path to the house. When their fingers became stiff they'd come in, drop their seal-skin boots and fox skin parkas by the door, and warm themselves by the stove. Then out again to shovel. With a cold wind flapping against the house, I'd hoped they'd stay inside after finishing the job, but after another brief warming, they set out to check their trap lines. Those two are a team. Where Nicky goes, Paulie follows. Nicky is like Paulie's papa even when Peter is home. Like Peter, Nicky doesn't train Paulie for the sea. He hates the sea. He teaches him to live off the land, instead.

Late in the afternoon, the door suddenly blew open and Nicky and Paulie blew in, their arms loaded with ptarmigan.

Alicia, Nadia, and I went right to work, clearing the counter and cutting up the birds and some lily bulbs for stew. A feast, I thought. It deserves candles.

I was just lighting them when the door opened again and Little Hunch came in, bearing a gift for Paulie— a box filled with flattened stones for his sling. He uses his sling to hunt small birds.

Soon after, the Old Man arrived, his beloved chess set under his arm. He laid the set on one end of the table, seated himself on the bench in front of it, then took a slab of tobacco from his pocket, cut off a wedge, and stuffed it into the side of his mouth.

"Aang, Mr. Herendin." Little Hunch greeted her nearest neighbor as if she hadn't seen him for a year.

The Old Man arched his brows and shifted his tobacco to the other cheek.

"A feast tonight, Mr. Herendin," Little Hunch said.

"About time. I'm hungry enough to eat a two-by-four."

"There was plenty to eat when you brought in a qawax for my thirty-first name day. The whole town celebrated."

The corners of his lips twitched in a small smile, maybe remembering that time when he was the best sea hunter in the village. But his smile died when he stared down at his knotted, crooked hands. Paulie went over to stand beside him. "Plenty of space over there by the counter," the Old Man crabbed.

Paulie didn't move away; instead he hung upside down on a ladder-back chair, his hands wrapped around the base of the legs and his feet curled over

the top rung. The Old Man drew in his breath trying to stifle a laugh, but it came out in a snort through
his nose.

Nicky sat down across from the Old Man and
moved a pawn. Paulie turned right side up to watch
the game. I watched, too, out of the corner of my
eye. The Old Man's antics tickled me. His head was
lopsided, so he had to look sideways at the chess
board or sit at an angle from it. After every move, his
eyebrows arched and he spit snuff into a tin can. I
wasn't sure if that meant he was glad or mad at the
turn the game was taking.

We ate in silence, but as soon as we finished,
Paulie asked the Old Man for a story about his chess
set.

"That story has grown a beard," the Old Man
chuckled.

We waited, knowing he'd tell it again.

"A long time ago, a Russian hunter, Vladimir,
brought a chess game to Akusha. No one here ever
saw one before. We watched him and another hunter
play. Their games sometimes lasted the night. After
keeping my eyes on many games, I finally figured
out why they sat so long without moving a piece.
Then I played with Vladimir. Others studied us until
they learned. We hunters liked that game. Then one
night at a town meeting with the Russian bosses,
Vladimir put his chess set in my hands and said to

the whole gang there, 'That's Afenogin's prize for being the best sea otter hunter in …' "

He stopped talking when Aunt Sophie and her husband, Bullshit John, showed up. John got that name from spinning yarns people didn't believe.

"There's news," he said before he even sat down. "A federal man showed up on the mail boat yesterday. He moved right into Elena Sistinkof's house. Right across from the church. And today he put bars across the door to the bedroom of that house. He's making a jail cell."

"Bullshit," the Old Man grumbled.

John ignored him, and plunked down on a box by the stove. "Innokenty and I were walking to church this afternoon when we passed this tall, fat promyshlennik with an unlit cigar hanging from his mouth. We stopped and watched him drag a door made of steel bars up the steps. After a while, the marshal laid the door down on the porch and came over to us. 'I'm Horace Gump, the marshal.' He took the cigar out of his mouth and snickered while he talked, but I didn't know what was funny.

"I told him my name and Innokenty did the same. 'I'm Innokenty Pushkin, first chief.' The marshal cleared his throat a few times and then, looking at Innokenty, said, 'I don't want to interfere with your business.' Innokenty nodded, puffed hard on his pipe, and said, 'First time the government sent a marshal here.' The muscles in Horace Gump's temples got tight, like he was mad. But, still smirking, he answered, 'You need someone to take care of things too big for the village to handle.' Innokenty and I stared at him, waiting for an explanation. None came. 'First time I ever heard of anything too big for us to handle,' Innokenty said. 'Things like murder and madness,' the marshal said. Innokenty was thinking and after a while, he said, "My grandfather told me about a murder here once. The community got together and sent that killer to another island.' The marshal looked puzzled, shrugged, then returned to the porch to drag the barred door into Elena's house."

The blood rushed to John's face. He stopped talking as suddenly as he'd started.

"Someone should go to that marshal and tell him the chief and elders are the law here," I said.

"Ah, Tatty, maybe we have to settle ourselves about the marshal," Aunt Sophie said. "Just like we do with the teachers and storekeeper. Sometimes we want them to leave. And sometimes they help us."

"But the teachers try to stop our language and now a marshal's here to stop our government. We should think of something to do."

Alicia was sitting on the edge of her seat like she does when she's tense. "Mama, what should we do?"

I searched my mind for an answer. I thought of my mama's teachings. "Your grandmother taught me, don't sit still when something's wrong."

"And you taught me it's wrong to fight."

"Doing doesn't have to mean fighting."

"What did my grandmother do?"

"She ran away from Umaka when she decided it was wrong to live with my papa."

"Why did she have to run away from Umaka? Why couldn't she just move to another house?"

"That would have set off fights, maybe explosions in the village. The council would have asked one or the other to leave. Mama left before anyone asked her to."

Alicia's face puckered into a frown. I waited for her to say what she was thinking. After a few minutes, she did. "Mama, I don't want you to run away from Papa."

I laughed. "Alicia, your papa is agreeable. Mine was mean. He didn't help Mama; he didn't help in the village. He was gone most of the year hunting sea otters on the *Sammy Jay*."

"But didn't all the men hunt sea otters in those days?" she asked.

"Before I was born, they did. But then there were plenty of sea otters near our island. Hunting trips lasted only a few months. Plenty of time left for the men to do their other work. After the sea otters disappeared from around there, hunting trips lasted most of the year. Our men stopped hunting them. Except my papa. Mama complained. She wanted him home to help with the church and community and fishing and training Alexi."

The Old Man spit a wad of tobacco into the tin can. "Your papa had a passion for his work."

"And Mama had a passion for the community," I answered, and then continued my story.

"They spoke harsh words when Papa was getting ready to go sea otter hunting again. That was right after my twelfth name day. Our barabara had only one room, so I heard everything. Mama usually spoke in a soft voice, but she made a loud command to Papa. 'I say, don't go, don't go.' Papa kept telling her to go to sleep. Mama's voice got louder. 'Hunt around here like the others. Alexi needs you here to train him. You don't have to hunt sea otters anymore.' 'Stop talking and go to sleep,' Papa said in a snappish voice. Mama's words came out fast. 'If you go, I go, if you go, I go.' Papa jumped up, grabbed his gear, and ran out the door. He slept in the shed that night and left early the next morning without saying good-bye to anyone."

Alicia's eyes grew wide. "Not even to your mama?"

"Not even to Mama. She was restless after Papa left, fluttering around the house like a bird hunting sand fleas. She didn't stop even when Gregory from Islik visited. Gregory was like Mama's aacha. He lived next door to her when they were children. And after he moved to Islik he kept visiting her, maybe a couple times a year. Gregory's aunt, Ekaterina, lived next door to us. This night she came over and told us a legend we'd never heard before.

"'This is a story about a girl who lived a long time ago,' she began. 'Her name was Varvara. She was young, fourteen, and had bright red cheeks and long black braids. Varvara was married to three brothers. She worked so hard many nights she didn't have time to sleep. After awhile she got tired of it. She walked off and hid in the hills. But one husband found her and brought her home. Time passed and she walked off again, this time to a cave high in the mountains. A second husband found her and brought her back. The third time she walked off many miles to the other side of the island. There were no people there. Varvara dug a barabara to live in. She caught fish in her hands. She ate the flesh of dead seals that rolled up on the beach. No one found her. She lived there always, in her own private village.'

"Mama told me she felt calm after Ekaterina's story, like something settled down on her insides. That's when she decided to follow Varvara's example and walk off from Umaka. She moved her chair close to Gregory's and the two of them talked in whispers. Then Gregory got up and left and Mama started running around doing strange things. First she pulled clothes out of storage boxes—boots, socks, parkas, kamleikas, sweaters. Then she started opening cupboards and taking out all the dried and salted fish and Pilot crackers. My stomach flip-flopped. I knew

something unusual was happening. Gregory returned
carrying empty boxes for packing. 'The boat is ready
to load,' he said. My heart started to jump around
like someone was kicking it. 'Boat, what boat? Where
are we going?'"

Alicia's eyes grew dark with fear. "Were you going to look for your papa?"

"That's what I thought until Mama spoke. 'We're
going to Islik with Gregory,' she said. 'And then
maybe on from there. We'll be gone a long time.' I
got dizzy thinking about Katya. She was at fish camp
on the other side of the island. All my life we saw
each other every day. She ate meals at our house. We
slept in the same bed many nights. We confided every thought. What would she think when she found
us gone? When would I see her? Would we be together for our thirteenth name day? Suddenly I had
an urge to hold my spirit doll, the one my godmother,
Matrona, made for my twelfth name day. I had left
the doll at Matrona's house. I started for the door.

"'Where are you going?' Mama asked. 'To get
my doll.' 'There's no time, Tatty. Alexi and Gregory
are loading the boat. Get Nicky and Sergie dressed.'
An hour later we were sailing away to Islik in
Gregory's powerboat. I'll never forget the sight of
the moonlit houses of Umaka and Matrona's and
Ekaterina's tiny figures on the beach growing smaller
and smaller until they disappeared."

Alicia was about to say something when I finished the story, but the Old Man didn't give her a chance. "Ha, who ever heard of packing a gang of children in a small boat 800 miles across the Aleutian Islands because you didn't like your husband? Maybe your mama got mixed up and thought you were a flock of geese."

Aunt Sophie's shoulders shook with laughter at the Old Man's remark.

"But Mama," Alicia said, "We can't run away from Akusha just because the marshal came here."

"No, we don't have to run away, but we don't have to sit still, either."

Alicia still looked puzzled. Maybe later she'd figure it out.

SEVEN

One day in late December, the sky suddenly cleared and I went to Rocky Point to fish. I caught five sculpin and rushed home to prepare them for lunch. The coals in the stove were glowing and two fish were sizzling in the pan when the children came in. Paulie ran over to the stove and looked in the pan. "Fresh fish," he called out to Alicia who was standing near the door. She didn't respond. "Sculpin," he said, trying to get her attention. Still, she didn't say anything. She didn't move, either, but stood frozen at the door with her jacket on like she didn't live here. I had never seen my lively daughter act that way before.

"Want some chai?" I asked her. No answer. I walked over and brushed her hair from her eyes with my hand. It fell there, just like Peter's. "Talk to me, little daughter."

"Can't."

"Can't?"

"Can't," she repeated. And then she bolted into the other room and fell on top of my bed.

I picked up my weaving, waiting for her to come out and tell me something.

I waited a long time. The light of the day dimmed. I called Alicia to the table for some crackers and fish. She came in and ate, but didn't speak and kept her eyes fixed on something over my head, though when I looked around, I didn't see anything. When she finished eating she went back to the bedroom. A sudden chill raced down my spine.

I decided to visit Nellie. Maybe she knew something. Her daughter, Agnes, was in Alicia's class. I hurried over there. Nellie and her sister, Anna, were splitting sea lion sinew into fine threads for making fish line. Anna was five years younger than Nellie, but she looked older; her hair was streaked with gray and she had worry lines around her eyes and mouth. Nellie got up, motioned me to a chair, and brought me a cup of chai. I noticed she kept peering into my eyes, so I told her about Alicia's strange behavior.

Nellie and Anna exchanged a quick glance. Then Nellie said, "She didn't tell you what Miss Parker did?"

"She didn't say one word."

Nellie's face colored. "Oh, Lord in heaven," she said, rocking her body back and forth in her straight-back chair.

My pulse started to throb. "Did Miss Parker cut out Alicia's tongue?"

"Agnes said Miss Parker put soap in Alicia's mouth, yes, soap in her mouth."

"Put soap in her mouth?"

"She kept washing Alicia's mouth in it even when it ran down her throat and gagged her."

My breath caught in my throat.

"Agnes said Miss Parker shouted at the children. 'And it will be soap in the mouth every time anyone talks Aleut in this school.' And then Miss Parker got real calm. She explained to the children, 'It's the fault of your parents you can't talk English right. It's because your parents talk Aleut at home. I want you all to stop speaking Aleut in your homes so you can learn English.'"

This wasn't the first time children were punished for speaking their tongue at school. Once when I went to American school, my teacher made me sit in the icy school corridor all day during the coldest part of winter for speaking Aleut. But putting soap in a child's mouth? It's an evil spirit who thinks up such an act.

Nellie was talking again. "Lordy, they brought in motorboats, and now no more baidarkas. They built frame houses, and now no more barabaras. They bring in the English language and soon, there'll be no more Aleut tongue."

Nellie spoke my fears. My mood grew dark.

Anna's face looked more pinched and worried than usual. "Terrible, terrible," she repeated. Then, looking at her sister, she asked in a high-pitched voice, "What can we do?"

"We'll talk to Evdokie," Nellie replied.

Evdokie was president of the sisterhood. We were used to following her wisdom. She lived only a few houses away from Nellie. We were there in a few minutes.

Everything in Evdokie's house is brown. Sometimes Evdokie blinks her eyes at my weaving when I use bright red and yellow dyes. She says brown is a calm color. Evdokie is calm, too. She hates feeling excited. And here we were bringing news that would surely make her pulse jump.

"Have you seen Simon or Akinia this afternoon?" I asked her. Evdokie has three children. Two of them, Simon and Akinia, are in Alicia's class.

"No. They're next door watching Papa repair their sled," she replied. And then her eyes questioned mine, Maybe she saw the red flush creeping up from my neck to my cheeks. So I told her what Miss Parker did in school.

"I don't want her to do that again," I said.

Evdokie sat quietly for many minutes, then said, "We should talk it over with Innokenty and the elders."

Nellie and I nodded, but Anna gave us news that changed my mind. "Innokenty and Ruff are at Unakeet checking their trap lines. They left this morning, so they won't be back for awhile."

"We'll wait for them," Evdokie said.

"I'm thinking about Miss Parker hurting other children while we're waiting," I said.

"We have to wait," Evdokie insisted. "The chief and elders know the laws of our ancestors."

My voice rose. "Did our ancestors know about promyshlennik teachers? Did they know about talking in two tongues?"

"The chief and the council are the suggestors about everything," Evdokie replied.

Nellie and Anna didn't say anything. I thought hard about Evdokie's opinion. It didn't feel good to wait. I thought of Mama, of what she'd suggest. She'd say we women should take care of the problem ourselves. Mama is right. I passed her advice on to the others.

Nellie agreed. "We don't have to turn to the elders for everything, for everything. We're sisterhood regulars."

Evdokie tightened her lips and the veins on the side of her forehead stood out. Before she could oppose me, I said, "We can talk to the council later. First, we women will go to the school."

"Go to the school?" Anna and Evdokie asked at the same moment.

"We'll go to the school," I repeated. "We'll go tomorrow and tomorrow and the next tomorrow. Then we'll see."

"To talk to Miss Parker?" Evdokie asked.

"Not to talk. To sit. In the seats at the back of Miss Parker's room."

Anna's skin paled. "She'll get mad at us."

We all nodded.

"But … but … if she's mad, she might not tend the sick. She's in charge of all the medicines." I shivered with the same fear. If we had sat in at the school before Peter got sick, would Miss Parker have helped him? I didn't want to fight with her. Maybe Evdokie was right. We should consult the council. But their deliberations sometimes lasted for days. Cold a minute before, my hands started to sweat as thoughts of Katya crowded my mind. I shouldn't have waited when she converted. I shouldn't have waited when she told me she was going to marry Buddy Thomas. I should have done something to stop her. The answer was clear. We had to stop Miss Parker from hurting our children.

"Promyshlennik are in charge of the radio communication and the store and cash jobs, too," I reminded Anna.

"So better not fight with them," Anna said.

"Sitting quiet isn't fighting," I answered her.

Nellie broke into a laugh that rumbled up from somewhere deep in her belly. "I like that—war without words."

Evdokie nodded. Anna sighed but went along with the decision.

Standing next to a dark, chipped, hardwood desk, her hands holding onto its edge, Miss Parker looked startled the next morning when she saw the four of us squeeze into empty desk chairs at the back of the room. I was just as surprised several minutes later when Sylvia South walked into the school room and took the seat next to mine. It was the first time a promyshlennik ever joined our protest, except Father Paul, of course. I wondered how she knew about our plan. Then I figured it out. Nellie had told her.

Miss Parker fixed her eyes on me. "Can I help you, Tatiana?"

I felt friendly toward this woman who saved Peter's life. But also confused. She was the same woman who injured Alicia. I shook my head slowly.

Miss Parker asked the same question of the other women, including Sylvia. All responded the same. Miss Parker frowned and pulled her bushy brows into the shape of a V. Turning to the children, she asked, "Is it some kind of a holiday that brings your mothers to the school?" The children didn't answer. They didn't know why we were there.

Miss Parker glared at the children for a few minutes. Then, throwing her shoulders back, she walked to the slate to start a lesson. When she talked, though, her voice cracked. She did lessons all that day while we women sat there.

The next day Anesia and Marie, the healers, joined us at the school. There were no empty seats, so they sat cross-legged on the floor behind us. Miss Parker did her lessons, but every few seconds she glanced in our direction. On the third day three more women came, older women—Little Hunch, Aunt Sophie, and Evdokie's mama, Parascovia. They sat on the floor with Marie and Anesia.

In the middle of the morning, something happened. Alicia wasn't afraid anymore. She turned around to face me. "Aang anax," she said.

"Aang asxinux," I replied.

I thought Miss Parker was going to have a fit, like a rabid dog. She turned her back to the room, but her hands trembled and her earlobes turned bright red. A few minutes passed. Then she spun around and looked at us. Her voice shook a little. "We don't allow Aleut spoken in the school. It interferes with the children's learning English."

I felt like shouting that Aleut was the language of our homes, the language of my mama and her mama and her mama before. But I decided to let our silence speak.

Miss Parker didn't seem to know what to do next. She walked to the back of the room. Then she circled around to the front. She folded her arms over her chest, and, speaking very slowly like we were deaf or maybe dumb, she said, "The children need to know English to have a better life. It's fine for husbands and wives to speak Aleut to each other. But if you speak Aleut to your children they'll never learn English. They'll never have a better life."

I didn't say anything. Neither did the other women.

Miss Parker pulled her upper lip down over her front teeth and began tapping her fingers on the back of her chair. "Do you understand?" she said. No one answered, but I think Miss Parker saw our tight lips.

"Will you cooperate with the school in this?" she stammered.

Not one of us said anything.

On the fourth day, Miss Parker made a statement. "I spoke to Miss Coombs." She was the teacher in lower class. "We talked it over. We decided you can speak Aleut to your children in your homes."

We left the school together, we nine women, our arms linked, our steps light, almost like we were dancing. "Let's go to the creek for some trout," I proposed in Aleut.

Nellie wagged her finger in my face. "Don't you want a better life? Better speak in English."

We all laughed except Sylvia, who didn't understand our language. Using English, I invited her to our fishing party.

"I don't have a fishing pole," she said.

Nellie laughed. "We fish with our hands."

"But …" Sylvia sputtered. And then I guess she decided to close her mouth.

We followed Icy Creek as it wound its way from the beach up into the hills behind the school. The sun had just scattered the clouds, and shadows played in and out of the creases in the mountains. A great calm washed over me.

Nellie caught the first trout. She pulled a knife from her pocket and started to clean it. We always carry knives in case we find fish. Soon five more trout lay filleted on the creek bank, enough for all. But Sylvia didn't take any. We kept munching anyway.

After a while Sylvia mumbled, "I don't eat raw fish." Red spots broke out on her neck like they did when Ralph upset her. I went over and stood close to her. I wanted her to know it wasn't important to eat the fish. She must have felt better. She started to talk. "I have some news. Guess what Ralph gave me for my fortieth birthday? A Steinway upright. It arrived yesterday on the *Elsie L*. I've played piano since I was five years old. It's the one thing I missed most living here." She paused, gulped some air, and went on. "Tell me what you think of my idea. I thought I'd give piano lessons. I wouldn't charge. I know most of you are poor. Do you think people here would be interested?"

There are so many things Sylvia doesn't notice. "I'm thinking about where they'd practice." I said. "There hasn't been a piano in Akusha since the Baptist missionaries left ten years ago."

"Oh, I'm sorry," Sylvia said, the flush returning to her neck. She left a few minutes later.

Anesia started to chant an Aleut song, and the rest of us joined in.

EIGHT

Early January. A big storm. Waves crashed on the shore and high winds pelted our windows and whistled through cracks around the door frames. But foul weather didn't blunt our excitement as we prepared for our ten-day Christmas celebration.

"Starring" marks the beginning. For three nights we parade around town singing and waving bright stars of our own making. There are eight star bearers, each with a hand-picked group of carolers. I sing with the sisterhood group; we've been rehearsing for a week. After every rehearsal, I hurried home to work on masks and costumes for the nights of masquerading that follow starring.

On this last day of preparations, coals burning hot in the stove, we all sat around the table putting finishing touches on our stars and masks. Gavril, Nellie's son, was helping Peter cut the deacon's star. He'd been living at our house for many days. That's the custom in our country. Children shift around to different houses. The village is their family.

Peter and Gavril were making a six-point star with a small cup on each end to hold candles. When Peter lights the candles and spins the star it looks like a flaming pinwheel. Gavril was pushing the candles hard into the cups, but they kept falling out. He looked at Peter for direction.

"The wax is too cool. Put it back on the stove," Peter said.

Gavril followed his suggestion, and after a while tested the heat of the wax with his finger. He howled. Peter tried to keep a straight face as he handed him a stick to use in place of his finger.

Alicia and I were working on the sisterhood star, shaped like a kite. She was painting a picture of the Virgin in the center of the star and white anemone blossoms around the edges. Alicia was an artist from birth. Before she could walk, she'd sit for hours watching Peter draw cartoons for our village newspaper and Nicky carve from wood and bone. And now a smile creeps across her face when she draws.

The first day of starring, a light, fluffy snow, like a curtain of gauze, fell on the carolers. Each group started at a different point. We laced our way along the paths, waving our stars, singing, and passing out gifts. Alicia paraded with the adults for the first time. She walked beside me in the sisterhood group. I watched to see if she was tiring, but she didn't flag for a second, her rich voice ringing louder as we went from house to house.

On the last night of starring, we caroled at Sylvia's house. She came out as soon as she heard us, beaming a smile, and swaying to the rhythm of our singing. After we finished, I handed her a gift—Christmas bread, fresh baked that day. Sylvia's emotions show easily. Her eyes misted over as she grabbed my hand and squeezed it.

On the fourth day, the masquerading started. The masks scared some of the children, but Alicia showed no fear until we reached the Old Man's house. Then, she stood as still as if she was nailed to the ground. The Old Man's door opened a crack and a long pole with a crab-like claw shot out toward us. Everyone laughed except Alicia; she backed away from his house, but her eyes stayed fixed on that claw until the Old Man finally yanked it inside.

On the final night of masquerading, we celebrated with a great feast at the community hall. It lasted nearly all night. As a finale, we dunked in the sea—our way of getting rid of evil spirits hiding in our costumes. Alicia jumped in first. "Eek, eek, it's freezing!" she shrieked as she ran out of the water. Others went into the water after Alicia. All except Nadia. She joined Aunt Sophie, Parascovia, and Little Hunch at the steam bath where the older women cleansed themselves.

I slept most of the next day. Then it was time for another high moment—our New Year's Eve dance. Nearly everyone in town, including the promysh-

lennik, came to the celebration. Wearing brightly
colored calico and gingham skirts and shirts, women
reeled around in large circles, doing Russian folk
dances that Father Paul's wife taught us the year she
spent in Akusha. When they finished, people imi-
tated the style of the ballroom dance—two people,
any combination, hugging and slowly moving their
feet. Alicia was my partner. She wasn't a star at dancing. She kept stumbling over her feet and finally her
her foot caught mine and we both landed on the
floor, laughing until tears came. "Enough dancing,"
I said. "Let's help serve the food."

We carried bowls of punch and platters of bread,
smoked fish, and fruit from cans to the tables. Peter
reached out and grabbed my arm when I passed him.
"Come sit with me, Little Wren. We're planning the
hymns we'll sing at midnight mass."

"I'll be back when I finish serving." Then, as an
afterthought, I went over and brushed a strand of
hair away from his eye.

Alicia and I were filling punch glasses at a table
in the rear of the room when we overheard a conversation at the next table. It was between James
Wilson, boss at the supply station, and Horace Gump,
the marshal. Horace's face was big and fleshy but
James's looked like a skull, the skin as taut as hide on
a drum.

"They're full of fun, aren't they?" the marshal
said.

"They like a good time, that's for sure. You know, they're a talented bunch. Who'd ever expect to find so many artists and musicians in a hole like this?" He paused. "But hard as I try, I just can't understand them."

"What do you mean?" Horace asked him.

"They don't care a fig about the future. They don't plan ahead for anything. Take that young man, Alexi, over there in the corner. He unloads supplies for me sometimes. A year ago last fall he brought in a 1,500 pound sea lion, nearly 1,500 pounds of meat. Think of that—more meat than all the cans in the NS store. But then I found out that his family had no meat at all that winter. He didn't save any for the cold months."

"You don't say. What did he do with it?" the marshal said, clucking his tongue against the roof of his mouth.

"He just gave it all away."

The blood in my veins turned to ice. I remembered how proud Alexi was the evening he hauled the qawax up on the beach. It was October. Dark came early. The sky was clear and the air was crisp and cool. People built fires to keep warm and light their work while they butchered the animal. When they finished, Alexi distributed meat, the largest shares to the Old Man and Little Hunch and others who needed it. He ran from one person and group to another, watching them prepare the various parts of the animal. They dried shoulder meat for winter, cleaned and dried the stomach as a poke for storing the meat, salted blubber for oil, cleaned the bladder for buoys, the throat for rain boots, the skin for baidarka covers, the tougher parts for the soles of boots. Parascovia and Little Hunch separated the sinew for thread and removed the thin tissue around the heart for carrying bags. Except for the head, we use every part of the sea lion. While these preparations were going on, before the meat spoiled, we boiled and roasted the ribs and breast for a feast. When the food was gone, we followed Alexi to the shore and watched him perform the final ritual— feeding water to the head before dropping it back into the sea.

Oh, how I wish James Wilson and Horace Gump had watched all these doings. Maybe then they'd see that what we have is like the sun—it's for everybody.

NINE

Big doings on this overcast day in the spring of
1939. Peter's not a hunter, but he's having a gathering with hunters from all over the Aleutians.
Innokenty and the elders and Father Burdofsky are
here, too. Sitting on chairs, the bench, or on their
haunches on the floor, the men are discussing buying a boat. Not a skiff or dory, but a vessel as large
and grand as the *Aurora*.

I was at the counter skinning seal flippers for
lusta and smiling to myself thinking of serving it to
Sylvia and Ralph. It's one Aleut food no white has
ever eaten that I know of. They can't stand the stink.
I can't either when the lusta is in the house. But we
keep it in the shed until we serve it. Then we spread
papers all over the table because you can't get the
stench out of the wood once it seeps in. But what a
feed. We roll sleeves to our elbows and chew that
delicious piece of fermented muscle clean. After, we
fill a pan with soapy water and scrub our arms and
hands. My stomach grumbles just thinking about
lusta.

Everyone's ears were cocked toward my cousin, Michael, Sophie's son. He and his partner, Ilarion, son of Anesia, were star trappers. "As it is," Michael said, the words whistling through the spaces where his front teeth were missing, "Ilarion and I can set fox traps on only one island a season. Then we wait many weeks to be picked up. Last year we were stuck on Unakeet for two months waiting for the *Elsie L.* to come for us. With a ship we could trap on several islands a season."

"The community would be rich," Ilarion added.

No one spoke for a few minutes. Then Ruff, third chief, pushing his glasses back from the tip of his nose where they always slid, expressed another view. "I'm thinking it doesn't matter how many places we set traps when the prices of fox furs are dropping so fast."

Alexi offered a more cheerful outlook. "I'm remembering that fox prices fell four years ago and rose again."

Father Burdofsky introduced another consideration. "Peter and I dream of visiting all the Aleut villages. But traveling by dory and skiff we get to only a few a year. A ship of our own, ah, it would bring joy to many villages." Father glanced at Peter as he talked, but Peter was looking out the window.

Evdokie's brother, Matfay, stood up and paced as he talked. "I've been doing sums. The kind of ship we're talking about costs thousands of dollars. Where will the money come from with fox prices now so low?"

Akuke Domasoff from Azian Bay jumped up from his seat. His face was flushed; his words came fast. "I have information on that subject. Our hunters and trappers have been putting money into a boat fund all year. We have nearly $1,500."

Zack Swenson, Alexi's father-in-law from New Harbor, grinned. "We have more than that in our New Harbor boat fund. We've already picked a name for the boat—the *Azian Bay Native*. That's because most of our cash comes from fox trapping near Azian Bay." Then, smiling wider, he added, "and the people across the bay from us in Kooney Pass are saving for the boat, too."

"Our community fund has $300. It could go in the boat fund," said an excited cousin Michael.

A lump formed in my throat. We'd been saving that money for an upright piano for the community hall. I hoped others put the piano first, too. But minutes passed and no one objected to using our piano money for the boat.

"With a ship of our own," said Cousta, Nellie's husband, "we could travel all over the Aleutians visiting relatives. They could come here, too, for visits and holidays."

His words set my imagination on fire. I saw myself traveling to Azian Bay to visit my brother Sergie. I hadn't seen him since he moved there for marriage eight years before. My temple started to throb. Maybe Azian Bay would be only a stopover on the way to Umaka. I pictured seeing Matrona and running in the hills and fields of lupine where Katya and I once played.

Innokenty spoke for the first time, and the warm glow inside me chilled. "When we started using putt putts instead of baidarkas, an evil spirit fell on us. Drownings came one after the other. And this boat you want to buy has an engine the size of twenty putt putts."

"We should heed that warning. Those drownings are a sign of our ancestors' anger," Leonty, second chief, warned.

Several men cleared their throats, and then, slowly, one by one, the men got up and left the house.

Later, when Peter and I were drinking chai and munching strips of dried fish, I asked his opinion about buying the boat.

"I don't know, Little Wren. No one understands those big engines."

"We learn many things."

"No one around here has the experience to teach us about them." He paused while he sipped his chai. "You know, Tatty, there are times I wonder if Kiril drowned because he didn't understand engines."

Kiril was Nellie's son. I remembered his excitement when his ten-foot skiff and Johnson engine arrived in town. He took off in it that very day. It was calm weather. We expected him back by evening. A couple days passed. Matfay and Alexi went after him. They found his boat; it was empty. They tried the engine; it was dead.

"Maybe our people should honor Innokenty's warning. Maybe we should offer reasons not to buy that ship," I said.

"People in other villages want it. Most of the people here do, too."

"I'm thinking about Katya turning away from our life. I'm thinking I should have done something to stop her. Maybe buying that ship means drifting away from our life, too."

Peter got up from the table and carried empty cups to the counter.

Then he picked up his pipe, filled it with tobacco, and fished in his pocket for a match. "Little Wren, we're one people, we're one community. It's not our way to split in two." Peter lit his pipe and went out.

The gloom that came over me during that conversation lifted when, on my way to the shed with the seal flippers, I saw that the sun had parted the clouds and the tide had run out. I grabbed a bucket from the shed and hurried to the beach to search the tide pools. In no time my bucket was full of snails, mussels, chitons, and sea urchins. Sea urchin eggs are Peter's favorite food. After a while I leaned back against a log and watched a flock of eider ducks skim across a calm sea. A putt putt approached them. The birds scattered. All except one. It was injured. The boat must have hit it. The *Azian Bay Native* might have killed the whole flock.

There were many visitors that evening—the *Azian Bay Native* was in everyone's thoughts. I served chai and my afternoon catch and listened to the talk.

Bullshit John, sucking a piece of fish from between his teeth, opened the subject. "Too bad we're not of one mind about buying that boat."

Innokenty ran his hand through his bush of white hair and fixed his soft, brown eyes on John. "The sea doesn't like engines. It fights them. Sometimes it destroys them."

Matfay, one of the few men in town who still hunted in a baidarka, nodded. "Our skin boats suit the sea. If they tip over we can right them in moments and climb back in. And they never run out of fuel. Our arms and paddles make them run."

I wanted to say, "Yes, yes, yes. We'll teach our boys to build baidarkas and our girls to sew skin covers for the boats." I wanted to say, "Let's forget all about motor boats." Yet, I trembled picturing our boys and girls traveling long distances in baidarkas.

"You sailed across the Aleutians in a baidarka, Mama. What was it like?" Alicia asked.

I got up and started to brew a fresh pot of chai. I didn't know if I wanted to set off the ache of that twenty-six-year-old memory. But everyone sat

quietly waiting, so I brought chai to the table and
began.

"There was one terrible storm after another. Sailing from Umaka to Islik, that part was okay. We were
in Gregory Mensoff's power dory. So we sat above
deck. And the trip was short. Maybe a day. But traveling from Islik to Azian Bay in Simeon Azinof's
three-hatch baidarka still haunts my dreams. I remember standing on the Islik beach waiting for Alexi
and Simeon to finish loading the boat. I sniffed the
fresh smell of the early morning air. I looked out at
the mountains, outlined in black against a pink and
violet dawn. And then my eyes rested on the sea. I
had the strangest feeling, like the sea was calling me.
My backbone tingled at the thought of our adventure. Later on, it stiffened in terror.

"Before we sailed we all squatted in the sand
around Simeon for instructions. 'Anastasia and Alexi,
you'll sit above and help me paddle. You young ones
will lie below. Sergie, get as comfortable as you can
against the supplies aft. Tatiana, sit at the other end
and put Nicky in the middle.' I asked how long we'd
have to stay below. 'Many weeks. Azian Bay is a long
way off. But we'll stop along the way,' I was told.

The sound of the Old Man spitting a wad of
tobacco into an empty coffee can interrupted my
memory. "That was a long haul to be cramped in
the belly of the boat," he said.

I nodded and caught up with the drift of the story. "It was eerie down below. Three pairs of legs dangling down from the hatches, and the sea surrounding us like we were in it. Only the width of a sea lion skin separated us from it. The water pounded against that skin so loud I feared my eardrums would crack.

"Our first stop was called Pilot Point. No one lived there, Simeon said, because there were no creeks and the harbor was no good. I was keyed up. I'd heard stories about islands with no people. But I never dreamed I'd be on one. My brothers and I ran around like we'd just been let out of a cage. Alexi climbed a small hill trying to get a good look at a strange-looking black and white bird. We learned later it was a magpie. We didn't have any of those birds in Umaka. I stopped near Alexi to look at a patch of tiny violet-colored flowers I'd never seen before. And right next to them I spotted a cluster of bright red berries that were also unfamiliar. I was wondering what I'd find next when Mama called us to a meal. I didn't want to stop exploring, so I pretended I didn't hear her. But she came and got me anyhow. I noticed Simeon staring at a bank of clouds piling up in the west. He was worried. As soon as we finished eating he told us to get ready to leave.

"On board, Simeon prepared us for the next stage of the trip.

'We'll be sailing through Sunotsky Pass. It's a rough passage under good circumstances. And storm clouds are gathering.'"

I paused again when Alexi got up and went over to stoke the fire. I waited until he sat down.

"I'd heard about treacherous Sunotsky Pass all my life. It earned its reputation. When the turbulence started, Mama yelled from above, 'Soothe your brothers, Tatty. Tell them a story.' Fear made me feel mean. I related the scariest story I could think of, about a stranger with bulging eyes and a huge hole for a mouth who'd sneaked into our village in the middle of the night, howled at the children, and finally stole one of them. Nicky screamed louder. Mama called to me again, 'Hold Nicky until he's calm.' My face grew red with shame. I pulled Nicky close and hugged him. I felt better when his body relaxed against mine.

"We were coiled around each other like that when suddenly we were thrust apart. The boat began to heave wildly. The dreaded storm had arrived. From below it felt like the boat was being tossed hundreds of feet into the air only to crash down deep into the sea moments later. It jolted every organ in my body. I retched until I thought my insides were coming out. Nicky was vomiting in my lap. His eyes were wider than an owl's. He started to scream that the waves were going to swallow us. I shivered, remembering Matrona's stories about angry ancestors and evil spirits. Were our ancestors punishing us for running away from Papa and from our people in Umaka? I wanted to protect Nicky from their wrath. I clutched him to my breast. He was stiff with terror. 'It's nearly over now, it's nearly over now.' And to my surprise, for I was certain we were all going to drown, the storm ended as suddenly as it began."

Alexi got up again, fetched a piece of driftwood from the porch, and dropped it into the stove. Alicia went over to the stove, sat down on a box next to it, and wrapped her arms around her shoulders.

I paused, wondering if I should stop.

"Go on, Mama," Alicia said.

"That night we landed on another island without people. The sun was just setting when we came ashore. Simeon said big tides were coming and he was going to carry the boat to high ground. Sergie ran off to look for clams, Nicky tagging after him. The rest of us stayed behind to unpack our gear. Simeon pointed to a protected area under an overhanging cliff as a campsite. After he secured his boat, he picked up his shotgun and set out to hunt birds for our meal.

"While I set up camp, Mama left to find a creek and Alexi went to search for wood. He returned with two armloads. I shredded one of the smaller pieces for kindling. Then Alexi and I tried to light the fire, but the wood was too damp. We lit more kindling.

Still, we couldn't get the fire to catch. We got down on our knees, side by side, and blew on every ember. I was thinking we'd never get a fire going when I saw a few tiny sparks. We blew soft breath over every one of them until tiny sparks grew into a flame that danced from timber to timber. Finally, the whole bundle blazed. We warmed up by that fire. But still Alexi and I stayed on our knees, close to each other, not wanting to break apart.

"The fire was burning hot when everyone returned to camp. Sergie had found no clams, but Simeon came back holding three Canada geese by the neck. Mama plucked and cleaned the birds, set them in a pot of water, and put the pot right into the fire. We sat around watching the pot boil until the birds were ready, our mouths watering for a taste of fresh meat. I gnawed that rich meat to the bone. As soon as we buried the bones Simeon said it was time to leave. The memory of that evening—the crackling fire, the fresh goose, and the nearness of my brothers kept me going through the awful time to come.

"During the third week we landed at Crater Island. Simeon hadn't planned to stop there, but a sudden, violent storm changed his mind."

I paused again when Alicia got up and came over to the bench I was sitting on, squeezing herself between Paulie and me. She was still shivering. But she nudged me with her elbow which meant she wanted to hear the rest.

"Everyone went into action. Simeon and Alexi carried the boat to a sheltered cove and tied her to boulders. Mama and I tried to put up the tent, but it kept blowing out of our grip. Finally, we tied it down. A few minutes later I heard a tearing sound. The wind was ripping the tent into tatters and scattering our food and clothes in every direction. Blades of rain slashed us at sharp angles like knives piercing our skin. It soaked through our sleeping bags and blankets. Nicky was screaming, 'Mama, Mama.' Sergie was crying, too. I didn't know any words for comfort. I was so scared I could hardly swallow. The tent flew off. Simon chased it, but it soared overhead and disappeared in the sea. Simeon ran back to us. 'Follow me,' he said. 'There's a cave nearby, in Crater Mountain.' He had sat out a storm there once before.

"We staggered after him, fighting the wind with every step. Alexi was holding Sergie upright. But gusting winds kept knocking Nicky down. Each time, Mama and I yanked him up. Seaweed and other debris hit us in the face and arms and legs, scratching and cutting our skin. Simeon ran ahead, but he kept coming back to check on us. Each time I asked him,' Are we close to the cave?' he'd say, 'It's a way, yet.'

"All at once my foot slipped on something slick and Nicky and I tumbled into a marsh. We were drenched in mud. The others, walking ahead, didn't notice. I couldn't lift Nicky. He had gotten stiff as a walrus bone. I didn't know how I was going to pull him out of that swamp. I was afraid we'd get left behind. With a strength that surprised me, I held Nicky by the armpits and jerked the two of us out of that mud hole.

"We pushed against wind and driving rain and rugged ground and marshes for hours. Finally we reached the cave in the flank of Crater Mountain. We had no outer garments. They had blown away. And the clothes on our bodies were sopping wet. We couldn't build a fire under those wet conditions. 'Keep active. Don't sit still or you'll freeze to death,' Simeon warned us. There wasn't much room to move around. But I kept rocking and stretching in my few feet of space. I took turns moving myself and moving Nicky. Alexi was doing the same with Sergie. I couldn't stop thinking about Katya. Before this day, even though we'd left her behind, I knew I'd see her again. But this night a vast fear surged through me. Then I heard Mama's voice. It cracked and trembled in the icy chill of the cave. I couldn't believe she found the strength to tell a story. But she did, and when she finished—"

"Tell us your mama's story," Alicia said.

"It went like this. 'After my papa died and Mama had to do everything, I decided to take over the fishing. I asked my uncles Philip and Ivan to teach me. 'Take me with you,' I pleaded, as they packed their skiff to fish for halibut. I wanted to catch a huge fish, enough to feed the whole town. They said no, hunting was for boys and that I had plenty to do helping my mama. And then the two of them pushed their skiff into the water, jumped aboard, fastened their oars, and rowed away. I ran after them and grabbed onto a coil of fishing line at the stern of the boat. The line was tough. It pulled me along in the water behind the boat. But that water was like ice. My toes and legs got numb. I knew I had to get out of that water fast. Using my arms I shimmied along the line trying to reach the boat. I began to scream my uncles' names, but a rising wind drowned out my voice. My chest felt like it was in the grip of a tight leather band. I started to gasp for breath. I clutched that line and pulled harder and harder until finally my hands touched the stern. My Uncle Ivan turned around and saw my fingers. He leaped to the rear and hauled me from the water. Without speaking a word, my uncles turned that boat around toward the beach they'd left just a few minutes earlier. Still, without speaking, Uncle Ivan lifted me from the boat and carried me home. After I warmed up by the fire, Uncle Ivan told me I was a goofy girl and in the next breath he said I could fish with them next day.'"

"My mama's courage kept me alive that night. And soon dawn came and the storm broke. I was still trembling from the biting cold of my wet clothes, but I smiled knowing I was alive, knowing I'd see

Katya again. Nicky didn't smile. He didn't speak, either. Not for the next month of hopping across more islands. Not for three months after we arrived in Akusha. And he never went out to sea again."

I looked around the room, expecting someone to tell a story that contradicted my message. Minutes passed. No one spoke. Not a single soul. Ay-yai, what have I done?

TEN

Nellie and I spent the morning wandering in the hills, rejoicing in the rich summer growth—moss green leaves sprouting from the buds of willows, spring beauties covering the gullies, and flowers studding the hillside like a painting: yellow buttercups, blue bells, white star flowers, lavender orchids, purple violets, pink primroses, and greenish-white windflowers.

The sight of windflowers always stirred memories of Katya and me as children rolling on the ground among them, feeling their silky texture against our skin. Sometimes on those days my edges blurred and I felt merged with Katya and the sweet-smelling earth around us. Oh, if only I could see her, touch her, hear her deep voice. Whenever Katya bursts from the back of my mind, anguish follows.

Nellie and I sat down on the crest of a hill, looking down to a turquoise-colored lake nestled in the valley. Nellie usually senses my mood, but on this day her thoughts were elsewhere. "Mr. Steele arrived on the *Aurora* this morning," she said. Mr. Steele was principal of Anton's school in Oregon. He'd never been to Akusha before.

I heard fear in her voice. I felt it, too. "I wonder why he's here," I said.

"Recruiting students. First thing, the very first thing he did was call the older students to a meeting. Tatty, he convinced Anton to go to his school; he might do the same with our girls."

"Well, Alicia won't go, that I know."

"If Alicia goes, Agnes will follow, that I know."

"Oh, Nell, my mind bends in two directions. I don't know what I'd do if Alicia left. But I do want her to learn. If my mama drummed one lesson into my head, it was the importance of school. You know she didn't read or write Russian or Aleut. There was no government school in Umaka and the Russian school taught only boys. I think she would have traded her arms for an education."

"Was it because of schools your mama ran away from Umaka?"

"She left Umaka to get away from Papa. But she picked Akusha because of the schools. I remember her eyes catching fire when her aacha, Gregory Mensoff, described the Akusha schools. He'd just returned from a trip there. That happened about a week before we ran off. Mama asked Gregory one question after another. 'Do all the children go to school? To both schools? How do they manage two schools at once? Do they go day and night? What subjects are offered?' After Gregory left, Mama turned to me. Her eyes were misty: 'I don't want you to grow up dumb in our tongues like I was.'

"I had been in Akusha only two weeks when the school term started, both schools—Russian and American. I don't think you were here then, Nell."

"I spent that year with Auntie Fedosia in Bolisof."

"Well, Mama's dream took strong hold of me. I was going to learn languages, read books, write letters to Katya and Matrona, read psalms in church. My heart sang that first day as I ran to school. Alexi wasn't with me. He had taken to staying with Matfay. But I met Alexi in the school yard and we went inside together. There were only five grades then, all in one room.

"Pastor Lowell, the Baptist missionary, greeted us at the door. He was head of the government school, too. 'Do you speak English?' he asked us in English. We shook our heads. Then he took us into the section for the younger students. He told Miss Long, the teacher, who was also a missionary, 'I'll send Catherine in to translate for the new students.' Catherine was an older orphan at the mission.

"Miss Long knew all the children but Alexi and me. She came over to us, patted our arms and pinched our cheeks. I winced. It felt like a bug bite. 'We're going to learn English,' she said with emphasis. 'And we're going to learn about Americans, how they live.' Then she returned to the front of the room and aimed a pointer at pictures on the wall with a word printed beneath each one—a boy, Dick, a girl, Jane, a dog, Spot, and a house with a white picket fence around it.

After that she pointed to other pictures—a bus, train, ambulance, fire truck, pineapple, and banana. I didn't know what they were. She tried to teach us the words for them. I was lost. And I felt even more confused when she gave us a book of characters. Those letters didn't look anything like the Cyrillic alphabet our Russian and Aleut books were written in.

"Near lunch time I asked Miss Long where the outhouse was. 'No Aleut spoken in school,' she said, smiling the while. I picked up her meaning. Catherine had already left. And I didn't know any other translators in the room. I thought I was going to shit my pants. But I held on. Finally the bell rang. I dashed home to our outhouse. Then I ran down to the creek and washed the stains from my pants. I didn't feel very cheerful when I went into the house."

Nellie cupped her face in her hands and swayed back and forth. "Lordy, lordy, why did we keep going? Why didn't we quit?"

"I had decided to that first day."

"But you didn't."

"Mama wouldn't hear of it. She'd prepared a special meal for me—sea urchin eggs and fried clams. She must have spent the morning gathering. Her eyes glistened as she watched me eat. When I finished, I said, 'I hate that school. I'm not going back.' Mama stepped back from me. She looked like I'd smacked her in the face. I told her everything that happened that morning, and repeated, 'I'll never go back.'"

"What did she say?"

"Not a word. I was afraid she was never going to speak to me again, she sat so long in silence. After a while, though, she sighed, a sigh so deep I could feel the air shimmer. 'We didn't get many letters in Umaka,' she said. 'But when one came I couldn't read it, not a word. I had to take those letters to my uncles to read to me.

"At church the men were able to read along with the service. I wanted to follow it, too. Many times I asked my uncles, 'teach me to read and write.' They smiled when I asked, but they never did anything about it. After I married I begged your papa to teach me to read and write. 'No time,' he always said. I appealed to the church reader, too, but he was busy training boys at Russian school. Mama sighed again and then stood up, took my hand, led me to the door, and said, 'It's time to go back to school.'

"I went. I learned those English characters. In six months I was bringing books home from school to read in the evenings after Russian school. Mama would sit close to me, looking over my shoulder. I started reading aloud to her, translating the English stories into Aleut. We had a lot of laughs when we read *Gulliver's Travels,* trying to find Aleut words for 'Brobdingnagians' and 'Lilliputians.' I think Alexi's and my school days were Mama's happiest times. Even after Papa came, Mama insisted I stay in school."

"Did your papa want you to stop going?"

"Papa wasn't interested in anything but his illness. He came here when he was dying from lung disease."

"You'd think she'd send him back to Umaka."

"She said she couldn't let him die alone. But she wouldn't let him infect us, either. So she took him to John's fox farm and tended him there. Alexi insisted on going with them."

"I remember—you had to handle everything at home."

"I was plenty busy with the boys and finding food and doing Mama's laundry jobs. I didn't have time for school. But when Mama came home to check on things during the week and I'd suggest quitting school, she'd say, 'Hold on, I'll be home any day now.' Of course, that made me think Papa was near the end. But months rolled by and he didn't die and she didn't return. And when winter came, I was even busier finding food and wood for the stove. It no longer mattered what Mama wanted. I simply couldn't keep up with school work. First I quit Russian school. That wasn't so bad. Peter, who taught Russian and music at the school, gave me lessons in the evening. But gradually I stayed home more and more from government school. By the time Papa died, I had stopped going altogether. Mama had wanted me to return. But I told her I was too old to be in lower class with the babies. Now I regret it. There was so much more to learn."

Nellie looked up at the sky like she does when she's thinking hard. Then she said, "Ah, Tatty, your mama would be proud if Alicia went to higher school."

"She'd smile wide," I answered.

"I'm smiling, too. Maybe higher school will teach the children about things like engines, yes, about engines. If Kiril had understood engines he'd still be alive."

"Nell, I can't stop thinking about Innokenty's warning. Yesterday, on my way to Rocky Point, I watched him try to appease our ancestors. He was kneeling on the ground scooping out earth to make a pit. And then he put two pure white ptarmigan wings in the pit, chanting all the while."

Several minutes passed before Nellie said anything. "Buying that ship doesn't feel wrong. No, it doesn't feel wrong. When I think of the *Azian Bay Native,* I see Mavra. It's like the two are one. The new boat means Mavra in my life. Can that be wrong?"

My brain felt like swamp mud. I wanted to move away from the subject. "Let's see if the mail's out," I

suggested. We got up then and set off for the school.
There were letters from both Mavra and Anton.
Nellie and I parted, knowing we'd tell each other
the news later.

Once home, something kept me from reading
Anton's letter. I laid it on the table and started to cut
up some dried fish for lunch. Alicia came in soon
after that.

"Mr. Steele met with us older kids all morning,"
she said.

"Must have been a lot of talk in all that time."

"It wasn't all talk. First he showed us pictures of
the Oregon school. The rooms, Mama. Beds covered
with colored quilts; drawings on every wall. And the
library must have every book in the world. There's
an art room, too, with easels and big white painting
tablets."

"What else did he show you?"

"Photos of the city near the school. Stores, movie
houses, eating places, and in one, taken at night, lights
danced all over that town. Oh, Mama, I want to see
that place. Agnes felt the same. Mr. Steele noticed.
He encouraged us to attend. 'High school is the path
to a good life,' he said. And when we didn't say anything, he went on. "You'll get a real education there,
not like the one in Akusha."

"So you're thinking of going to that school?"

Alicia looked sorrowful. "No, Mama. My English
isn't good enough."

Those words made me catch my breath. Was Miss Parker right after all? Did speaking Aleut at home hurt my daughter?

Alicia noticed the letter lying on the table. "Mama, a letter from Anton!"

I opened it and read aloud.

"June 5. Friday evening. I was growing used to thinking bad news every time I saw Mr. Steele. So I was feeling low when he called us Alaska students to a meeting in his office. You can imagine my surprise when he gave us good news. 'I found money to send you all home for summer vacation. The *Aurora* leaves in a week.' I felt like jumping up and dancing, but I didn't. I just ran out of his office and grabbed every student I passed to tell them the news. A gang of us decided to celebrate. We got passes into town and spent the evening at the Indian bar. That's a merry place. Not home, but it feels more like it than any-place else in Oregon.

"June 11. Thursday afternoon. I can hardly write these words. They stick in my throat. Mr. Steele came to my class this morning to tell me there was no room for me on the *Aurora*. 'I won't take up much room,' I told him. He shook his head. 'There's noth-ing I can do. There's not an extra inch of space on the boat.' I never felt so bad. I don't know what to do. If only I could fly like a raven."

Blood rushed to Alicia's face. "Mr. Steele is a liar. He said he sends the high school students home every summer and sometimes at Christmas. And all the time he knew Anton couldn't come home. I'll never go to that school. I don't want Anton to stay there, either."

She stopped talking then because Peter, Innokenty, and Cousta came in, looking weary. Innokenty took a pipe from his pocket, and then, very slowly, he filled it from a pouch and tamped it down. After that he went to the counter for a match to light the pipe. He puffed slowly and deliberately.

"It's decided," he said. "We're going to buy the *Azian Bay Native*."

I wanted to feel something—glad, mad, scared. But my blood froze. I looked at Peter. The color of the scar above his lip turned deep red like it does when he's upset.

Only Cousta showed a spark of cheer. "Seven of us are going to Seattle to shop for the boat. Maybe we'll have one built. Nothing like this ever happened to our people before."

"Who's going?" I asked.

"Four from other villages. Three from here."

"Who from here?"

"Peter, John, and me."

"Peter?"

"We'll need him to go over the written material—contracts, instructions, things like that."

"When do you leave?"

"As soon as the *Elsie L* shows up. She's expected in a few days."

Eleven

A wet July, but there was lush growth and berries everywhere. Maybe I was more stirred up than ever in my life. There must be twenty-five people here from all over the Aleutians to greet the *Azian Bay Native*. She's due any day according to what Captain Akuke Domasoff reported on the ship's radio. Marina Domasoff, the captain's wife, her mama, Agapin, and her two sons, Mathew, twenty, and Little Akuke, twelve, are staying with us. They're from Azian Bay where my brother Sergie lives with his family.

I was busy in the kitchen making perok and seal stew for the evening meal. People were telling stories, laughing, everyone in a festive mood. I had been, too, but suddenly, a fear, lying deep, fouled my mood. I had to get off by myself. I left the rest of the food making to Nadia, picked up a basket for fish, and set out for the creek.

Sloshing barefoot through the cool, spongy ground, sniffing the fresh smell of wet dirt and leaves, I felt overcome with love for our town, for our life. I started to sing Aleut chants that Katya and I learned in Umaka. I wanted to recall every song we knew, every story we heard together. I tried to picture Katya in the here and now—how she'd look and think, how she'd react to the *Azian Bay Native*. I knew the answer in an instant. She'd scoff at Innokenty's old fashioned beliefs. I found myself wishing I could feel as she would, but I couldn't purge my dark misgivings.

The creek was crowded with trout. I returned home with a bucket full—twelve fish. Everyone was sitting at the kitchen table. Nadia, too. I never saw her in such high spirits. She and Mathew had their heads close together in a lively discussion. I figured she had curiosity about these people from the town of her birth. I served the trout and made fresh chai.

After a while, Nadia surprised me. Usually so timid, she actually suggested showing the Domasoffs the inside of the church.

"All my life I've heard about the Russian church in Akusha. I've heard it's like a palace," Marina said as she got up to leave. Everyone else joined the tour.

I stayed behind to make sweet bread. My hands were dusty with flour when the group returned, talking in excited voices.

"I never dreamed there were so many icons in all the Aleutians," Marina said.

"And those glittering chandeliers and sunbeams sparkling on the stained glass windows," Agapin added.

I glanced at Little Akuke, the only silent member of the group.

There was a question in his eye. I let him know I noticed.

"We only have one church in Azian Bay," he said.

I nodded.

"I saw another church here at the end of the beach. Who goes there?"

"That's the Baptist mission. It's closed now," I explained.

"That's not an Aleut church," he said, looking confused.

"They came here on their own, uninvited, to take care of orphans, they said."

I was spared more questions about that unwelcome subject by Paulie, who came running in to announce a salmon fry on the beach. The others left. I stayed behind to finish the bread. But my last remark—"they came here to take care of orphans"— chased itself around in my head. Katya was one of those orphans.

The memory rose and wrapped its icy fingers around me. We'd been parted for two years when, without anyone saying anything, I knew she was on her way to Akusha. For three nights, I saw her in my dreams, traveling by boat, by foot, by sled; and in the last dream, on the back of a walrus. I thought I was still dreaming when on the fourth day I watched her come down the gangway of the *Aurora*. I ran to her, but before I reached her side, Pastor Lowell whisked her away. I didn't know then that she'd been orphaned. The lung disease that attacked Papa also killed Katya's papa and aunt, her only relatives. Others in Umaka died from it, too. There was no one to care for Katya, so the council decided to send her to the Baptist mission orphanage in Akusha.

I walked past the mission three times the day Katya arrived, hoping to catch a glimpse of her, but the yard was empty. That night, even though I'd never been inside the mission, I knocked on the door. Thelma Lowell, the pastor's wife, answered. "Good evening."

"Katya from Iliaka is my aacha."

"I'm sorry, no visitors tonight."

I returned the next night and the next and the next, and always the same message—"No visitors tonight."

I was no longer in school, but I went to the schoolyard at recess one day, determined to see her. "The hills are calling to me," I said in the way of an invitation.

"Too busy," she replied.

I arched my eyebrow.

She went on to describe the constant round of activities at the mission. She and the other girls got up at five every morning to do laundry. They had to boil sheets in a big tub and then beat them clean with a wooden paddle. Some mornings they didn't finish the wash in time to get to school. After school she and the others did chores. Evenings were taken up with sewing, crocheting, embroidering, and knitting things to sell to the crews of visiting ships. That's how the mission got some of its money. Late in the evening, right before bed, there were readings and music in the mission parlor.

So, it was a while before I set eyes on Katya again, not until the day of the water blessing ceremony in January. Father Paul, wearing a long, flowing white satin robe, led the procession. He was followed by the chiefs, elders, banner carriers, male singers, and then the rest of us. Father waved his scepter and blessed every house he passed—except the mission. There, he paused for a second, crossed himself, and made a wide detour around it. We wound our way up the hills to a tiny lake nested in a deep valley. At that spot, Father Paul blessed the frozen water while the others waved brightly colored banners.

I remember wishing Katya was with me. Looking around, I was surprised to see her standing on a distant hillock. I was puzzled. Why was she watching the ceremony rather than joining it? I walked over to ask her, but a strange look in her eyes, maybe it was fear, made me hesitate. Instead, I invited her to walk on the beach. On the way, we heard the high-pitched call of emperor geese, reminding me of the many autumns in Akusha when Katya and I watched these geese fly in from the north at the same time the Canada geese were winging it to the south. I think her heart pounded like mine to see the sky alive with the sight and sound of the birds.

"Watching the geese makes me feel like I'm back in Umaka," Katya said in English.

"Why don't you speak in Aleut?" I asked her.

"They want us to speak in English at school."

"It's the same for everyone. But when we leave school, we speak in our tongue."

"They want us to speak English all the time," Katya explained.

I felt like shaking her. Why did she have to do everything the missionaries told her? She even let them cut her hair ear length with bangs across her forehead, her beautiful long hair that she used to let hang loose and when she'd run against the wind, it would billow out behind her like a sail. Pretty soon, Katya wouldn't feel like my aacha anymore.

Katya hadn't said a word about her absence from the water blessing ceremony. I was thinking of opening the subject when the clouds darkened and moved toward us. We jumped up and started for home.

As we neared Leonty's house, I heard the familiar ping of his hammer. "I wonder what Leonty's making now," I said as I motioned Katya to follow me into his yard. He was building a box shaped like a coffin, child-sized. Parascovia came to our side and said there'd been a death. It was Tanya, a mission girl. Katya knew Tanya had been sick, but she never expected her to die.

Katya and I didn't talk on the walk back to the mission. But as we neared the door, she said, "Tanya isn't Russian Orthodox."

"I never heard of an Aleut who wasn't Russian Orthodox," I said.

"Pastor Lowell preached a sermon. 'You're Americans,' he said, 'and you should have an American religion, not a foreign one.'"

I closed my mouth until I calmed down. Then, in a soft voice, I asked her, "What was the religion of your mama and her mama before?"

Katya's eye started to blink. That tic started after she moved into the mission. "Pastor Lowell said that baptism in his church will teach us about Jesus. It will save us from sin. It's the path to a good and moral life. That's what he preaches."

"That's no different from what Father Paul tells us."

"Pastor Lowell said Father Paul is ignorant. And the Russian Orthodox religion has no soul."

A great fear took hold of me. "Katya, will they baptize you?"

Her silence sent tremors down my spine.

My head ached when I left Katya and the pain got worse a few minutes later when I saw Makary, another mission orphan, also building a child-sized casket. "It's for Tanya," he said when I walked over to watch him.

I wondered if I heard right. "For Tanya?"

He turned his eyes away from me when he next spoke. "I'm just following Pastor Lowell's instruction."

Why two coffins? I wanted to ask someone who could explain. I decided to visit Aunt Sophie.

A council meeting was in progress at her house. Father Paul was there, too. I sat down on the floor and listened. Leonty was talking. "I was building a box for our departed child, Tanya, when Pastor Lowell came to see me. He said that because Tanya converted to his church, he would bury her. Tanya is an Aleut child. She should be buried in the Aleut way, by a Russian priest."

Usually the elders are silent for a while after someone expresses an opinion. Not this day. Everyone had something to say.

Ruff whipped off his glasses and said in a hoarse voice, "They deny our church the right to bury our own member because they baptized her."

"And to make matters worse," Leonty said, "Pastor Lowell is going to bury her in our Russian graveyard."

I thought the Old Man was going to burst a blood vessel. "If they say she's Baptist, why don't they bury her in the Baptist cemetery?"

Leonty pursed his lips when he answered the Old Man. "The Baptist cemetery is promyshlennik ground."

I remember Innokenty sitting quiet through the whole discussion. Then he told a story.

"My grandmother used to tell us about a time when the ravens were the only birds on our island. Then magpies came and stole the ravens' eggs. The magpies couldn't lay eggs here because they weren't from this country. That's why they stole the ravens' eggs. When the eggs hatched, the magpies taught the young ravens to fly with them. The grown ravens were upset. They chased the magpies out of this country. Not the young ravens, though. Those they carried back in their beaks. So the story goes."

Everyone sat in silence. After a while, Innokenty spoke again. "We'll send a petition to the chief of the Baptists, to their main office."

"That won't stop Pastor Lowell from burying Tanya tomorrow," John said.

"Maybe it will stop him next time," Innokenty answered.

The following morning, the chief and elders composed a petition.

"We Aleuts in Akusha regret that the Baptist mission enticed an Aleut girl to convert. We regret that in exchange for a bit of bread, they claimed her soul. We regret that they wanted to deny our church the right to bury our own member because they had baptized her. They wanted to desecrate the place of rest of our fathers and mothers by burying their convert in our churchyard. They wanted to violate the

Aleuts' right to decide who is to be buried in our own cemetery. They made a game of the sacredness of our cemetery." The petition ended with a plea to restore all Aleut children at the mission to the Aleut community.

The next day, we carried that petition from house to house and asked everyone, adults and older children, to sign it. All did, except seven mission children. Katya was one of those seven. She and I were standing in the mission yard when I handed her the petition. She gave it back, shaking her head. I turned and walked away from her. She ran after me, and when she caught up, she said, "Tatty, Sunday at church, Pastor Lowell is going to baptize me."

I felt like someone had split my head open with an ax. "I'm wondering why you're doing it."

"The people at the mission are my family."

"Katya, I'm thinking about how you feel when your mission family insults our Aleut people."

Katya's eye began to blink again.

I didn't say more. I didn't want to fight. Ah, Katya, why did you turn away from us? Why didn't I do something? Why didn't I say something to stop you? Suddenly, the *Azian Bay Native* was on my mind. Should I have spoken up? Should I have tried to stop our people from buying that ship? Innokenty, I wish I could forget your warning.

TWELVE

Our town buzzed like a hive of bees on this warm summer afternoon—everyone outside doing this and that. Wandering on the beach, Alicia and I stopped to watch Sophie, Bullshit John, and their son, Michael, load their skiff for a trip across the bay to fish camp. Near them, Matfay was getting his baidarka ready for a hunting trip. We strolled past him to Ollie Larsen's herring dock where Nicky works. Ollie has red hair and with his excitable nature his cheeks often match. Nicky was gutting the fish and removing the fins and Ollie was salting and packing them in barrels. After a few minutes, we walked on, stopping in front of Evdokie's house. Evdokie's family was pulling in a seine net full of jumping salmon. Alicia and I pitched in, tugging on the net until we hauled it ashore.

Then everyone went into action—Evdokie and her mother, Parascovia, cleaning the fish; her daughter, Akinia, Alicia, and I carrying them over to Simon; Simon filleting them on a big flat rock, leaving them connected at the tail so they'd hang on the drying rack; Leonty and us girls hanging the filleted fish in neat rows on the drying rack. A whole gang of us working together, our movements blending like voices in the church choir, no sound except the soft swish of water against the shore. Then, like a blast of wind, Cousta whooshed into the yard, breathless, pointing to a vessel sailing into the bay. Evdokie and Leonty stayed with the fish; the rest of us ran to the pier. On the way, I heard the ship's horn. It was different from the low muffled whistles I was used to. This one was high-pitched, shrill, like someone screaming. I felt suddenly cold and huddled my shoulders. But a few minutes later, on the dock, I was spellbound, watching the slow approach of the *Azian Bay Native*. She was big, too big, maybe more than four dory lengths long. She had a pilot house and two sails, one forward, the other aft. Her sides were high, shiny brown, with the name *Azian Bay Native* painted in bold white letters. When she anchored, I saw the narrow planks of the deck shining like mirrors. I wanted to cheer our new boat, but I turned my back on her, trying to get rid of a heavy feeling in my stomach. Then I heard the sweet ring of Peter's voice—"Little Wren, Little Wren." I swiveled around and saw Peter waving from the side of the boat.

"Who's that standing next to him?" Alicia asked.

It was a man with dark skin, the color of seal liver, like Anton's. And his hair was shorter than most of our men's, like the students at Indian school. My breath caught in my throat as I tried to tell Alicia, "It's Anton."

He had grown so thin and his eyes had become dark with pain rather than light with dreams as they were when he left. When he leaned over and hugged me, I ran my hand along his forehead, trying to erase the furrowed lines.

Anton didn't speak on the way home; he just peered intently at everything around, as if he was trying to etch it into his brain. Once home, visitors came one after the other. I busied myself putting up clam soup and cutting up a smoked salmon Matfay had brought over. The conversation was slow. I think people were waiting to hear about the Indian school. But Anton was mute on that subject. He needed time to get used to things. He'd tell us about Oregon another time.

I didn't have a chance to talk to Peter until we went to bed late that night. Then I asked the question that had been on my mind all day, how Anton came to be on the boat.

"Little Wren, I collected Anton at his school."

"You went to his school?" I was amazed. My mind blurred when I tried to imagine traveling around the world looking for Anton's school. "How did you find it?"

"This is how. A captain at the boat harbor in Seattle gave me directions to the train that goes to

Salem. He said, 'Get off the train at the Salem stop, then ask someone the way to the trolley into town.'"

"A trolley?"

"Every time I turned around in that place, I'd see something strange. A trolley is a single train car that's powered like our light bulb."

"If it's as dull as our light bulb, that trolley must travel very slow."

"It moves as fast as an engine dory. I was in Salem before I had time to look around. Then, I asked a clerk in a cigar store for directions to the Indian school bus. He pointed to a corner a couple blocks away. I waited on that corner so long I began to think the clerk was mistaken. But finally a bus came and drove straight to Anton's school."

My eyes grew wide. "What did it look like?"

"First thing I saw was two huge red brick buildings, one for classes, the other for sleeping. I went into the first one. I walked down a long narrow hall. Classrooms on both sides—so many classrooms. At the far end of the hall, I came to a door with a sign that read, 'Principal.' I walked right in. Mr. Steele was sitting behind an old, shabby-looking desk. I wondered why he didn't mend it. He looked up. I told him my name, but he didn't remember me. It didn't matter. 'It's time for Anton to visit home,' I said. He cleared his throat and gave me that missionary look, like he'll do anything in the world for me. But his words didn't match. 'I'd like to send Anton home this summer, but the Bureau ship doesn't have half an inch of extra space.'

"Anton will travel home with me on the *Azian Bay Native*," I told him. He looked suspicious. 'What kind of a boat is that? I don't want our boys and girls taking dangerous trips on small craft.' I smiled then and took photos of the boat from my backpack. Mr. Steele cocked his head and squinted at me. 'I never saw that boat before. Whose is it?' 'Our Aleut people bought it.'

"Mr. Steele's face turned bright red. Oh, oh, he's mad at us for buying the boat, I thought. But no, he stood up and gave my hand a vigorous shake. Then he motioned me to follow him to the library at the end of the hall. I told him Anton would be returning for the fall term. He nodded as we walked into the library. Tatty, books line every wall from floor to ceiling. I'd like to spend a season in that room. Then Anton ran up to me. That's the end of the story."

I had no words. I was too choked up. We lay quietly in each other's arms for a few minutes. Then, something else came into my mind. "Peter, did you have this plan in mind before you left for Seattle?"

"Yes."

"I'm thinking you never mentioned it."

Peter didn't answer me. But I figured out, his silence on this subject was his way of protecting me from disappointment if the plan didn't work out. I put my arm around Peter's waist and slept in that position all night.

In every letter, Anton expressed longing to come home. But he seemed so restless. He'd go out, come back in a few minutes, then turn around and leave again. Same thing when he was in the house. His eyes darted from here to there, but settled on nothing. Sometimes he'd examine a chess piece, but he didn't play a game with anyone. Other times, he'd whittle on a piece of driftwood. That, too, didn't hold his attention. I tried to understand what was troubling him. Maybe the space seemed tight after the big school in Oregon.

One morning, I said, "Maybe you'd like to build a room for yourself."

It was like he came suddenly awake after a long sleep. He glanced at me, then down at his hands. His thin, graceful fingers looked like they were made for holding books. Was he wondering if they could turn to carpentry? After a few minutes, he laughed. "I've never built anything. But when I was a little kid, I used to dream about being like Leonty. Maybe building my own room is a beginning." He jumped up then and ran out, probably to tell others his plan.

I guess he hadn't let Simon and Simon's uncle Matfay in on it, for next morning they called for him to go fishing on the *Azian Bay Native*. He gave them a mysterious smile. "I'm busy," he said. Simon looked puzzled. Then Anton explained. "I'm taking up carpentry. To start, I'm adding a room onto our house."

After the *Azian Bay Native* left for fishing, some of the brotherhood members came over to talk to Anton about the new room. They knew the NS store had a supply of lumber. The problem was paying for it. "There's no cash in the community fund. We used it all to buy the boat," Ruff told him.

I knew we could buy the lumber on credit, but I hated being in debt to the store. I've felt that way ever since Tom Jones, the store manager before Ralph, took Ilarion's house away. He called it a foreclosure, a trade for Ilarion's store debt. We thought it was a joke. No one believed Tom Jones would steal Ilarion's house. But he did. When we complained to the captain of the revenue cutter, he told us it was legal. After that, many of us refused credit at the store.

But this was different. Anton's happiness was reason to break my rule. "We can buy the lumber on credit. I'll pay it off by selling baskets."

Parascovia and Aunt Sophie, who were visiting, said they'd do the same. I knew we'd get the money together. Anton looked like he was going to leap from his chair and dance the way Leonty used to.

His pleasure sparked my desire for him to forget about school and stay home for good. But moments later, I felt ashamed for putting myself before him. But was I? Was Anton's mind as divided as mine? I had a chance to find an answer that evening when

Alicia and Anton were talking about his school. They were squatting on the floor by the stove and I was sitting in the rocker across the room from them weaving a basket for Little Hunch's seventieth name day.

"You sounded lonely in your letters," Alicia said.

Anton bit his lip and then took a deep breath. "Many times I thought I'd die from it."

"Did you feel like that when you spent a summer with Mavra and Sasha in New Harbor?"

"I was used to things there. Everything in Oregon is strange."

"Strange?"

"The food. Like bleeding cow meat and fish that smelled funny. I think it was old. And dessert, the usual dessert, ugh, tapioca pudding, pale yellow and lumpy like vomit."

"I'd hate to live someplace where the food was bad."

"Oh, I liked some things—the bread, canned peaches, and apples, there were always plenty of apples. Maybe the worst part was the insults."

"The insults?"

"Mr. Steele told us education was the path to respect. So I expected the teachers to honor us. But when I'd talk in class, they'd act disgusted and criticize the way I spoke. Those criticisms felt like a fish hook in my soul. The other students got corrected all the time, too. So we just stopped talking in class. Then the teachers got mad at us for our silence."

"At least you students were together on this."

"That felt good. And then again, it felt bad."

"Well, which was it?"

"Good to feel close to the other students; bad to be … well, there are no easy words." He paused, looked at the ceiling, his brow wrinkled in thought. "It's like all boats heave in a storm at sea but that doesn't make dories identical to skiffs and baidarkas to fishing vessels. Yet, our teachers and the books they give us to read treat all of us—Hopis, Navajos, Peublos, Papagos, Cheyenne, Eskimos, Aleuts—like we're carbon copies of each other. No mention of the different ways we live, believe, hunt, eat. That's what poisoned my interest in school."

"Then you're not going back there?" Alicia asked, a hopeful tone in her voice.

"I don't know about that. There was a good side, an excitement, something always going on, guys visiting in each other's rooms, playing cards, telling stories about our lives. And on weekends, we got passes into town. We'd walk around looking in different shops and if we had money we'd buy gifts or go to the movies. Here, in Akusha, we show the same movie over and over again, but in Salem, there are eight movie houses and each one shows a different picture every few days. That was fun, but the high point was the church choirs."

Afraid I'd miss something he was going to say about the choirs, I went over and sat on the floor next to him. Anton turned toward me.

"Mama, I wish you'd have heard the Methodist church choir last Christmas. It had as many singers as there are people in Akusha, and they sang the most beautiful music I ever heard—the *Messiah* it was called."

Anton was wound up. Even without prompting, he kept talking. "Sometimes, I left the others and walked by the Willamette. I swear, that river looked like it flowed forever. I'd watch the current and dream I was a raven following its course all the way to Akusha. Then, when I'd get back to my room, I'd weep with desire to see my people, eat my food, walk around my village. Sometimes, I'd stay awake all night living in those dreams. One of the dreams was about you and Papa, your eyes smiling when I graduated from the seminary." Then looking at the ceiling, he said, "That's why I have to stick with high school. If only I can."

"Maybe someone else can train as priest. You don't have to," Alicia said.

"Many times when I listened to Simon and Matfay describe their hunting adventures, I thought I'd like that life, too. Then I'd remember how bored I was when I went to sea in Alexi's baidarka, hour after hour sitting and waiting, all for a few minutes' excitement. My heart never beat fast about those trips like it does when I imagine being priest of the Aleutians."

Alicia started twisting her braid. "Let's go down to the dock and look at the new boat."

"Okay. Say, Mama, come with us," Anton said.

I shook my head. Innokenty's and Leonty's warnings were still nagging at me. I didn't want to acknowledge that boat. I wished she'd disappear.

Anton didn't know much about carpentry. When we had a Russian school here, all the boys learned to work with wood. Now, like Anton, most of them have no training in that skill. Victor, Marie's son, who was the same age as Anton, offered to help him build the room, but he had no experience, either. Others who might have helped were away. So Anton and Victor started the job themselves. The first day, the Old Man and Leonty ambled over to watch them. Those two showed up every day after that. And in their quiet comments and demonstrations, they trained Anton and Victor.

The boys finished the room in ten days. Then Anton turned his attention to building bookshelves for it. "I don't know if I'm more pleased with the room or the bookcase," Anton told visitors who came to admire his work. I admired it, too. But I was puzzled. I wondered—maybe hoped—that the new room meant Anton planned to stay home. But the

bookshelves? He owned no books. He must be thinking of making space for seminary books.

As the days went by, Anton's interest in the new
room waned. He grew restless again. He couldn't sit
still and nothing held his interest. He crabbed at Alicia
and Paulie. And I noticed him biting his lower lip a
lot. One night when Victor was visiting, I heard
Anton say, "This place is so damn boring. Nothing's
going on."

"It's slow in summer when so many are gone."

"It's slower in winter when everyone's inside,
slower than a snail climbing a steep rock," Anton
muttered, biting harder on his lip.

So, he was going back to school. A scream was
rising in my throat. I felt like crying out, "Don't go,
don't go." I remembered Mama saying those very
words to Papa before his last trip on the Sammy Jay.
I remembered all the times Papa left and stayed away
most of the year. And now Anton, doing the same.
Don't go.

The *Aurora* was in port, due to leave the next
day on its last trip to Oregon before the fall term.
Where was Anton? He'd left early in the morning
and no one had seen him by nightfall. I went to bed,
but I couldn't sleep. I listened for his step. A couple
of times, I got up and looked out the window to the
main path in town. No Anton. It started to grow
light. Where was he? I couldn't stay in bed any longer;
I dressed and sat by the window watching. Someone

in the distance was staggering down the path. He came closer. It was Anton, so drunk he had to run to keep from falling. He fell anyhow, right after he opened the door to the house. I went to him; he didn't speak; I covered him and sat in a chair nearby, my stomach knotted with fear. Maybe Anton didn't fit here or in Oregon. What would become of him?

A few hours later, Anton woke up, looking pale. But he was cold sober. He didn't say a word while he packed his gear. He didn't have to. I knew his decision. We walked together to the pier. Right before he boarded the *Aurora,* he put his arm around my shoulder. "This time I've figured out what I want, Mama."

After the *Aurora* left, I gazed for a long time at the *Azian Bay Native.* She'd just returned from her first fishing trip. It was hard to believe that we Aleut people owned this splendid vessel, more beautiful even than the *Aurora.* I pictured Anton as priest sailing on her to all the Aleutian Islands. I saw myself at his side when the ship sailed to Umaka.

Thirteen

The summer bloom was fading fast—paths cluttered with willow leaves, the air saturated with downy fuzz sent out by the open sheaths of fireweed, and the mountaintops dusted with snow.

The bloom in our house paled, too, after Anton left. Reminders were everywhere—his tools on the porch, the empty bookshelves in his room, the low stool he built to sit next to the fire. But no Anton. Keep busy, I told myself, as a I started weaving another container for cigarette packs. Ships' crews bought as many as I could make. We were still paying off the store debt for Anton's lumber.

Nicky and Paulie kept themselves busy, too—collecting driftwood for the stove, filling the coal bin, and, to Paulie's delight, finding heavy stones to use in his first bola. For many hours during the past week, Paulie sat on the floor watching Nicky drill holes into the stones and tie them to lines. When that job was done, Nickie trained Paulie to swing the bola hard enough to land in the center of a flock of birds. Paulie practiced for three days. On the fourth, today, Nicky invited Paulie to hunt eiders with his bola.

Paulie shrieked after looking under his sleeping mat where he stored it. "My bola—it's's gone!" He turned around and faced Alicia. "Where is it?"

Alicia had been salty as sea water since Anton left. It seems like taunting Paulie was her only interest. She shrugged, a big smirk on her face.

"Maybe the eiders will decide not to wait for us," Nicky said.

I gave Alicia a hard look. She started to laugh, wildly, like people do when they're trying to stifle tears. She pulled his bola from inside her paint box, laid it on the table, and rushed out of the house.

After everyone left, I picked up my weaving but my mind was on Peter, due home from Bolisof any time now. He was there helping Father Burdofsky with two marriages. A funeral was scheduled for the day after the weddings. Two Bolisof brothers had drowned when their dinghy crashed into a boulder. I wondered how people could laugh at a wedding one day and weep at a funeral the next. I'd ask Peter about it when he returned. I sighed, picturing his homecoming. The door flew open and there he was.

We sat quietly together drinking chai. Then Peter lifted a piece of weaving from his duffel bag. He knew my enthusiasm for new patterns and brought them to me from other villages. I stared at the pattern trying to figure out how to duplicate it.

"Everybody is away?" Peter asked.

"Paulie's hunting eiders with Nicky. Nadia went berry picking. And I don't know where crazy Alicia went. She left in a fit."

There was a note of hesitation in his voice when he spoke next.

"And Anton?"

I choked back a sob, so Peter knew Anton had left. "Last night I dreamed about Anton," I told him. "In the dream, Anton turned into Constantine Churginoff, the Azian Bay boy who killed himself at Indian high school. I lay under the covers shivering, thinking maybe Anton will despair like Constantine did, thinking maybe he'll never come back, like Daria Snigerin from New Harbor."

Peter rose, picked up his violin, and played a tender song we'd heard in the NS store. "I Wanna go Home," it was called. I joined in with my guitar. When we finished, Peter sat on the floor by my chair, his head resting on my knee. "Little Wren, I'm afraid for Anton, too."

"You never said anything."

"I think I've been afraid since the day I told Innokenty … uh, the day I pledged Anton's life to make up for failing his dream of me as priest."

I was stunned. I thought all the worry about Anton lived in my heart.

"Foolish thoughts," he said. "Forget them."

John walked in at that moment, and seeing us sitting so close he started to leave, but Peter jumped up and greeted him. And then John said, "I've got some putty to plug the cracks around the church windows before it gets any colder." Peter put on his parka and went out with John.

I felt restless after he left, so I went to see Nellie. No one was home. I went next door and knocked on her sister Anna's door.

Anna's husband, Big Shot, answered. He got that nickname from acting like he was always owed something. "I'm looking for Nellie," I said.

"It's hard to get rest when people keep rapping on your door," John grumbled.

I started to leave, and he yelled after me, "I heard them say something about lingonberries."

I knew where to find them. There's a large lingonberry crop in the hills behind the mission. Just as I expected, Anna and Nellie were there, hidden among the tall grass and lupine. I sat in the grass with them. No one could see us, but we could see the goings-on below. Matfay and Alexi were loading their baidarkas for a hunting trip. Ruff was helping Innokenty repair the siding on his house. Sophie and her neighbor, Pletanida, were cutting grass in the churchyard with long scissors. And children were gathering shells and rocks on the beach.

"I was telling Anna what happened last night when I visited Sylvia," Nellie said. "You know

Chester Brown? He lives in the house next to Sylvia's."

"That bearded fellow who's second boss at the supply station?" I asked. Our Aleut men don't grow heavy beards; they don't have enough hair on their faces.

Nellie nodded and went on. "I looked out Sylvia's window and saw right into his house."

What could Nellie have seen? Her voice sounded mysterious.

"Akinia was in there."

"Akinia. In Chester Brown's house?"

"In Chester Brown's arms."

It felt like a cold wind blew through me. I wrapped my arms around my shoulders.

"Tatty, what's wrong?" Nellie asked.

"Nell, I'm thinking we should warn Akinia about Chester. Tell her what happened to Katya after she married Buddy Thomas."

"Lots of young people fool around like that, Tatty. Let's wait and see, yes, wait and see. Besides, Katya and Buddy happened so long ago." Nellie stood up. "I'm going to look for some blueberries."

Anna followed her, but I stayed in the grass thinking about that time twenty years before when Katya first told me she was going to marry Buddy Thomas. We were sitting at this very spot. I was stricken. "A white man?" I'd said.

"Tatty, for six years I've been living with whites. I go to a white church. I'm baptized in a white religion. In the evenings I listen to white stories."

"Your heart is Aleut, Katya."

Katya looked away, her brow puckered in thought. After a while, she said, "You know I had nightmares after moving to the mission, every night. Well, it was Thelma Lowell, pastor's wife, a white woman, who comforted me every time I woke up sweating. It was Thelma Lowell who tutored me in English, who taught me to knit and crochet and play the piano. Thelma Lowell was like my godmother."

I should have answered her. But I couldn't find words. I had a terrible feeling. I had to get away from her. Without a backward glance, I dashed to my house, opened my sleeping mat, buried my head under a cover, and tried to blot Katya out. Mama knew something was wrong. She knelt beside me and waited until I told her about Katya's marriage. She reminded me of Father Paul's sermon the Sunday before when he had said, "Don't live for yourself. Follow the path of righteousness and give to others." I felt rotten, like I'd spit on my aacha's celebration. I wanted to make it up to her.

"Mama, I'm thinking about a special wedding gift for Katya, not a a bird skin parka, not a grass weaving, something unusual. But what?"

Mama thought a while. "I saw some beautiful golden stones, shining like little suns, at the foot of the waterfall, the one near the blackberry patch. I told Sophie about them. She said they were amber, very rare, and very beautiful for a necklace."

"Oh, Mama, let's go after them." I was so excited about the stones, I forgot for a while about Buddy Thomas. Mama and I set out that very day, and found several handfuls of amber, enough for a necklace. First thing, back at home, I started weaving a fine band for stringing the stones.

I worked on that string of stones like I had a fever and finished it in time for the wedding, set for the following week. The night before, I helped Katya attach lace collars and cuffs to her organdy wedding dress. "Try it on, Katya. I want to see how it looks." And then, as she twirled around showing me her gown, I went over and coiled the amber beads around her neck. She made a low buzzing sound like a milling swarm of bees. Her eyes glistened when she looked at me. "This necklace will be my charm, my aacha bringing luck into my life. I'll wear it always." I'd shuddered. And a quaking in my stomach never stopped all through the wedding. She was wearing those beads when I found her.

Fourteen

It seemed like winter flew through our country on the wings of an eagle. The snow melted fast and by early April every path in town was a sea of mud. Nellie and I sloshed through it, ankle deep, searching for driftwood to heat the rocks at the steam bath. It was Thursday, the day the sisterhood women meet there. The wood was wet, but with the gift of patience, we nursed embers into flames until the fire was hot enough to heat water. We had just finished pouring water over rocks to make steam when Anna, Evdokie, Parascovia, and Anesia showed up. They piled their clothes on the porch, came into the steam room, and sat down with Nellie and me on benches lining the walls. The warmth and the soft sound of the women's voices made me drowsy. I leaned against the wall, half asleep and half listening.

Nellie was telling tales on Anna's husband, Big Shot. "Anna was sick, had the dripping shits all night, too weak hardly to move. And in the morning that big strong husband of hers told her to get up and gather wood for the stove. So she did. And when she returned, he sent her right back out to catch fish while he warmed himself by the fire."

Anna had a twinkle of triumph in her eyes as Big Shot's shame was exposed. She stretched, yawned, and then began to chatter about this and that—her child's losing a tooth, Ilarion's home brew party, the arrival in town of the marshal's bride.

"Nothing but talk, talk, talk," Nellie said in a gruff voice, imitating the Old Man. She was about to say more when the door opened and Sylvia walked in, wearing one of those bathing suits I'd seen in movies. Her neck flushed when she saw we were bare. I figured she'd remove the suit, but she didn't. I wondered why she was there. I don't remember any promyshlennik ever visiting the steam bath, except Father Paul, of course.

Nellie explained Sylvia's presence. "I went over to listen to her new Victrola yesterday and when I mentioned our Thursday steam baths, she asked if she could join us. So okay, I said. But I forgot to tell her we steam our skin, not some material wrapped around it."

Nellie was talking in Aleut. None of us switched to English for Sylvia because Anesia didn't understand it. As we talked, Nellie sometimes interrupted to translate for Sylvia. But even when she didn't, Sylvia looked contented. I think she just wanted to belong somewhere.

School was out and Alicia and Agnes came in, followed by Nadia. After the girls undressed, everyone's eyes fastened on Nadia's fat belly. No one said anything about it. We were waiting for her to open the subject.

But she never mentioned it. Not one word. I'd been waiting for weeks, wondering about it. Peter, too.

"Maybe you should say something to her," he'd said to me a couple days before.

"She'll tell us when she's ready."

"Maybe she's afraid to tell us."

"Afraid, afraid of what?" Something made my mind fly back to the time of Marie's pregnancy eighteen years earlier. It was the result of a rape by a sailor on a navy ship. Marie was living at the mission then. "Peter," I said, "when Marie was pregnant from that rape, the missionaries, even Father Paul, kept at her like a gull pecking at the flesh of a dead fish. 'Who's the father? Who's the father?' She didn't want to talk about it. But they wouldn't stop. Then, one night, Pastor Lowell went into Marie's bedroom and asked again about the father. Marie didn't answer. He shook his finger in her face and said, 'Tell me, Marie, who is that prince of the night that you protect beyond your good name and your child's good name and the good name of our mission?' That was when Marie decided to leave the mission. I don't want to nag Nadia like that." A chilling thought came into my mind. "Peter, do you think Nadia was raped?"

"I don't know what to think, Little Wren."

The women in the steam bath looked equally puzzled. But they kept quiet, except Sylvia. She mentioned it right off. "Say, Nadia, I didn't know you were pregnant. That's swell."

Nadia smiled, but still said nothing.

"Are you getting married?" Sylvia asked.

Nadia didn't answer.

Nellie interrupted the cross-examination. "You've had enough for your first sweat bath," she said to Sylvia in English.

Sylvia nodded, but didn't move, so we ended our bath to get her out of there.

On the way home, we noticed people going to the schoolhouse. I stopped Ruff and asked if the mail boat was in.

He bobbed his head and then moved it in the direction of the school, meaning the mail was being sorted.

"I'll go after it," Nadia offered. The rest of us went home.

We had just started to eat when Nadia walked in clasping a letter in her hand. Her cheeks were flushed and tiny flecks of light danced in her eyes. "The Domasoffs are coming on the next trip of the *Azian Bay Native*. She's due next week."

The Domasoffs had only visited here once, when they came to greet the *Azian Bay Native*. They had no relatives here. No celebrations were planned that

I knew of. "The whole Domasoff family is coming here for a visit?"

Nadia laughed. "They're coming to talk to Innokenty."

"To talk to Innokenty?" I was puzzled.

"To talk to Innokenty about a wedding."

A light dawned. Nadia wasn't raped after all. Mathew Domasoff was the baby's papa. Mathew was coming to ask the council for Nadia as wife. I waited to hear more, but Alicia couldn't hold her tongue.

"Whose wedding? "

"Maybe mine," Nadia answered.

I felt the sweet sensation of warm tears on my cheeks.

The Domasoffs arrived on a Friday. The wedding was set for Sunday, nine days later. Father Burdofsky traveled here with the Domasoffs, so everything was ready. Nadia's stomach was ready, too. Two days after the Domasoffs showed up, she gave birth to Ignaty, named after Nadia's papa.

I prayed for clear weather on Nadia's wedding day, but rain was beating against the house so hard I thought the clouds were angry. We didn't have enough oil skins and rain coats to cover our wedding clothes on the way to the church, so we took turns. Peter, Nicky, and Paulie left first. Then Paulie ran back with rain gear for Alicia and me. I carried Ignaty inside my oil skins.

I'm used to being short, but I always felt tall in church, in the presence of the gilded ornaments, the candlelight, and the grand rituals. A soft warmth flowed through me when I looked at Nadia and Mathew standing side by side, their cheeks glowing like they'd been polished, their hands trembling. Mathew wore a black broadcloth suit and Nadia, a white organdy dress. White against black like snow-flakes on sand.

Nicky, the best man, stood beside the wedding couple, but his eyes and smile were fixed on Marie. I glanced at her. Her eyes sparkled like the bride's. What was this? I always looked on Nicky and Marie as brother and sister. They lived at each other's houses plenty of times in earlier years.

There was a hush in the room as Father Burdofsky and Peter made an entrance through the central door of the inner sanctum. Reminding himself of his responsibilities, Nicky handed Nadia and Mathew kerchiefs for their heads and candles trimmed with ribbon bows. Then the three of them approached the altar. Father held a large crucifix in one hand and a book of services in the other. Peter carried a silver salver on a small gold tray. As Father placed the wedding rings on the tray for a blessing, one fell to the floor. Peter smiled at me as he bent over to pick up the ring, maybe remembering, like I was, how our wedding rings fell off the tray, too.

Peter went back to the inner room and returned with a huge candelabrum holding a single lighted candle. After handing the lighted candle to Father, he rested his eyes on me again. My face colored, like I was a bride, too.

Father lit the wedding couple's candles while he chanted the service. The choir answered his chants. Father put the rings on Nadia's and Mathew's fingers, waved incense from a censor around them three times, and handed Peter and Nicky decorated crowns to hold above the couple's heads for a procession around the church. Nicky and Peter had to hustle to keep those crowns poised in the air.

When they returned to the front of the church, Father gave Nadia and Mathew a ceremonial cup filled with wine. Oh oh! Marie spilled some on her dress. Red wine on a white dress, like a spatter of blood. She stared down on it, frowning, but Father distracted her by whispering something first in her ear, then in Mathew's. Following his instructions, Nadia and Mathew walked to opposite sides of the church and prostrated themselves, Mathew before a picture of Christ, and Nadia in front of the Virgin and child. The ritual ended after they touched their heads to the floor three times. They rose, joined hands, wrapped themselves into their rain coats, and left the church.

The rest of us did the same, running against the rain the fifty yards to the community hall for the reception. No whites attended the service, but Sylvia and Ralph, Horace Gump, the marshal, his new wife, Serena, and Mr. Tulliver, Paulie's teacher, were waiting at the hall when we arrived. The atmosphere at the reception was merry. Alicia had decorated the hall with streamers and balloons; the table was crowded with dried fish, sea urchin eggs, seal oil, and home-baked bread and cakes. Old-timers danced and sang and played their instruments, and some of the young people jumped up and danced with them. Nicky and Marie did a Russian folk dance they learned from Father Paul's wife, swirling, stamping their feet, throwing out their arms, and laughing all the while.

Alexi was trying to pull the bride from her chair. "C'mon, little sister, I'll twirl you around the room."

Nadia wouldn't budge. After Alexi moved on, she and Mathew started to whisper, looking very solemn. My heart skipped some beats. Was something wrong? I watched them closely. Nadia was chewing on her bottom lip. Mathew was twisting his long black necktie. I was about to go to them when Alexi asked me to dance. I smiled, remembering the time in Umaka he had asked me to teach him the dances Matrona showed me. I got up and we stamped around the room. But I kept glancing at Nadia and Mathew.

When I sat down, they came to me. "Mathew and I have no house in Azian Bay," Nadia said. "We'll be living with his parents and their five children. It'll be crowded."

I understood her sideways communication. "Ignaty can stay with us," I said.

The strain drained from their faces.

Alicia, standing beside me, couldn't stop laughing. "Yes, yes, yes," she kept repeating. Alicia had hardly left Ignaty's side since he was born. She hovered over him, day and night. I was surprised because she never liked taking care of Paulie. But she was a schoolgirl then. Now, no longer in school, she took a new interest in babies. The idea of having charge of him made her eyes light up. Peter walked over to us.

In a voice shrill with excitement, Alicia announced, "Papa, Ignaty's going to live with us."

So, we have a baby in our family.

Fifteen

The lantern-lit deck of the *Azian Bay Native* was crowded with revelers watching fireworks flush the summer sky with color. We were celebrating the end of her first season. Until now, she'd sailed only to near islands, but the men were preparing for a long trip to the distant islands. Peter and Father Burdofsky knew of a dozen marriages and as many baptisms awaiting their arrival. Others from our village were also going—my brother Alexi and Aunt Sophie's son, Michael, to fish halibut; and Marie's son Ilarion, to check his trap line at Unakeet. The prices of fox pelts had fallen so low, few were trapping anymore, but Ilarion clung to trapping like Papa did to sea otter hunting.

"Will you be sailing as far as Umaka?" I asked Peter after we left the party and headed home.

"Maybe next summer," Peter said.

"Peter, I want to go on that trip."

"I hope you can. I hope I can, too. When you talk about Umaka, I close my eyes and see every curve of the shoreline, every barabara, the creek where you and Katya fished and your mama washed clothes. We've realized other dreams, Little Wren. We'll make this one happen, too."

Next morning at breakfast, Peter told me I had hummed in my sleep. I wasn't surprised, for I'd dreamt about sailing to Umaka all night long. A few minutes later, I felt like humming again when I heard the foghorn of the mail boat. For sure, there'd be a letter from Anton.

Two hours later—the time it usually takes to sort the mail, I hurried to the school. On the way, I met Father Burdofsky standing in the yard of the parish house. His eyes twinkled when he greeted me. "Tatiana, I've just received confirmation from the bishop to bless you as a reader. I want to announce it tonight at vespers." I grew six inches in that moment, proud of my strength in language. I thought of those many nights after I left school, studying churchbooks and Sergie's schoolbooks, too. But I paused, wondering why we needed another reader. We had three already. I asked Father about that.

"Two of our readers, Alexi and Peter, will be away for many weeks on the *Azian Bay Native*. That puts too heavy a burden on Innokenty. He'll need relief in offering services."

I grinned my answer.

The mail wasn't ready and the time dragged. I had an urge to hop from foot to foot like little kids do. But finally, Mrs. Parker handed me a letter. I knew it was from Anton. He's my only correspondent. At home, Peter and Alexi were packing gear to load on the *Azian Bay Native*. Seeing the letter in my hand, they sat at the table waiting to hear me read it.

"June 11. Thursday evening. Mr. Steele called me out of class yesterday. One look at his face told me the news was going to be bad. He said there was no money to send me home this summer. I just stared at him because I knew I was going to go home whatever he said or did. I had to or go crazy. Then I told Mr. Steele, 'I'm quitting school.' 'Haste makes waste,' he said. 'I'm going to find a job and earn my fare home.'"

"'Jobs are scarce,' he answered. I walked away and hiked into town to talk to the men at the Indian bar. They gave me the same message—jobs are scarce, especially for Indians. But I'll find something. I have to. I don't know how long it will take. In the meantime I cheer myself by imagining I'm a Canada goose fattening up for my flight home."

I gripped the edge of the table to steady myself. I think my face lost its color. Alexi, always seeing the light side, reassured me, "Anton will be home soon." Then, looking at Peter's anguished expression, he added, "And he can return to high school next year." When neither of us said anything, Alexi got up and moved toward the door. "I'll take a load down to the boat."

"I'll go with you," Peter said.

A chill traveled from my finger tips, up my arms and down my backbone. I fetched the sweater Nellie knit for me. And then Nellie came in holding a grass bag. She pulled cormorant and puffin skins from the bag, sorted them on the table, and sat down to sew the parka she was making for Mavra. We often worked side by side, but this day my hands were still. She waited expectantly, and after a while I told her the news.

"Nell, my chest hurts when I think of Anton alone in that city. He could lose heart like Constantine Churnigoff did. He could go downhill like Katya did."

"Trouble, trouble, trouble," Nellie said in a voice so mournful I figured she had sorrow, too. It was my turn to wait.

She laid her sewing aside, wiped the moisture gathering in the corners of her eyes, and told me about Akinia's trouble.

"Chester Brown asked her to marry him. And that goofy girl was pleased, downright pleased. Then he said they'd move to Seattle after they were married. And Akinia became confused. She's like a top, spinning in circles."

"Nell, it's time to tell Akinia about Katya."

"Yes, it's time, it's time," she said as she stuffed her skins back into the sack.

Evdokie and her brother, Matfay, were sitting on the floor when we walked in, she scraping the blubber from a sealskin and he, untangling kelp for fishing line. Akinia, the only other person in the room, was sitting at the table, an untouched cupful of chai before her, her hands idle, her eyes looking far off. Evdokie got up to brew fresh chai for Nellie and me. After she served it, I began my tale.

"Many years ago, before you were born, my aacha, Katya, married Buddy Thomas, a white man and a liar. That marriage was one of the things that destroyed her."

Akinia turned her body away from me. I waited for her to turn around, but she kept her eyes fixed on the window as if it was a picture show screen. Finally, she shifted her position halfway between me and the window. I figured she was ready to hear more.

"Before Katya had agreed to the marriage, she told Buddy she'd never move away from her people. He said okay, he liked living in Akusha. And truth to tell, when we'd visit them after they married, he was friendly, offering us coffee and sometimes booze. He liked to drink. But soon, we noticed he never returned the visits. Katya always came alone. A couple of times she mentioned that Buddy hung around with the people at his end of town. But at least we could still see Katya. Those first months were like the lull before a storm."

Akinia shifted her eyes away from me again. I paused until I saw the stiffness leave her body. "One night, I stopped by to bring Katya some salmon eggs.

She loved caviar. "A treat," Buddy said as he brought some crackers to the table to go with the caviar. He also brought a jug of whiskey. He was drinking with his neighbor, Clarence Collier, boss at the supply station. 'Have a drink,' Buddy said, offering me the bottle. I said 'no' and started to pour myself a cup of chai. 'Come on, have a real drink,' he pressed me.

"'She doesn't want one,' Katya told him. Buddy took another swallow, a large one. I felt like leaving. But I didn't want to walk out on Katya. So I turned my back on Buddy and talked to her. 'The lupine are in flower.' Those were her favorite plants. But before she could say something, Buddy's slurred words stabbed the air.

"'I hate it here.' He was talking to Clarence Collier. 'The sun never shines. Wind, rain, storms, fog—it's the shittiest climate in the world.' Katya's eye started to tic. I glared at Buddy, hoping to stop him from saying more. But he continued. 'I'm amazed that you can stand this climate, Collier. I can't take it any longer. It's like living in hell. Why should I take it? It's no place for Honeybunch, either.' That's what he called Katya. Katya's face turned gray like a gathering fog. I wanted to get her out of that house.

"'Katya, let's walk to the lupine field,' I said as I rose to leave. 'Stay with me, Katey, we're having a party,' Buddy said. Katya didn't move from her seat. So okay, nothing more to do there. I went home.

"I didn't see Katya for a week, not until she stopped by to tell me Buddy was gone. This is what happened. The day after my last visit to Katya, she reminded Buddy of his promise to stay in Akusha. 'I can't stay here any longer, Honeybunch. I've been looking for a job in Seattle or San Francisco. If I don't find one soon, we'll move to one of those places anyhow. You can choose either one, Katey love." Katya was frightened. She didn't say anything to him that day or for several more. Then, on mail day, Buddy came running into the house, laughing and excited. Locking Katya in his arms, he said, 'Celebration time, Honeybunch. I have a job in San Francisco. They want me to come as soon as possible.'

"Katya said she wasn't going with him. 'I'm your husband. You have to come. You'll get used to it. And you'll have shops and movie theaters. And we'll visit my brother and his family there." He took her silence for consent and wrapped his arms around her. Katya broke away and ran to her bed. Buddy followed, maybe thinking she wanted to couple. But she wanted to be alone to grieve his leaving. He lay down beside her and started to kiss her neck. Then, one last time, she asked Buddy if he'd stay in Akusha. Buddy packed his gear then and left the house. The next day, the night before I saw her, a tender called to load cod fish. Buddy left on that boat."

Akinia walked over to a corner of the room and sat down on the boot bench, her back to me. It was quiet, except for the sound of Evdokie's knife scraping fat from the sealskin. I don't know how long Nellie and I sat there waiting to tell Akinia the rest. But finally, she came back to the table.

"You said the marriage ruined Katya, but Buddy left and she was still all right."

"It wasn't just Buddy. She had turned away from our life in other ways. When she lived at the Baptist mission for four years, she converted to their religion, their language, their customs. Her marriage to Buddy was like a graduation into their world. But I think she was ashamed for what she did. And sorrowful, too, for having lost the promise of a family. She was orphaned by her mama at birth and her papa when she was fourteen. And though they were good to her at the mission, she always hungered for her own family. After Buddy left, she fell into a black mood. It didn't lift until she realized she was pregnant.

Akinia smiled and relaxed her body.

"After Dmitri was born, Katya seemed like my aacha again. We did things together. She wanted to create every stitch of clothes Dmitri wore. I taught her how to make kamleikas and boots from qawax skins and diapers from grass. Then she wanted to teach me things she'd learned at the mission—crocheting, and embroidering. We were together all the time, teaching each other. We were together like we were in Umaka."

"Then her life wasn't wrecked," Akinia said.

"A boat can take on only so much water before it sinks. Katya couldn't survive Dmitri's death."

"I don't remember Dmitri."

"You were a baby. It happened the year I thought winter would never end. Then, one day the sun broke out and the children went tobogganing in the hills. All but Dmitri sledded on a gentle, gradual slope. Dmitri picked a steep one. He was speeding down that slope when the avalanche buried him. The children began to claw through the mountain of snow deposited by that avalanche. Except Anton, who raced to town with the news. Word spread fast. Nearly every adult in town, including the whites, ran to the mountain. It was hopeless. There must have been four feet of snow. A few with shovels dug. The rest of us tore at the snow with icy hands. We cried and scooped and gouged the snow. That's what we did—all afternoon, all evening, into the night. About midnight, Innokenty told people to go home. Most left, filing down the mountainside in a slow, halting procession. But Katya kept trying to rip away layers of snow, calling Dmitri's name over and over again. Peter, Alexi, Nicky, and I stayed with her to make sure she didn't freeze to death. We worked in relays, taking time out to run home and warm ourselves by the stove.

"Light began to creep above the mountains. And soon, the whole sky cast an orange glow over the white capped ridges. Katya's hands were still burrowing in the snow. Suddenly, she toppled over in a heap. Alexi and Nicky carried her to our house and put her to bed. She stayed there two days. She wouldn't eat anything. But she drank some chai. When she rose, she mumbled, as if forming words took more energy than she had. She got up to leave. 'Stay here,' I begged her. 'I have to go home. Dmitri may come,' she answered."

My heart still hammers my chest when I recall that time. I should have made her stay. I should have kept her by my side. Ah, Katya.

Akinia's eyes filled with tears.

"Katya sat in her house, one week, two weeks, three weeks, waiting for Dmitri. Then one night, she got roaring drunk. Ilarion, her neighbor, brought her a jug of home brew. When Katya sobered, she started to live again. Well, I don't think that's right. Maybe she acted like she was living, but her spirit was dead. She fished and trapped and ate and slept. But she didn't make anything. She didn't join in the talk around her except to answer questions. I watched and waited for a spark from her. Nothing. Not until she started drinking. She was pretty lively then. She kept herself drunk day after day and when there was no more home brew in town, she got booze at the dock. Sometimes she'd drink with men on fishing vessels. Once, a boat took off with Katya aboard. She didn't return until the next day. I watched for her all night. I turned my eyes away from her for two days. I wanted her to know she was never to do that again.

"But she did. It happened ten years ago. Katya and I went to the community hall to see a picture show, a silent film called *Love Story*. That was before the NS store donated sound equipment to the community. The picture told the story of a woman who rescued her nearly drowned lover from a raging rapid. My heart thumped hard, watching him struggle to keep his head above water, seeing it go under time after time until finally the woman pulled him onto a bank. Katya squeezed my hand so hard it stopped the flow of blood. After the show, before we parted, I saw Katya talking to a sailor. Next day, I couldn't find her."

Suddenly I stopped talking. I felt overcome. Parascovia noticed and put some smoked fish before me. My head was spinning. "Let's get some air," I said, starting for the door. Nellie joined me. I was glad to see Akinia do the same.

There was a light breeze, just like the night I found Katya. We walked by the edge of the sea in silence. After a while, I continued the story. "When I couldn't find Katya at her house, I called at every one of the forty houses in town. No one had seen her. Then I hiked around the bay to old man Grigori's place. He hadn't seen her. My panic grew so large I thought I'd fall over. But there was one more place to look, John's fox farm. John hadn't seen her, either.

Two days and nights I searched. Sleep was impossible. On the third night, I woke Peter and told him I was going to find Katya.

"'There's nothing to do tonight, Little Wren. Try to sleep.'

"A dread too big for words filled me. I could hardly breathe. Gasping for air I said to Peter, 'Katya's calling me. I'm going.' I could hardly walk, I was trembling so hard. But I was sure of my direction. I headed straight for the shore, and waded into the water at the south end of the beach. I ran my hands through that black water, up and back, up and back, up and back. Then I shifted a spear length to the north, moving my hands in ever wider circles, around and around and back and forth and frontwards and backwards. My legs began to ache with cold. I ran to the beach and rolled in the sand until the soreness was gone. Then I went on. I was determined to cover the entire waterfront. I started to call her name, and tears splashed down my face into the water. After a couple hours, something caught my eye. A yellow glow in the water. I thought the pounding of my heart was going to crack my chest. I reached toward the gold glitter. I grabbed onto something. It was Katya's amber beads, the ones I gave her for her wedding gift, wound around her neck. I tugged Katya out of the sea, pulling hard for she was waterlogged."

Nellie, Akinia, and I were standing next to a large, cone-shaped rock. It was the spot I dragged

Katya to. "This is where I found her," I said, point-ing to the water in front of us.

Ten years had gone by, but I felt as overwhelmed now as I did when it happened. I fell down onto the sand next to that rock and imagined cradling Katya in my arms. I started to moan and rock back and forth.

"Stop it," Nellie barked.

I kept rocking.

"It's time to let it pass on, Tatty."

I stopped rocking, but my heart still cried. "I should have kept her from going off with that sailor. I should have done more. Oh, Katya, I always thought you deserted me, but it was me, your aacha, who didn't do enough."

"Tatty, there was nothing you could have done," Nellie said, her sharp words piercing me like needles. "Nothing, Tatty. Nothing, nothing, nothing."

I stood up then and we set out for home, but the heavy feeling, like a boulder in the pit of my belly, didn't ease. I was afraid—for Akinia, and for the rest of us, too.

SIXTEEN

High winds seeping in through cracks around the window and door put an icy chill in the house. I sat in the rocker by the stove knitting the sleeve of a sweater for Anton. Nicky and Paulie were huddled together on the floor making snares and traps for fox hunting. Watching those two makes me think of a circle. I was Mama to Nicky. Now, with Peter gone so much, Nicky is Papa to Paulie. Maybe Paulie will enlarge the circle with Nicky's and Marie's child.

Yes, the news nearly knocked me over. After her rape, Marie swore she'd never couple again, and, for sure, she has avoided it all these years. "Victor is all the family I need," she'd often say. And I don't remember Nicky ever showing an interest in taking a wife. Our family seemed enough for him. I should have known, though, after the looks they exchanged at Nadia's wedding. So now, Nicky will have another family. I'm glad about that. But not glad that ours will shrink. I'm used to seeing him every day. And

Marie's house is so far away, in the foothills, hard to get to in foul weather.

Alicia came tearing into the house. "Word from Anton," she announced, handing me a letter. We hadn't heard from him in weeks, not since he wrote that he was quitting school. My hands shook as I read aloud.

"July 7. Seattle. Good news. I'm in Seattle after having looked every place for a job in Salem. I couldn't find a regular job, not even washing dishes. I couldn't even get hired on as a day laborer. One of the men at the Indian bar told me it was because my skin is as black as a Negro's. But Tiasook's skin is golden like yours, Alicia, and he couldn't find work, either. Last week, Tiasook said we should try our luck in Seattle. I was getting used to Salem, and Chrissakes, Seattle is one of the biggest cities in the world. 'That place is too big for me,' I told Tiasook, but he said we had no choice, so we hitched a ride in the back of a moving van and arrived in Seattle last Sunday. We put our money together, enough to rent a room for a week. It's near the wharf and seeing those fishing boats anchored out there made me feel at home. We had no money for food, but a mission near our rooming house serves soup and bread once a day. The good news came on the sixth day in Seattle, when I found a job as night watchman in an office building not far from our room. Tiasook wasn't so lucky. He's still looking."

Alicia clapped her hands. "He'll be home soon."
I held the same thought until I read on.

"July 15. Seattle. Mama and Papa, I have a plan. I
never heard of an Aleut teacher in our schools. Maybe
I'll be the first. There's a college near my rooming
house. It's bigger than the Indian school. And not so
bare. The yard's shaded by large trees and edged with
bright green shrubs and tall flowers that look like
monkshood and fireweed. I had a good feeling in
that yard. I went inside, to the registration office. A
chunky woman who reminded me of Nellie sat behind the counter. I told her I wanted to be a teacher,
but I didn't graduate high school. She asked me a
bunch of questions about my life in the Aleutian
Islands. She was really interested. So different from
the people who worked at the Indian school. After a
time, she said if I passed the entrance test they'd probably let me attend. Then she gave me a booklet list-
ing the courses I'd need for teaching. I walked around
that campus for the rest of the day, thinking, thinking, thinking. The next day I enrolled."

Anton's words fell on my heart like a stone. But
that heavy feeling was the devil's work. I turned my
thoughts to Peter. I could see the smile break across
his face when I told him about Anton's decision.

Peter was due any day. He'd been gone on the
Azian Bay Native nearly two months.

Nicky didn't speak after I finished the letter. He
moved over to the table and began to whittle on a

piece of bone. Alicia looking glum, sat down beside him and watched. I didn't know what I felt like doing until I heard Ignaty wake up from his nap. I lifted him from his crib, put him on the pee pot, and blew softly in his ear. It worked. He peed in the pot. After I put him down, I picked up the sweater I was making for Anton. I shuddered, wondering when he'd be home to wear it.

Alicia carried colored pencils and drawing tablets to the table. She had a habit of telling Ignaty a story as she drew even though he was too young to understand. Holding him in one arm and drawing with the hand of the other, she said, "This big bird is an eagle. And these lines are the wind chasing the eagle. It chased the bird so far it was lost. Its sisters are flying around looking for the bird. Whoosh, the wind switched direction and blew that bird back to his family."

Nellie walked in just as Alicia finished the story. I always expected to see her on mail day. "Wind's died down," she said. "Sea's calm. But my heart's flopping around like a fish just caught." She sat down and pulled a letter from her knitting bag. "Mavra. She's coming home for a visit next trip of the *Azian Bay Native*. I'm glad I have two pokes of dried fish. And I'll tell Cousta to forget cod fishing, yes to forget cod fishing until he brings in a qawax. I wonder when the *Azian Bay Native* will call at New Harbor." Nellie got up and walked over to the window above the counter that looks out to the sea. She stared out for many minutes. "That boat's been gone too long," she muttered.

Nicky looked up from his carving. His jaw was tight. Nicky's always edgy when someone in the family is out to sea. "Sea time isn't clock time," he snapped.

But something else attracted Nellie's attention. "A lot of people, yes a lot of people are walking on the beach. Something's going on."

I went to the window and saw a crowd moving toward the north end of town. At first I thought they were going to church, but they passed right by it. "They're heading for the community hall," I said. We all ran out then to join them.

The community hall was packed like a keg of herring. I didn't know some of the people there. "We need homes for everyone from Bolisof," Innokenty was saying when I walked in. I was afraid. Did a tidal wave destroy that village?

"As soon as we find lumber, we'll put up houses for our Bolisof neighbors. Until then, they'll honor our beds," Innokenty said.

I wanted Innokenty to tell us why the Bolisof people were here, but our villagers were already inviting them to their homes. So I made an offer, too. And so it went until every one of the thirty-four Bolisof migrants, all the people in that village, had places.

Vassa and Vasili Boroff, an old couple, both crippled with arthritis, were my guests. They're the couple who lost two sons when their dinghy crashed into a boulder last summer. Their only other child, Lupp, twenty-four years old, went home with Evdokie.

On the way home, I paused and stared at the pass to the open sea. All that met my eye was a vast expanse of white, empty space.

"No, no," Vassa protested when she saw me ready my sleeping room for her and Vasili. "We'll sleep in the kitchen. We're used to small spaces. Our barabara is only ten by twenty feet."

I pretended I hadn't heard and carried their gear into the bedroom. After that I started to boil some salmon Nicky had caught earlier. Then I sat down at the table waiting to hear why the entire village of Bolisof moved to Akusha. But when the Boroffs's heads drooped, I suggested they go to bed. They welcomed the idea.

Later, Innokenty, Nellie, and Agnes stopped by. After drinking a cup of chai, Innokenty told us what happened in Bolisof. "There was a mystery in that place. It is not understood. About seven days ago, two of the finest sea hunters in that town, Bill Soporinsky and Radion Kozaken, went out in their dory to hunt geese. They headed for the other side of the cove, the side with the lighthouse. They didn't take camping gear. They expected to be home that evening. They didn't show up, but no one was concerned. The sea was calm and they were top rate sailors. Concern came the next afternoon when there was still no sign of them. A search party went out." He paused and took deep breaths before going on. "They found some pieces of the men's dory—an oar and some fishing line. They found bullet holes in two of those dory parts. Bullet holes. Bullet holes."

Innokenty's voice cracked. We waited. "Everyone knew it was foul play. Everyone knew that Eddie Smith, the lighthouse keeper, murdered those two men. Everyone knew that Eddie Smith was violent. When he was drunk, he'd wave his shotgun around and brag that he'd shot men before. The Bolisof people believed him. They'd heard stories about his having shot at a couple of New Harbor fisherman when he ran the lighthouse there."

"That's why they all left their village?" I asked.

"A different reason," Innokenty said. "Bill Soporinsky's brother sent a radio message to the marshal here. We didn't know about that, the marshal never said a word. But he went to Bolisof to investigate the murders. He stayed there two days. All the people there told him about the lighthouse keeper and the bullet holes. But the marshal decided there was no evidence. He came back here and still said nothing about the murders. He must have sent a message to the Coast Guard. Three days later, the captain of the Coast Guard vessel showed up in

Bolisof. Like the marshal, the captain made an investigation and all the people there told him about the lighthouse keeper and bullet holes. And again like the marshal, the captain decided there was no evidence. But he didn't really believe it because he gave an order to the Bolisof people. 'You people are in grave danger. You must all leave here at once. Pack your belongings and move to Akusha where you'll be safe.' That's all."

"Why don't they just go back to their village?" I sputtered.

"It would be a hard life if the government refused to deliver supplies or mail or keep the school open."

I wanted to do something, maybe send a petition to the boss of the Coast Guard telling him to arrest Eddie Smith, maybe ask him to get rid of the marshal at the same time. I wanted to discuss this subject with Peter. My stomach muscles tightened. Where was the Azian Bay Native?

Vassa slept for fourteen hours. Vasili was still asleep when she got up. Paulie had left for school. Alicia was bathing Ignaty in the sink. I was putting cold salmon on the table when I heard Vasili move around.

"Is that you, Vasili?" Vassa asked.

"No, it's not me," Vasili answered.

"He jokes," she said, a big grin crossing her face. Moments later, Vasili walked over to the table. "What's the news, Vassa?"

"What could be new? I just saw you before we closed our eyes."

"What's new is this salmon on the table and a beam of sunlight coming through the window." Vassa patted Vasili's arm and the two of them turned to the business of eating. When they finished, the three of us got acquainted. Neither of them had visited Akusha before.

"What kind of berries grow around here?" Vassa asked.

"Salmonberries are plenty."

Her eyes flashed. "Ah, the juiciest of all berries." She was even more buoyed up when I mentioned blackberries, blueberries, strawberries, nagoon berries, and lingonberries. "Ah, my stomach will be content." Then, after a few minutes, she gave me a tender look. "Maybe we'll like it here."

Vasili's mind was on other matters. "In Bolisof, we have only a small chapel in a barabara. I've heard about your Russian church, but I never pictured anything so grand. It's like the tsar's palace. I peeked inside on the way over here last night. I saw three altars and icons everywhere and hundreds of candles. Those candles must cost a lot of cash."

"We have a church fund, and when it gets low we sisterhood women sell baskets or brotherhood men give earnings from selling fish. The church is our glory." We sat at the table drinking chai and exchanging talk all morning. Their eyes became hooded with grief every time they mentioned Bolisof. But not once did they groan about it. Maybe the berries and church softened their sorrow.

Vassa's treadle sewing machine was standing against a wall in the kitchen. Where Vassa went, so did her machine. It was like her blood. Her hands were too crippled for fine work, but she was able to feed material into the machine and keep it going with her feet. The Bolisof men had carried her treasured machine across those eight miles separating our villages.

Vassa pulled a chair over to her machine and started to feed it a large piece of gingham. "Lupp, my son, bought this machine with cash he earned fox trapping. It's the only sewing machine in Bolisof."

"What are you making?" I asked her.

"Dresses for the girls to wear to church. I can sew clothes while the other woman get the new houses in order."

The brotherhood was going to build one-room houses for the new arrivals. And Leonty and Matfay had already started digging a barabara for Vassa and Vasili at their request.

Two days later, their barabara was nearly finished; only roof work remained. We started to haul things over there—a table, chairs, a kerosene lantern. We stopped before going in, to watch Matfay and Leonty securing the roof with grass and dirt. After a while, we walked down the four steps that led to the inside room. It was about the same size as Vassa's Bolisof barabara. All day, people dropped in with gifts—grass mats, a bucket of paint, a curtain for the window, a mattress and quilt. Nicky brought Vassa's sewing machine in. And soon after that, Little Hunch arrived with a gift tied to our past, a hollowed out stone for burning seal oil and giving light.

Sitting in that snug room surrounded by my people, I felt protected like a clam in its shell under warm sand. Then, Nellie came in with Sylvia. Nellie explained right away. "Sylvia asked to see the inside of a barabara. She's never seen one before."

I noticed Sylvia staring at the lamp sitting in the center of the table. "It doesn't look like much. But it gives heat and light," I said.

"Heat?" she asked.

I demonstrated, putting the lamp on the floor and squatting over it.

Sylvia continued looking around that small ten-by-twenty foot space. "Where will you cook?" she asked Vassa.

"We don't cook much," Vassa answered with a smile, knowing that whites are disgusted with the idea of eating raw fish. "And if we want to," she added with a twinkle in her eye, "we use the seal oil lamp."

Others came, making a crowd. So, Nellie, Sylvia, and I left. Walking down the path, we saw three men putting up an above-ground house for another family.

"Why didn't the men build a house like this one for that old couple?" Sylvia asked.

I wanted to defend our barabaras. "I was born in a sod house like theirs. I wish I had one now in my backyard. I could live in it during winter. I could be warm all winter. I wouldn't need cash for coal."

"If those dirt houses are so great, why don't your people still live in them?" Sylvia asked.

Nellie tried to explain. "Lordy, people from out-side our country were disgusted with our under-ground houses. Pastor Lowell said they stank. He said they smelled like dead fish. Helen Long, the govern-ment teacher said our barabaras were filthy, not fit for pigs. The doctor on the Coast Guard cutter said the same. 'Get rid of these filthy holes in the ground, they're the reason you have so much sickness.'"

"Is that true? Did they cause sickness?" Sylvia asked.

"Outsiders brought those sicknesses to us," I said.

Sylvia puckered her brow, trying to understand. "But if you didn't agree with those outsiders, why did you move from your barabaras? No one made you move."

The back of my neck felt tight. I decided to end the conversation. But Nellie wanted Sylvia to un-derstand. "We felt ashamed. So when the company built above-ground houses as prizes for the best sea hunters, people began to move into them. Little by little we were lured away from our barabaras. Next generation, the shame was deeper and barabaras fewer. My generation, no more barabaras."

Sylvia looked bewildered, but dropped the subject.

I heard a boat horn. The others heard, too. Nellie and I had the same thought. We left Sylvia and hurried to the pier. Fog covered the water. My eyes roamed the bay, but could see nothing. I heard the soft swishing sound of a bird's wings on the beach below me. An injured sea gull stood on the water's edge, uselessly flapping its broken wing. I started cheering for it. Lift your wing higher, just a little higher. It tried, as if it heard me. I cheered it on. Why did I feel so strong about that wounded bird? I took a deep breath every time it tried to fly. And each time it dropped to the ground, a shadow fell over me.

The boat came into view. It was not the *Azian Bay Native*.

Seventeen

It wasn't the noise of the storm that woke me, it was the ringing silence when it ended. I sat up in bed, my pulse running wild. During the storm, I figured the *Azian Bay Native* was waiting in a sheltered cove. Now in the wake of the storm, I realized that the boat was probably on its way to Akusha and Peter would be home anytime. I dressed, and after putting water on the stove to heat, I lifted Peter's violin from its rack and blew the dust from it. I did the same for my guitar and Alicia's accordion. I saw the three of us playing together, maybe that new Polish dance Peter learned right before he left. I hugged the guitar to my chest, hummed the melody, and danced around the room.

I stopped when I saw a bird crash into the window. It reminded me of the wounded gull I saw on the beach a few days before. I didn't want to think about that gull. I wanted to think about Peter's homecoming—playing music together, hiking on the beach, chanting at vespers, and talking in bed at night.

I'd ask about his trip and he'd say, "First tell me the news." I'd tell him about Anton's training to be a school teacher, Alicia's hovering over Ignaty, and the Bolisof folks making fish traps and fishing in kelp for mackerel and pogy. I was so carried away by my vision, I thought I heard Peter whisper my name, Little Wren. I guess I was still smiling when someone rapped on the door. In our country, people just open the door and walk in, except the promyshlennik. Who was this calling before the children were even up? Paulie sat up on his sleeping mat, rubbed his eyes and tried to press tufts of hair flat. Alicia stuck her head under the covers. I opened the door.

Sylvia and Ralph stood there, looking stiff and grim. A cold sweat broke out on my neck and rolled down my chest and back. They sat down at the table. I sat across from them. Ralph slumped down in his chair, dark circles under his eyes as if he hadn't slept in a week. Sylvia's eyes were filled with a kind of dreary sorrow. Ralph opened his mouth to say something, then closed it and looked at Sylvia.

"Bad news," Sylvia said. Her voice sounded gravelly, like she needed to clear her throat. Ralph took over.

"I was listening to the shortwave radio. There was an SOS." Bile rose in my throat and gagged me. Alicia jumped up and came to my side.

"The *Azian Bay Native* ran into trouble." Ralph had a coughing fit that lasted a few minutes. "I heard

Captain Domasoff call the Coast Guard for help. During the night the seas got rough and the wind hauled and blew a furious gale and the engine failed. Captain Domasoff said they worked on it for hours, but couldn't get it going again. They drifted into Unakeet Bay, on the side where there was no beach, just huge boulders. They started to drag ashore and then their radio went dead and there were no more sounds, nothing. I listened all night, waiting, hoping for word, and then Tatiana, about an hour ago, I heard the Coast Guard operator report, 'The *Azian Bay Native* sank. All hands lost.'"

I hit my head against the wall, trying to empty my brain. It's not true, I told myself. It's some kind of vicious mistake. Alicia took my arms and steered me to my bed. On the way, I caught a glimpse of Paulie's face, his mouth open wide, his eyes glazed over.

I was trembling. Alicia threw covers over me. I knew Peter wasn't dead because I heard his sweet voice calling me—Little Wren, Little Wren.

I don't know how many hours or days passed before awareness returned. I opened my eyes to see Alicia standing by my bed holding a bowl of soup.

"Drink some fish soup, Mama. Please eat something. You haven't eaten anything for two days."

I didn't want to frighten Alicia, but my throat was so tight I couldn't talk and my bones ached so bad I couldn't move. I motioned Alicia to leave me. She shuffled out of the room.

Suddenly, my head cleared. My daughter lost her papa. I don't want her to feel she lost her mama, too. I should leave this bed, this room. I should go into the kitchen with the others. I should work on the basket I'm weaving for Parascovia's name day.

That was my last thought before falling into another stupor. I awoke to the sound of voices in the kitchen. I cocked my ears.

John was talking. "It was the engine. The fellow who sold us the boat told us we didn't need the brand new engine that was in it. He said it was an unnecessary expense. And then he replaced the new engine with a used one. I think it was damaged. That's why it failed."

A tremor started somewhere deep in my stomach. It stole up my chest and down the insides of my groin and legs. I curled into a tight ball and scooted down under the covers to the bottom of the bed. And then I could hear Peter's soft voice calling me. I could see his half smile and the scar above his lip. How many times I ran my finger over it. And sometimes, when he wanted to play, he'd bite my roving finger.

For a moment, I felt calm. I realized something. Peter's death didn't end Peter. He was inside me, all over. The next minute, a sob broke from me. I saw huge roaring waves crashing over Peter. I called his name over and over again as the waves blotted him from my mind's eye.

I must have spoken his name aloud. Alicia came to me. "What, Mama?" Alicia's fifteen-year-old brow was wrinkled like an old woman's. Her cheeks were pulled tight with the effort of trying to hold back tears. I got up. Alicia handed me my parka to put over my sleeping gown. I went into the kitchen then.

Nellie was filling a soup pot with greens and teal ducks. Her eyes rested on me and stayed there until I spoke.

"What day is it?"

"The day of the funeral services, Tatty."

"Funerals?" I couldn't keep track of all the threads in the tangled web of my thoughts.

"For everyone on that boat."

"Is Father Burdofsky here?" I asked. Then I remembered that Father was on the *Azian Bay Native,* too. "Who will offer the service?"

"You and Innokenty."

"Nell, I can't."

"I will," Innokenty said in a faint voice. He pulled himself out of the rocking chair, walked over to Peter's pipe shelf, lifted out a pipe, packed it with tobacco, and puffed slowly, as if he were inhaling Peter rather than tobacco.

"Where's Sophie?" I asked. I didn't remember hearing her voice in the house since the accident. Maybe I forgot. No one answered me. Then I re-

membered. Her son, Michael, was on the boat. I
thought about other voices I hadn't heard. During
mourning, everyone usually calls. Anesia, where was
Anesia? Who did she lose? Her son, Ilarion, was on
the boat. Who else? Who else? A vise tightened
around my heart.

"Have Alexi and Tessa been here?" I asked Nellie.
The grave look in her eyes answered me. I groaned.
Alexi lost! I started to faint. Nellie and Evdokie
helped me back to bed. "I'm freezing," I said.

Nellie lay down beside me, warming me with
her body. I kept shivering. Evdokie brought another
cover. I curled up again at the bottom of the bed.

"Little Wren, Little Wren."

Even in death, his voice filled my black heart
with a moment of calm. Before falling asleep, I imagined my hand brushing a lock of hair away from his
eye.

A few minutes later, I snapped awake. Who will
put out the community paper? Peter had been the
inspiration ever since the paper started ten years ago.
At first it had only one sheet. It grew, year by year,
to six pages. Even the school children wrote stories
for it. They interviewed elders—the Old Man, Little
Hunch, Parascovia, Pletanida, Anesia. They wrote stories about our ancient cures and hunting adventures
and anything else elders recounted. Sometimes the
brotherhood and sisterhood wrote something. Peter

prepared Aleut translations of Russian hymns and psalms. There were announcements of community doings and movies. Nicky drew cartoons, wonderful cartoons. And since Ralph became manager of the NS store, the paper had a paid advertisement. We used the cash to buy a typewriter and mimeograph machine. In recent years, Alicia and Agnes joined Peter, Nellie, Nicky, and me doing the typing, lay-out, pasting, and copying. And Paulie, Gavril and two other boys delivered the papers to every house and extra ones to the store and school. Peter was the only one who knew every step in the publication process. Would the paper die?

Who would teach Russian? Peter's been the teacher always. Would the Russian language die, too?

My chest couldn't hold the pain. I tried to go numb, imagining myself under a frozen pond. But the shaking didn't stop. Alicia and Nellie were by my side.

"Get up, Tatty. It's time for the service."

"I can't."

"Time to get up," Nellie repeated.

I shook my head.

Nellie pulled me to a sitting position. Then she shifted my body so my legs hung over the side of the bed. Meanwhile, Alicia brought me a skirt and blouse. I think those two dressed me. With Nellie and Alicia, one supporting me on each side, I walked to the church, chilled by the cold gusts of wind from an early winter storm.

People were standing in small groups near the church door. Their dark rimmed eyes looked hollow, like those of a Halloween pumpkin. Grief lined every face, grief for the loss of our men, grief for the death of a dream. Innokenty and Leonty approached us. Leonty was leading him, as if Innokenty was the blind one.

I shook off my chill and straightened my shoulders. "I'll start the service," I announced. The others followed me inside. I kept my eye and mind fixed on the acolytes lighting candles with long matches. Candles were everywhere—before the icons, in the hanging lamps and high candelabra, and in the central chandelier hanging from the dome.

I called up a memory of Father Paul, the priest here during my childhood, in a black robe coming in from the inner sanctum. I closed my eyes and pretended I was him. Then I walked over to the prayer desk and started the memorial service. "Give rest O Lord, to the soul of thy servant, Ilarion Sorokin ... Give rest, O Lord, to the soul of thy servant, Michael Ilianof ... Give rest, O Lord, to the soul of thy servant, Emil Burdofsky." My voice cracked. I cleared my throat a couple times and went on. "Give rest, O Lord, to the soul of they servant, Alexi Popoff ..." My tongue turned to dust. Innokenty shuffled up to the prayer desk and lifted the service from my hand.

I went over and stood between Alicia and Paulie. On the way I noticed Sylvia and Ralph and Selena and Horace Gump standing in the rear of the room.

"Give rest, O Lord, to the soul of thy servant, Peter Pushkin …" I was afraid Innokenty was going to faint when he uttered those words. But he kept going. "Give rest, O Lord, to the soul of thy servant, Akuke Domasoff … Give rest, O Lord, to the soul of thy servant, Igor Mensoff …" He was the son of Gregory from Islik. "Give rest, O Lord, to the soul of thy servant, Simeon Azinof …" Simeon, who took us in his baidarka from Islik to Azian Bay. "Give rest, O Lord, to the soul of thy servant, Fred Swenson…" He was Tessa's brother from New Harbor. Tessa also lost a husband and brother on that boat. I'd visit her after the service. Innokenty ended the service with these words: "And bless, O Lord, our Aleut boats made from qawax skins that fit our bodies like gloves and sail by our own hands."

Next day, sitting at the table in my kitchen, I felt warmed by the silent presence of my visitors. Innokenty came by every day to smoke one of Peter's pipes. After a while Alicia came in with a letter. It was from Anton, returned with the words "Not At This Address" stamped across it. The blood rushed from my head. I clutched the back of a chair. When I opened my eyes, I found Alicia squatting beside me. She helped me to my bed.

It seemed like I lay in a numb state all night. Next morning, I gave myself a talk. Get up. Do something. Cook something. Make something. But I continued to lie there, an unnamed thought nagging at me. I don't know how long I tried to catch it. Finally I did. I had to visit Tessa. The thought exhausted me, but I couldn't rest. I rolled over this way and that way. I was cold one second, hot the next. Images of Peter, Alexi, my cousin Michael, and Ilarion blazed across my mind. I tried to push them away— I'd never see them again. Maybe I'd never see Anton, either. I tightened my insides against the pain. Ignaty was crying. I heard Little Hunch talk to him in a soft voice. Where was Alicia? She's like his mama, his little mama, just like I was Nicky's little mama. "Where's Alicia?" I called out.

Little Hunch hobbled into my room. "She's fishing at the creek. She brings food every day."

Poor Alicia, burdened like I was at her age with the care of a whole family. I felt ashamed. I got up then. I kept repeating Father Paul's words: "Forget yourself and follow the path of righteousness." I knew where that path must lead. "I'm going to visit Tessa," I announced.

Little Hunch began to rub her finger against the arm of her chair. "I'm wondering if it's a good idea," she said. I wasn't sure what she meant. I waited for her to go on, but she said nothing more. So I left for Tessa's house.

I hadn't seen Tessa in a couple months, not since her twenty-ninth name day party. Tessa was more than ten years behind Alexi. She was only seventeen when they married. Alexi met her one summer when he fished on a New Harbor boat. New Harbor was her town. Tessa wanted Alexi to move there. She didn't want to leave her mama alone with the care of six children younger than she. I remember Alexi telling us about it. He liked New Harbor. "It's a beautiful place," he told Peter and me. "And there's a cannery and good fishing around there. The men can afford to buy big fishing boats." My heart had dropped into my stomach when I heard those words. I didn't want Alexi to leave Akusha. He thought about moving for many weeks. Then, one day, while he was giving out the skin and meat from a sea lion he'd shot, he turned to me, and, with a big grin, said, "Tatty, I don't have to leave you and Nicky. I don't have to leave Akusha where I know every trail, every pond and pool, every curve on the shore." So Tessa moved here. But I don't know that she ever liked it.

Walking to Tessa's, one question after another tumbled around in my mind. Who was watching her children? Did Tessa need food? Coal? Tessa didn't have Aleut skills. Her Norwegian papa wanted her to learn modern ways—English language, books, knitting, and embroidering, but not how to prepare clothes and food from seals and sea lions. How would she manage? She had stayed apart from the others in Akusha, except my family. I'd take care of her. My next thought—I won't have time now.

Nicky was at Tessa's, sitting at the table talking to Zack Swenson, Tessa's father. Nicky looked sick. His eyes were filmy like an old man's. His skin was the color of a gull's wing. His voice caught in his throat when he told me that Zack was going to take Tessa and the children back to New Harbor.

"Oh no," I said without thinking. The children were all I had left of Alexi. Nicky must have felt the same. His eyes searched mine for a solution.

Tessa was busy packing clothes. I walked over to her. She turned her head away when she talked to me. "I gave our house to Ephraim and Marla Kochutin from Bolisof."

So she wasn't planning to come back to Akusha, and I might never see Alexi's children again. Nicky got up and shot out the door so fast I knew he couldn't bear watching Tessa prepare to leave. I brushed Tessa's cheek with my lips and rushed out after him.

EIGHTEEN

The dream seemed endless. Anton and I were sailing to Umaka in a dory when a fierce wind blew us out of the channel toward a rocky outcropping on the shore. I paddled with all my strength away from the beach. Anton rowed directly toward it. I screamed. We're going to crash on those rocks—crash, crash, crash. The louder I shrieked the more Anton's figure faded until it turned into vapor like steam from a wood stove. My eyes searched. I could see only a huge, jagged boulder moving closer and closer. It was upon me, crushing me.

I awakened slowly, listening to the keening of the wind and the thud of snow falling from the roof. I tried to move my mind away from that dream but it stuck like it was glued. I counted the months since Anton's last letter. One, two, three, four. A pain stabbed the back of my head. I rolled out of bed, slipped into my dress, and went to the kitchen. Alicia, at the stove, stirred a pot of porridge. Ignaty was crawling across the room chasing a ball Paulie had rolled to him.

"Paw, Paw," he said, repeating his name for Paulie. Ever since he'd started saying words, Alicia had been talking to him in English. It sounded strange inside an Aleut house.

"He might forget he's an Aleut," I murmured.

"Oh, Mama, I don't want him to have trouble in school."

I didn't know what to say. I wanted him to do well in school, but not so well he'd go off like Anton did.

"Stinky, stinky," Ignaty said, pointing to his diaper drooping with shit.

"Why don't you clean him?" I snapped. Alicia looked startled. She wasn't used to me talking to her like that. I realized fear drove those words, fear that Ignaty would turn away from our life.

I picked up a rag and took Ignaty's hand, planning to tidy him at the shore. I changed my mind the instant I opened the door. Waist high drifts of snow blocked the way to the main path. I'd have to clear a trail before the children could leave for school. Paulie was in the upper class now. Alicia was no longer a student, but she went to school most days to help teach art in the lower class.

I lifted a diaper from the rag box and filled it with water from the water bucket. I stopped using grass for diapers when Sylvia South gave me old sheets to cut up. Ignaty squirmed on the floor and tried to pull away from me, chuckling every time he thought he outwitted me. Of course, I won in the end. I always did.

"Path needs shoveling," I told the children as I put on my sealskin parka. When I looked in the boot box, I remembered something.

The soles on my boots had broken open last time I wore them. If Alexi was here, I'd have sea lion skin to make new ones.

A rage rose inside me. I tried to tamp it down with reason. I could buy boots at the store. Then I reminded myself I had no money, not even for coal. Everyone was poor this winter. The prices for fox skins were so low the men seldom trapped. And the cod were disappearing from our waters, just like the sea otters did. The tender, *Northern Pioneer,* that used to pick up salted cod hadn't been here all year. Some of our people were so discouraged they didn't even go to fish camp. So now, in the beginning of 1941, we were not only short of cash but of dried and salted fish, our winter staple.

How would I shovel snow without boots? Paulie's were too small, and Alicia's, too big. Well, I could stuff rags in Alicia's boots. She couldn't leave for school anyhow before I cleared a path. I'd worry later about what to wear when I went after some fish.

I dug snow all morning, hurling it several feet in the air to reach the top of the snow pile. When I was so tired I thought I couldn't lift another shovelful, I pictured Peter on New Year's Eve before last clearing the main path in town after a blizzard so people could get to midnight mass. Peter didn't look strong like the others, but he could shovel for hours on end. That thought kept me going until I finished.

I felt ornery as I went into the house. I tried not to speak so it wouldn't show. And after drinking a cup of chai and eating a couple of Pilot crackers, I felt better. The snow had stopped and Alicia and Paulie were getting ready to leave for school. I started thinking about the evening meal. There was nothing to eat but crackers. I had to catch some fish. So what if my tennis shoes got wet? I bundled Ignaty, picked up my fishing line and basket, and carried Ignaty over to Evdokie's where he often stays when Alicia and I are away from the house.

The room was alive with smiles—from Evdokie and Akinia sitting at the table drinking chai, Parascovia standing at the counter mixing bread dough, and Simon and Matfay on the floor repairing a seine net. I dropped my gear on the porch, put my shoes next to the stove, and sat down at the table, waiting to hear good news. No one spoke for a long while.

Finally, Parascovia said, "Lupp is at the council meeting. He wants a wife. He's asking for Akinia." Lupp was Vassa and Vasili's only remaining child. Parascovia's announcement was followed by another long silence full of faces beaming smiles like quarter moons in a black sky. I should have jumped with joy, but a grim thought occupied me. Peter and Father Burdofsky wouldn't be here to perform the ceremony. Think of something else, I told myself. I focused on the glow in Akinia's eyes.

The council approved Lupp's application in less than an hour, Leonty told us when he returned from the meeting. "All that remains is your answer," he said to Akinia. She smiled and blushed. Then, suddenly, a hush fell over the room. Maybe the others, realizing the absence of Peter and Father Burdofsky, also wondered who would offer the ceremony.

As if he had heard our unspoken thoughts, Innokenty suddenly appeared at the door. He shuffled in and sat down without a word or nod of greeting. Akinia brought him a cup of chai. He sipped in silence. He was there, yet it felt like he wasn't. I wanted to wake him up. "Innokenty, who will marry Akinia and Lupp?" He looked perplexed, disoriented, and no words came. I felt an uneasy quiver. Is our chief of thirty-two years getting too old to lead? Too old to advise? I looked around. Everyone had turned their eyes away from Innokenty. Shortly, he stood and made his way to the door.

I wanted to get out of there, too. My shoes were dry. I picked up my gear and headed for the dock to fish. Might as well not have bothered drying those shoes, I thought as I slopped through ankle-deep snow on my way to the pier. I threw out my line and watched it bob in the waves. Many minutes passed without a bite. My hands were turning blue and my shoulders ached from shivering. Keep going, they're bound to start running, I told myself. Sure enough, they began to bite and in no time I filled my basket with flounder.

We had a feast that night—Little Hunch, the Old Man, and the children. And there were leftovers to take to Vassa and Vasili. Those two gobbled the food fast, like they hadn't eaten in a long time.

Later, lying awake in bed, I discussed the wedding service with Peter. "There's no Russian priest here. Who will marry Akinia and Lupp? Who will baptize Nicky's child?" I waited. I heard no answer. I repeated the questions. And waited again until sleep claimed me. It was a deep, dreamless sleep, but I think Peter stroked my mind while I slept, for I awakened with an idea. We'd petition the bishop at the seminary in New York to send a priest to our village.

After the children left for school, I visited Innokenty. He was dozing in the rocking chair, but woke when he heard me bustling around the stove boiling water for chai. His eyes were watery and tired looking. I waited to see if he'd say something about the upcoming marriage. When he didn't, I opened the subject. "I was thinking about the marriage ceremony."

He clenched his hands a couple times before answering. "The marriage and baptism will have to wait."

I wasn't used to challenging him or other elders, but I had to say something. "I wonder if we should petition the bishop to send a priest here for a while."

Innokenty looked surprised and then smiled and then stood up and headed for the door. His step was sprightlier than the day before. "Time to round up the elders for a meeting," he said on parting.

The council members gathered around the table at Innokenty's house that very afternoon. Nellie, Evdokie, and I sat on the floor near the door listening in. "I'm reminded of a time twenty-five years ago," Innokenty started out. "We sent a petition to the head of the Baptist mission to stop converting our Aleut children." He paused, wormed a pouch of tobacco from his pant's pocket, filled his pipe, lit a wooden match with his thumbnail and blew smoke rings for a while.

Everyone waited. "We should listen to our young people"—his next words. Leonty and Ruff nodded. "Tatiana advises another petition, this one to the head of the Russian Orthodox church, to send a priest to the Aleutians."

The councilors nodded approval. Then, Leonty suggested sending a letter instead of a petition.

Another long silence. Ruff disagreed. "A petition has more power." Innokenty rested his pipe in a razor clam shell. "The *Aurora* is due any time, maybe tomorrow," he said. "Not enough time to get a petition going, but enough for a letter." The others nodded. Ruff reached for a pen and tablet in the center of the table. Innokenty spoke the letter. "To our Bishop of the Russian Orthodox Church. Father Burdofsky, the Russian priest in New Harbor, drowned last summer when our Aleut ship, the *Azian Bay Native,* sank. There is no other priest in all the Aleutians. Meanwhile, we have a wedding and a baby coming up in Akusha. We, the people of Akusha, request a priest to visit us soon."

I felt a glow like warm embers in my heart, proud of Innokenty, proud of our council, proud of our people.

In the days that followed, I forgot about the letter to the bishop. I was too busy fishing. Every day, wet or dry, wearing only tennis shoes, I went to the dock for flounder or to Rocky Point where I fished for pogy and sculpin. When I got some fish, then I'd go after firewood. Our coal supply was nearly gone.

One day I interrupted my fishing for a wonderful reason. Marie went into labor. Nicky rushed over to me at the dock. "The baby's coming!" That's all he said, but I think I heard his heart pounding. We ran all the way to his house.

Victor was heating water and Nellie was laying pieces of clean sheet in the drawer of an old dresser to hold the baby. Marie was sitting on a grass mat on the floor, Anesia behind her, pushing with her hands against Marie's hips to help the baby out. Marie made no sounds at all, but pain showed in every muscle of her face. She pulled her lips inside her mouth and bit on them. I took her hand in mine. She dug her fingernails into my hand so deep it bled. It was not her first child, so the baby should come easy. But minutes turned into hours and still Marie sat there, tight, tense, biting her lips, squeezing my hand so tight it turned white.

Nicky walked from one spot in the house to another. He couldn't sit or stand still for long. And finally, he turned to me and his troubled eyes asked, "What is wrong?" I reached out and touched his shoulder with my spare hand. Was Marie going to die? I remembered the time Peter was dying, saved by the doctor on the Coast Guard cutter. I started to dream about a doctor or nurse living in our town permanently.

People drifted in. Parascovia, Evdokie, Anna, Vassa, and Little Hunch were sitting around waiting, looking dismal. At one point, I left Marie's side to go to the outhouse. More than thirty people were gathered in the yard.

It was near dawn when Marie howled. Feet showed. That was why it had taken so long. Anesia was in front of Marie, gently maneuvering the baby back and forth out of Marie's body. All the while Marie kept screaming. Nicky sat down on the floor, his hands covering his ears, and rocked. Suddenly, the room became silent. Anesia and I helped Marie to her bed. She lay back drenched with sweat, her face lined from the struggle. After removing the afterbirth, Anesia and I washed the baby.

Nellie, wiping Marie's face, asked, "What will you call your son, Marie?"

"His name is Peter."

NINETEEN

March. We call it the time of year we eat leather straps. Most of our supply of salted and dried fish was gone, and it was still too cold and stormy for fishing and hunting at sea. So when we didn't catch fish through holes in creek or lake ice or at the dock when the water was open, we were hungry. It was a hard time, made worse by the shadow that fell on my heart. I'd console myself by thinking about life as a circle, an arc over which Peter's spirit flows into Little Peter. Sometimes, when shadow shrouded the arc, I'd visit Marie and cradle Little Peter in my arms.

But lately I had little time to dwell in sorrow. This week we all pitched in to fix up the parish house for Father Joseph's visit. Yes, our petition brought results. Father Joseph was due to arrive any time.

A gang of us worked together—Evdokie cutting material for curtains; Vassa hemming them on her sewing machine that Nicky had carried over for her; Nellie, Anna, and Parascovia making a rag quilt for the priest's bed; Vasili, on his knees, scraping paint from the floor; and I, weaving a brightly colored rug.

"Better find a sticky paint for this floor," Vasili said one day near the end of the project. Everyone looked at him, wondering about his meaning. "I hear that Father Joseph has wings. A sticky paint will fix his feet on the ground." Vasili cheered everyone's mood. Even though it was cold in the parish house, I felt warm inside, working and joking with my people.

Father Joseph arrived on a Friday. The weddings were set for Sunday. A double wedding—Akinia and Lupp and Nicky and Marie. That gave us two days to get ready, to prepare food and fix up the community hall for the reception. Nearly everyone was short of food. But we combined what we had. Nellie and I made the wedding cake with her sugar, my flour, Evdokie's eider eggs that she'd preserved in water, and canned blueberries that Sophie bought at the store. We cooked up a great pot of stew with puffins and murres that John and Big Shot caught at Bird Island and ptarmigan that Nicky and Victor snared in the hills. Others gave dried and salted fish. For some, it was the last of their winter supply.

Alicia was in charge of decorations. She showed the children how to cut streamers from thick colored paper and paint a sparkling wall mural. The children also hung balloons that Ralph South donated.

The memory of that party is etched in my brain. I felt drunk with a belly full of food and the feverish singing and dancing. I guess everyone reveled in the release from our winter of hell. I left the reception at dawn, carrying sleeping Ignaty in my arms.

We had no store of cured fish and though the weather had been foul, I had to fish every day. The sun finally broke out three days after the wedding. In the midst of gathering mussels, I paused to gaze at the pattern of light and shadows in the folds of mountains. I never tire of that sight. But I didn't linger; I had work to do. When I finished collecting mussels, I hiked along the shore past the north end of the beach to a rocky outcrop where I fish for pogy. I dropped my line, and waited. One hour. Two hours. I caught only two pogy. Enough for the children, but not for Little Hunch or the Old Man or Vassa and Vasili.

The stove was cold when I reached home, and the coal bin was nearly empty. Too bad. I'd been looking forward to warming my feet by a hot fire. So, I set out again to search for wood. Walking toward Grigori's place, I met Anna's husband, Big Shot. He was after wood, too. "Ah, I see you're taking Anna's place as wood gatherer," I teased him.

He turned away from me, then spun around and started grumbling. "Some people in our town start scavenging for wood at dawn and don't leave any for the rest of us. Now I'll have to get my coal on credit at the store. You may have to do that, too, Tatiana."

I didn't answer, but I knew I wasn't going to buy anything on credit. We were already in debt for church supplies. I had no prospect for cash other than selling baskets, and lately I was too busy to weave. I didn't even have time to train my children— to tell stories about our ancestors or teach Alicia gut sewing or Paulie the plants and herbs that keep us alive during hard times.

We ambled along the beach in silence, our eyes fixed on the shore. Finally, we reached Grigori's house. Big Shot went in to visit, but I turned toward home, still hoping I'd find wood before the day's end. I didn't.

I used the last of our coal to heat the stove. When it was burning hot, I fried pogy. After eating, the children moved their sleeping mats near the stove. We kept our spirits up by singing church hymns. I loved hearing Alicia sing. She had Peter's rich, melodic voice.

The following day, a storm that started during the night piled snow around the house. The snow was blinding so we stayed indoors. To keep warm, we wore our parkas. And to keep our spirits up, we made a drum. Peter had been saving a hoop and sealskin for that purpose. I fetched the materials stored under my bed. Then Paulie and Alicia stretched the sealskin tight around the hoop and I sewed it on.

Paulie sanded a willow branch for a stick and then started to beat a rhythm. Alicia and I jumped up and danced, Ignaty crawling after us.

Next morning, I said to Alicia. "Stay home from school and help me find driftwood."

"I'll watch Ignaty," Paulie offered. Paulie was thirteen, old enough to help. I carried a sled, ax, baskets, and fishing line, hoping for a fish feast in front of a warm fire, but it was not to be. On the south end of the beach, beyond the dock and warehouses, I met many others with the same idea—Nellie and Gavril, Simon and Lupp, Marie and Nicky, and Sophie and John. So Alicia and I turned around and headed north, past the mission. Others were searching for wood in that area, too. I went next to the beach below the fox farm. Luck came. We found a log the length of Sylvia South. After cutting the wood and tying the pieces onto the sled, Alicia and I started singing again. Our voices blended like Peter's and mine used to. We were in high spirits when we returned home.

But who was that sitting in the rocking chair? A white woman I'd never seen before. "Paulie, help Alicia carry in some wood," I said, eager to heat the stove so I could make chai for the visitor. I pulled a wooden chair next to her and nodded a greeting. She was huddled into a gray wool overcoat that matched her watery eyes, magnified by thick glasses.

"I'm Matilda Witherspoon, a social worker, here on government business," she said, in a voice that sounded like it needed sanding. "Your name is Tatiana Pushkin, is that right?"

"Yes," I answered. I started wondering what she was doing in my house, what she wanted. Paulie had started the fire but I didn't feel like making chai.

"The Alaska Territory has just set up a public welfare department," she said. "This is my first visit to the Aleutians." She paused and scratched a big brown mole next to her ear. "My job is to locate families that need help or children who need protection."

"Protection from what, eh?" I felt suspicious.

"Protection from poverty and neglect."

My suspicions grew stronger.

"I think your children may be a case in point, Tatiana. I found your young son and baby alone in a freezing house with bare cupboards. Why did you leave them alone? Why did you leave them without food or heat?"

I wanted to answer, but my voice refused me. I got up, stoked the fire Paulie had started, sat down on a bench across the room from her, picked up some grass that was on the table next to me, and started to braid. When I settled down, I explained. "My daughter, Alicia and I were looking for driftwood for the stove and fish for dinner."

"Speak up. I can barely hear you."

I repeated my explanation.

"You need a man in the family."

Alicia was standing near me, and Paulie, who had been sitting on a box by the stove, came over and sat beside me.

I laid the grass aside and held my arms tight against my sides. I never hit anyone in my life. But I had a sudden urge to strike that woman. I was too mad to say anything. But Alicia did, fighting tears all the time. "Papa drowned last year when the *Azian Bay Native* sank. So did my uncle, Alexi. And my cousin, Michael."

Knowing our tragedy, surely the social work woman would stop her questions. But, she kept on, smiling as if she were my best friend. "Have you got any prospects for remarriage, Tatiana? Your family is starving and freezing. Your children need a father."

No one, not anyone I ever knew, crashed into my insides as this stranger was doing. I felt like running out of the house. But mostly I felt alarmed, frightened. I couldn't figure out what any of this talk meant. I decided to explain to the social worker why I would never marry again. "Truth to tell, Miss Witherspoon, my husband and I had a love marriage."

She scratched her mole and stared at me as if I had suddenly sprouted an ear on the top of my head. I thought she'd understand. My people learned about love marriages from her people, from American teachers and missionaries and movies and magazines. Didn't she see the same movies, read the same magazines, hear the same sermons about loving forever? No, she didn't see.

Miss Witherspoon pulled a form from her carrying case. "Tatiana, I need some information from you. Tell me, how many children do you have?"

"Four. Anton, my oldest, doesn't live in Akusha."

"Tatiana, I've been told that in your culture people feed others who aren't family members. How many people do you feed?" Had my ears betrayed me? Did she think we counted our visitors? She asked again. "Tell me, how many people eat at your table?"

I shrugged.

"Well, can you name the people who eat here regularly?"

I tightened my lips, so she dropped the subject.

"How old is your oldest child, the one who doesn't live here?"

"Nearly eighteen."

"Hmm, maybe old enough to provide for your family. Can you bring him back here to Akusha?"

"I don't know where he is."

"You don't know where he is? Doesn't he communicate with you?"

I didn't answer.

"Tatiana, we could assist you with money for food and coal for a few months. But our program is for temporary relief. We can't give financial aid for an indefinite period. If you had a plan that included marriage, I could send you money for three months.

Without such a plan, the Territory will have to protect your children.

"Protect them?" My voice shook.

"Yes, place them in the orphanage in Anchorage
until we find foster homes for them."

I thought I missed her meaning. The Territory
was our Alaska government. I didn't believe it stole
children. I decided not to say another word until I
talked to Nellie and Evdokie.

The social worker stood, walked over to my side,
and touched my arm. My stomach lurched. "I'm
going to discuss this matter with your chief," she
said as she turned away from me and left the house.

"Mama, what was that woman talking about?"
Alicia asked.

Before I could answer, the door swung open and
Evdokie, Nellie, Anna, and Marie walked in. They
knew about Miss Witherspoon's visit. It seems everyone in town knew about it. Before Miss
Witherspoon came to my house, she was seen at the
house of Natalia, Ilarion's widow. And before that, at
the house of Michael's widow, Christina. I pinched
myself to make sure I wasn't having a bad dream. In the
middle of our mourning, that social worker threatened
to steal our children. No, no, I must be mistaken. I
waited for one of my friends to explain. They didn't
have answers, either. They didn't understand. But they
were angry. They wanted to do something.

"Anesia is watching the chief's house. She'll tell us when the social worker leaves," Nellie said.

But Anesia didn't have to alert us. Maybe an hour after Miss Witherspoon left my house, we saw her making her way toward Sylvia's end of town. She was staying with James Wilson, boss of the supply station.

I was building a fire and filling the teapot with water when Innokenty came in. His head kept jerking to one side and his hand trembled when he held a match to his pipe. He puffed on it for many minutes before speaking. "They heard about our ship sinking and sent their social worker here to investigate." Then, after two long puffs, he said, "So, they've decided to pay attention to us. It was better when they didn't."

"She wants to steal my children," I said, feeling hot all over.

"There's a new law about welfare and charity, something about putting children in families without a permanent provider in orphanages or foster homes."

"I don't see what it means—permanent provider."

"Miss Witherspoon says it means having a man in the family. She checked the three families who just lost their men. She is satisfied about the other two. Natalia is going to move in with her in-laws. And Christina's son, Philemon, is old enough to provide, she said. You're her only worry, Tatty. She told me that unless you have a marriage prospect, she'll take Paulie and Ignaty away from Akusha."

"My husband is Peter." My voice quaked in saying the words.

No one spoke. Many silent minutes passed, interrupted only by the sound of lips sipping chai. It felt like fists were thumping against the walls of my chest. Ignaty climbed onto my lap and I pressed him to my heart. Paulie stood next to Alicia's chair, his body touching hers. Anna made no attempt to hold back tears. But there were none in the eyes of Nellie and Evdokie. I thought I saw blood in Nellie's eyes.

"Tatty, we won't let Miss Witherspoon take your children," she said.

"The marshal will do her bidding. He's the law," Innokenty answered. Then walking over to my chair, he placed his hand on my shoulder and said, "I'll find a husband for you before Miss Witherspoon shows up here again."

TWENTY

"It is said that Stepan Shemikin is a good man."

I nearly choked on Innokenty's words, even though I expected them. Two months after Matilda Witherspoon's visit and a year after the Azian Bay Native sank, Innokenty visited Kooney Pass to find me a husband. I felt sick at the thought of replacing Peter. Most of the time. Once in a while, though, I felt warmed by the idea of enlarging our family, grown so small lately.

A gang of us, sitting around the stove, waited for Innokenty's visit the night he was due to return from Kooney Pass. He came directly to our place, and after going through his pipe-lighting ritual, he sat down next to me at the table and related the news.

"He's about your age, Tatty, your size, too. Short, but his chest is filled out. He was trained for hunting in the old way."

Alicia, serving chai, spilled some on Innokenty's bare arm. Maybe this conversation was making her nervous. It was having that effect on me. After she dried his arm, he continued.

"I stayed with Chief Theophon. He lives in one big room with cots along the walls—plenty of space for meetings and celebrations. Stepan came over right after I arrived, like he knew my mission. His wife, Rosie, died from pneumonia two years ago, same year eight others in that town died from drowning or lung disease." Innokenty paused to relight his pipe. "Hate to see a town go under like that. Government even closed the school last year."

A shiver slid down my spine, thinking the same could happen to our village.

"I asked Stepan if he thought of marrying again. He shook his head up and down, vigorous shakes. I said I had you in mind, Tatty. His eyes lit up like our Christmas stars. Before anything definite was decided, people started coming in, glum looking. I think they figured out why I was there and didn't want me to lure any villagers away. They sat on the cots staring at the floor, but their ears were cocked. Chief Theophon came up with a suggestion. 'Tell Tatiana the people in Kooney Pass would welcome her here.'"

"I'd die first," I blurted out.

"I was aware, so I told the chief, 'Stepan and Feckla—that's his seven-year-old daughter—should honor our village.' The chief didn't answer for a while. Then he suggested you move across the bay to New Harbor so Stepan and Feckla could live close to their home. Before I could say anything, Stepan held his hand in the air. 'Feckla and I will live in Akusha. Feckla needs a place with a school.' So, it was settled."

A week after Innokenty's visit to Kooney Pass, the *Phalarope,* a New Harbor fishing boat, carried Stepan and Feckla to Akusha. No one knew they were on their way, but word traveled as fast as an eagle on the wing after they came ashore. In no time, Innokenty was at the dock to greet them and lead them to my house.

It was a festive evening. Evdokie, Nellie, Sophie, and Little Hunch brought sweet bread and smoked fish and fish pie to welcome the newcomers. I could see Stepan was a good listener, the way he leaned toward whoever spoke, the way his eyes came alive with interest. But he never volunteered a word.

Feckla, her cheeks as pudgy as Ignaty's, resembled her papa—shy, quiet, with big, black, knowing eyes that seemed to take in everything going on around her. Only unlike Stepan, who sat among us, Feckla chose a corner of the room far from the rest of us. She sat on the floor, twisting her hair around her fingers, sometimes chewing on it. I brought her some bread when she started to eat her hair, but she refused the food and sucked harder on a lock of hair.

Ignaty thought she was playing a game. He went over to her and yanked her hair, too. She pulled back from him. He tugged at her then, trying to bring her to the table. She resisted. He tugged harder, saying,

"Da, da." Ignaty, only a year and a half old, understood everything said to him, but "da" was one of the few words he spoke. When he wanted something, he'd pull some big person to an upright position and lead them to it, pointing and repeating his command, "Da, da." I figured he didn't talk because he was confused hearing two languages in his house. Anyhow, his tugs and commands didn't work with Feckla, so he tried something different, climbing onto the chair and trying in vain to hang upside down like Paulie does. Everyone laughed except Feckla. She just stared at him, without expression.

A week later, Stepan and I married. We didn't know when to expect a visit from a priest, so we married like our ancestors, blessed by the chiefs. I didn't want a party at the community hall afterwards. It would have felt like I was celebrating Peter's death. But we made a big pot of ptarmigan stew for everyone who dropped in.

Before then, Stepan and Feckla had both slept in the main room. But the morning of our wedding, Stepan carried his duffel bags into my bedroom. I knew he wasn't a talker; in fact I don't think he initiated a single conversation before that time, but I figured on that night, he'd surely open up. After the guests left, he headed straight for the bedroom, mumbling something about "time to turn in." I followed him, undressed with my back to him, pulled on a flannel night dress, climbed in beside him, and waited.

He lay on his back, still as a stone, but I knew he was awake from his irregular breathing. So okay, I'd think about Peter. He was the one I wanted beside me anyhow. He was the one I'd love forever. My union with Stepan wasn't a love marriage. A thought jarred me. Was Stepan stretched out beside me thinking about Rosie in the same way? I don't know how long we lay side by side in our separate worlds before sleep came.

The sound of Stepan's voice woke me early the next morning. He was standing by the side of the bed, fully clothed. It was then I realized he stuttered. "I'm thinking about finding something to do." I knew he was used to hunting in a baidarka with spears and throwing boards. His eyes filled with thanks when I suggested he fix up Alexi's baidarka for himself.

"It's in a boat rack next to Ollie Larsen's herring station. There are three herring stations on the beach. Ollie's is the one closest to the pier."

"Um, um, see ya," he said, a smile in his eyes, as he left the room.

I knew the boat needed plenty of repair after sitting around without use for a year. I got dressed, searched the storage boxes under my bed for gut thread and pieces of sealskin to patch the baidarka cover, and went out to help him. Matfay was there already, shaping a piece of wood to replace the damaged section of frame Stepan was removing. Soon,

Matfay's nephew, Simon, joined us. Those two, Matfay and Simon, were the only baidarka hunters left in Akusha until Stepan arrived. Stepan talked so easily with them. I hoped he'd become as comfortable in our family.

I finished patching the baidarka cover in one day, but the men worked several more repairing the frame. Then, after I sewed the cover on, the men left to hunt sea lions, Stepan in Alexi's baidarka and Simon in Matfay's. They were gone many days.

In Stepan's absence, I had a chance to get to know Feckla. She wasn't lively like Ignaty, but she stopped sitting in the corner. And she looked forward to her English lessons with Alicia. Feckla had never been to school and Alicia took on the job of teaching her English.

One day, Alicia announced to Feckla, "You're ready to start school."

Feckla looked frightened and shook her head.

I didn't press her. She wasn't ready. "We'll wait a while," I said to Alicia.

And then I turned to see who'd come in. It was Nellie, out of breath, with news the hunters had returned. We all followed her to the beach. Maybe half the town stood at the shore watching the hunters haul in a sea lion and two seals. My imagination was impatient. I started planning the sewing of mukluks and kamleikas and skin boots for Ignaty and Feckla.

We stayed up half the night skinning and butchering the animals. Then, after a few hours' sleep, the celebration started at my house.

We feasted on liver, heart, and shoulder. Feckla was more spirited than I'd yet seen her and at one point, instead of resisting Ignaty as he pulled her around the room, she pushed him down to the floor and tickled him under his arms until he laughed so hard tears came. Feckla had joined our family.

Later in the evening, when people's bellies were bulging, Stepan broke his silence and spun a yarn about an adventure at sea. "I had never seen Una … Una … Unakeet before, the island we … we … we landed on our first day out. The island was loaded with birds, there were birds everywhere." Stepan paused, maybe trying to rid himself of his stammer. He pulled a wad of snuff from his pocket, stuffed it between his bottom teeth and lower lip, and went on. "Matfay and I weren't interested in birds. We had our minds set on a sea lion. So we left Simon hunting birds at Unakeet while we got in his baidarka and headed for the qawax rookery at Oloff Point." He paused again to spit in a can. "It was a fine morning, a light wind and high clouds. But later in the day, a heavy fog rolled in. Pretty soon, I couldn't see Matfay sitting three feet in front of me. I couldn't make out his figure. And then I lost sight of the water a finger's width below me. 'I can't see a thing,' I

yelled to Matfay. 'I don't know which way we're going. I can't even see you.'

   "'Stop paddling. I'll get us there,' Matfay assured
me. I tried to understand why he said that. If I
couldn't see, then he couldn't, either. How did he
know we weren't spinning around in cir … cir …
circles? But I knew we weren't. Matfay's strokes were
sure and I sensed he was following a direct course. I
concentrated my eyes on what lay ahead, hoping I'd
pick up an outline of a headland or a cove. But I saw
only thick, dark soup. Suddenly Matfay started to
sing, 'Hey dee dee, hey dee dee.' I thought he'd gone
goofy. But by God, I heard the boat scrape against
rocks. We were close to a beach. And then he jumped
out of the boat and hauled her ashore. We were at
the rookery. 'You have magic sight,' I said. He chuckled and said it wasn't magic at all, he'd just followed
the smell of sea lion piss."

   Everyone laughed, and maybe I laughed louder
than the rest to discover that Stepan was a lively sto-
ryteller. That encouraged me, later in bed, to confess
something.

   "Sometimes I think about Peter when we're lying
here together."

   After a while, he said, "I don't want to forget
Rosie either."

   "How long has she been gone?"

   "She died the winter before last."

"Longer than I've been without Peter. I wonder if I'll ever get used to it?"

"I don't want to get used to it. If I forget Rosie, who'll remember her? Feckla was so young when she died."

All at once, something became clear to me. "Stepan, we don't have to forget them or stop loving them to like each other."

"Ah, Tatiana, you're a wise woman."

I turned my full body to him then, and for the first time he put his hand to me.

Twenty-one

Winter storms started early in 1941. The wind blew so hard it made the window panes bend and sway. And the low fog was so dense it blotted out the midday light. But on this December morning, the heavy cloud cover cracked and shafts of sunlight shone through the seams. I stood at the shore watching Stepan load his baidarka for a hunting trip. Alicia was with me. She'd taken to hanging around Stepan lately.

Shortly after the hunters sailed off, a fishing boat came steaming down the bay. It was the Phalarope from New Harbor. I went to the dock to check the passengers. Nellie was there, of course, hoping to see Mavra. We didn't talk as we watched the Phalarope tie up, but we kept our eyes glued to the boat ladder.

The first person to come down was wrapped in oil skins. I couldn't tell if it was man or woman. The person turned around. I felt hot and cold at the same time. It was Anton. Ai. Did he know about the sinking of the *Azian Bay Native*? About my marriage? In moments, Anton was beside me. "I heard the news in New Harbor," he said as he held onto my arm on the way home.

Visitors usually show up when someone returns to town, but no one dropped in that afternoon. I figured they knew Anton had to get used to the changes in our family. He'd never seen Stepan or Feckla, or, for that matter, Ignaty. Anton and I just arrived home when Paulie came running in, out of breath. He stopped suddenly when he saw Anton, staring at him as if he was a ghost. Maybe Paulie lumped Anton and Peter together; both had disappeared from his life about the same time.

Anton had just dumped his gear in his room and come back to the kitchen when Ignaty began to tug at him. "Da, da," he said as he pulled him toward Anton's chess set on a wall shelf. Anton handed him a couple of pawns to play with. "Da, da," Ignaty repeated, pointing to the queens. I don't know how long he negotiated with Anton but finally he succeeded in having the whole chess set on the floor in front of him. But, after all that effort, he tired of playing with it in a few minutes. He tried another tack to get Anton's attention, hanging upside down on the back of a chair. Anton didn't notice until Ignaty started to chant, "Da, da, da." Then, Anton laughed. So did everyone else. Except Feckla. She was sitting off by herself watching this stranger. I noticed Anton glance in her direction a couple of times, and when he finished eating, he went over and sat beside her. Like Peter, Anton knew when to keep his mouth shut. Feckla seemed to like his quiet presence. After a few minutes, she moved closer to him and was about to say something when Alicia scolded Anton for not having written.

"We were scared. We didn't know if you were dead or alive."

Anton leaned his head back and sighed, but he didn't say anything. Alicia stopped pressing him then, maybe thinking, as I was, that he missed his papa. He'd never been home when Peter wasn't there or expected. Anton sat in a tight silence that entire afternoon, except when Ignaty tugged at him.

He unfolded that evening with Alicia and his pals, Simon and Victor. Simon was a hunter, but Victor, Marie's son, worked as a clerk at the NS store. He was the only Aleut who ever worked there on a regular basis. Maybe Ralph South didn't know Victor was Aleut. Victor has blue eyes, inherited from the sailor who raped his mother.

Alicia and the men were sitting on the floor in front of the stove listening to Simon describe the Bolisof migration when Anton suddenly interrupted: "I've stopped drinking."

I moved from the rocker to a chair close to Anton. I wanted to see and hear beyond his words—his sighs and hesitations and changing expressions.

We all waited for him to go on. In a while, he said, "I found out I couldn't go to that teachers' college. The program takes four years and costs more cash than our village earns in a year. So I went after a job and found one. I was a night watchman in a building fourteen stories high. Chrissakes, it was eerie in that building, so quiet I could hear the sound of my breath. After work, I'd go to my room and sleep until midday, then get up to the same damn silence. The people in my rooming house were away at work. I was surrounded by silence, like in a tomb. I thought I'd go crazy if I didn't see people or hear voices. I'd walk all over Seattle—in the parks, on the streets, to the harbor. It helped until I'd return to that empty house or that morgue where I worked. And then that feeling would overcome me, that I wasn't alive, that I was a ghost. I knew I had to talk to people. That's when I started hanging out at the Indian bar on Pier 7 where there were guys like me. We'd drink and talk and gripe and pretty soon my heart would feel lighter. I started to look forward to seeing those guys every day. One night I guess I drank more than I realized. Someone called me a dumb Eskimo. The rest of that night is hazy. I think I threw a glass of beer in his face and he lunged at me. Others joined the fight. Then the bartender called the police and five of us landed in jail."

Sweat was rolling down Anton's cheeks, onto his neck and under the collar of his shirt. I dropped my kerchief beside him. "If only you'd written," I said. "If only we'd known."

"My shame was too deep to speak of, too deep to write about."

"How long were you in jail?" Simon asked.

"I'm not sure. I lost track of time, but it was many weeks. When they set me free, I knew I had to get out of that place fast, and get home to my people. I haunted the wharf looking for a fisherman I knew. One day, I spotted a familiar-looking boat. I talked to the owner, name of Swede, and learned he was from New Harbor, getting ready to go back and fish salmon. That wasn't home, but it was close. I let him know I was from his country and was trying to get home. We talked together a long time. By evening, I had a job on his boat. I felt pretty good about that.

"When did you get to New Harbor?" I asked Anton.

Waving his hand as if he was swatting at pesky thoughts, Anton said, "Enough talk."

So that was the end of the story that night.

Anton didn't mention New Harbor the next day or the next. On the third day when he and Alicia and I were fishing for sculpin at Rocky Point, I asked about it. "I suppose you fished in New Harbor, eh?"

Anton didn't answer right away. He untangled his line and hooked some bait to it. Then, in a voice so low I had to strain to hear, he said, "Mama, my shame is eating at me."

I swallowed a sob.

"I stayed with Mavra and Sasha. Sasha was busy getting his boat ready for salmon fishing, but he had a full crew so there was no job for me there. I walked around town asking everyone if they needed a hand. No one had a place for me. Every day, I watched the men work on their boats. I wasn't part of anything. I felt invisible, cut off, useless, living in a ring of silence like I did in Seattle. I started drinking again. Every night I drank until there was no more kvas in town."

I wanted him to stop talking. I wasn't sure I could bear to hear more. I dropped my line in the water, but he went on, his eyes darting around like he was scared. His next words sounded forced.

Maybe he thought that in the telling, the memory would melt.

"After the kvas was gone, I was afraid I was crazy or afraid I'd go crazy if I didn't keep drinking. But I had no cash. One night when Mavra and Sasha were away, I started ransacking their house looking for money. I emptied drawers and cupboards. I ripped floorboards loose, remembering that Ilarion once hid his money under the floor.

"You fouled Mavra's house. She's like your sister." I hadn't meant to condemn him. The words just fell out of my mouth. Anton started rubbing one hand hard against the other until his knuckles looked as if they were bleeding. I took his hand in mine and massaged it until he calmed down.

"Mama, it gets worse."

I felt like plugging my ears. I didn't, of course.

"When I found three dollars in the pocket of Sasha's winter parka, I ran to the store and bought every bottle of hair tonic, cough syrup, and Sterno. I learned about the alcohol in those things at the Indian bar in Seattle. One after the other, I drank them until the bottles were empty. Ugh, my stomach revolted. I tried to get to my bed, but before I did my gut split open and I vomited and shit and pissed all over the floor. Then I passed out."

"Holy Moses!" Alicia exclaimed. What happened when Mavra and Sasha found you?"

"As soon as I woke up, I got out of there fast before they returned. The cannery wasn't operating yet, so the watchman let me stay in the bunkhouse. After that, Mavra and Sasha looked the other way when I'd pass them on the street. They never started a conversation with me. Oh, they'd answer if I said something first. If I'd greet them, 'aang,' they'd answer, 'aang,' and when I'd say no more, they'd walk off." He looked away from us and in a hoarse voice, said, "I was killing myself. So I stopped drinking. Only thing, it left a huge hole where the booze used to be. I don't know how to fill that hole, Mama."

I touched his arm. "You're home now. We'll figure out something."

The next day, high winds kept Stepan indoors. He spent the morning in the kitchen untangling kelp for fishing line. Then, after lunch, he went to the shed and returned with a large piece of driftwood. Sitting in a corner he seemed to have claimed for himself, he started carving a new throwing board for his spear. I was sitting in the rocker nearby, sewing a pair of mukluks for Feckla. A couple times, Stepan glanced at me. He must have noticed that something was on my mind. So I told him. "If Anton doesn't figure out what to do—oh, Stepan, I'm afraid, afraid he'll go downhill like Katya." I had told Stepan about Katya.

"Such a gloomy view, Tatiana."

"Where does hope lie? He drank until he was crazy. He betrayed Mavra. He can't hunt like the others."

Stepan looked thoughtful. He laid his line aside and looked up at me. "I always wished for a son," he said. "If Anton was my son, he'd love the sea. Tatiana, maybe later when he knows me better he'll become interested. That's where hope lies."

At that moment, the door opened and Anton and Victor came in. "My mouth started to water when Anton told me you brought in three king salmon yesterday," Victor said to Stepan. He and Anton went to the counter and filled plates high with the fish.

"I never tasted fish like this at boarding school," Anton remarked.

Maybe Anton was feeling proud of Stepan. Maybe this was a beginning, I thought.

"It's been a treat for me, too," Victor said. "I don't fish much since I started working at the store, and I don't have a seaworthy boat, only a little dinghy."

"Alexi's baidarka is very seaworthy," Stepan commented.

Anton gave Stepan an intense look, but he made no comment. He got up and went over to the counter for another piece of fish.

Victor moved his chair close to Stepan. "What are you making?"

"A throwing board."

"Why don't you use a rifle?"

"Yes," Anton chimed in. "If I had a gun, I could hunt seals and sea lions. I can't hunt the old way, I wasn't trained for it."

My pulse skipped some beats. Was Anton thinking of learning from Stepan?

"You lose a lot of animals with rifle hunting," Stepan explained. "They sink and you can't find them. But spears mark the animal and keep them afloat. That's why I use them." And then, looking at Anton, he said, "My brother didn't train for hunting at sea until he was a man. And he brought in as many fish, seals, and sea lions as anyone else."

Sitting forward in his chair, Anton was about to reply when the Old Man, Little Hunch, and Matfay came in. They were hungry for king salmon, too. A while later, Aunt Sophie and Bullshit John showed up for the same reason.

"Ah, that salmon is good, " Bullshit John said. And then, leaning back in his chair, he spun a yarn about his recent trip with Matfay trapping birds on Bird Island. "Matfay was checking traps at one end of the beach; I was at the other end. I got to my first trap. Nothing but bits of a mallard's carcass. But where was the mallard? I looked around the area. I couldn't find a sign. Then, I saw a track in the sand. It wasn't the print of a creature from the sea. It was shaped like a man's foot, but it was too big for a man. It was the print of a giant. I was scared out there alone, but I was curious, too. I followed those prints along the creek bank. And about two dory lengths ahead of me, I saw a huge brown bear, as high as the NS store. It was the first bear I ever saw outside of pictures."

"Bullshit," the Old Man grumbled.

I could see why the Old Man questioned John's account. We never saw bears in the Aleutian Islands. We knew about them only from books and legends.

John was determined to convince the Old Man. "I heard that big brown bears like this one live on the mainland. This bear must have swum across the strait to Bird Island. I wanted to watch him, but when he started to run in my direction, I got out of his way and raced back to the boat to wait for Matfay. When I told him what I saw, he said I had good dream powers. I took him back to my first trap to see those tracks in the sand. Matfay didn't say another word about my dream powers."

"Bullshit," the Old Man repeated.

"Better be careful," Stepan said with a twinkle in his eye. That bear might swim across the channel and show up here."

The Old Man frowned, but the rest of us laughed. Anton, too. Then, turning to Stepan, Anton said, "Maybe I'd like to learn to hunt at sea."

Stepan sniffled and drew his hand across his nose.

I felt a surge of joy. But next minute, fear gripped me, fear for Anton. He had no experience as a sailor or hunter. He wasn't used to icy water. His shoulder muscles weren't developed enough to paddle a baidarka for long stretches. His arm wasn't strong enough to throw a spear any distance. Maybe Anton was making a mistake. Maybe he was setting himself up for another sorrow. I wondered if he'd survive.

The next morning, I felt lighthearted seeing Anton and Stepan head for the door. "We're going to search for wood to make me a spear," he said, grinning.

Anton was determined to succeed. Not once did he complain during weeks of strenuous training. Stepan made Anton dunk repeatedly in the sea to accustom him to freezing water. He bent his arms back as far as they'd go and made him run holding heavy rocks in his hands to strengthen his arm muscles. He pressed down hard on his knees to develop his back muscles for long hours of sitting in the baidarka. The workouts were so demanding that Anton often fell asleep in the middle of a meal.

Finally, Stepan judged Anton ready to go to sea with him or Matfay or Simon. All had two-hatch baidarkas. Anton was excited preparing for his first trip with Simon. But he returned sullen and silent. And so it was after every trip. Not once did he bring home a seal or even a large fish. I didn't ask questions. I didn't want to add to his anguish.

But Alicia pressed him one night on his return from a fishing trip with Matfay. "Did Matfay catch anything?"

"He hooked a hundred-pound halibut."

I was puzzled. Why didn't Anton bring some of that fish home with him?

A short time later, Anton explained. "I couldn't keep the boat steady enough for him to play his line. He lost the fish."

At that moment, we were all distracted by a great noise. It sounded like a hundred dory engines revving up at once.

"If this weren't Akusha, I'd swear I heard the sound of trucks," Anton said.

We ran to the shore, Ignaty and Feckla trailing behind us.

"Chrissakes," Anton exclaimed as we watched twelve large green trucks roll off scows onto the beach. "The army's coming here?"

We knew about the war, but like the last one, it seemed very far away. What were those trucks doing here in the Aleutian Islands? In our village? One of them smashed Stepan's baidarka rack. Another ran into Ollie Larsen's herring dock. A third was leaking oil near the place I dug clams. I dashed to that spot and saw hundreds of smashed clam shells.

TWENTY-TWO

It had the quality of a dream, too unbelievable, too dreadful to be real. Yet, there it was before our eyes, Alicia's and mine. Military trucks grinding their way up the hill behind the mission, gutting our paths and berry patches and creek beds. We were standing in the yard when Nellie and Evdokie hurried by followed by other villagers, all heading toward the dock. We followed, wondering as they probably were—what next?

Two huge, gray vessels—"transport ships" they were called—were tying up when we arrived. Men dressed alike in soldier suits the color of winter grass poured down the gangway.

Alicia's skin paled. "Mama, is the war coming to Akusha?"

I had no explanation. Victor, who heard daily reports on the radio in the NS store, had been posting us on war news. Like the last war, this one seemed very far away. That is, until trucks and ships and soldiers swamped our town.

Two hundred and fifty men came ashore, more people than lived in Akusha. We stood around waiting for an explanation. But Alicia wasn't gifted in patience. She walked over to someone she thought was in charge. "What are the soldiers doing here?" she asked. The officer glanced at her and then walked away without answering.

As he passed me, imitating my daughter, I tapped his arm. "I wonder where all these men will stay."

Pausing for a moment before moving on, he said, "Most of them will camp in the hills in the rear of the village."

I was relieved to learn that the men would live out of town. But I wanted to know why they were here, how long they'd stay, and most of all, if war was coming to Akusha.

Those questions chased me for many days. One night, after listening to the Old Man tell a tale about invaders destroying his grandfather's village, I lay awake, trying to quiet the tremor in my heart. I closed my eyes and created a peaceful vision—Stepan, the children and me on a boat sailing away from Akusha to Umaka. The dream fired my imagination. I wanted to do it. But how could I run out on my people in Akusha? Oh, I felt torn, I had to go off by myself and sort things out.

"Where are you going, Tatiana?" Stepan was propped on his elbow, watching me dress.

"I have to breathe cold air. I'll be back soon."

"But … but Tatiana …"

I was gone before he finished his sentence. The wind was blowing hard, maybe hard enough to wash away my distress. I ran with it until I came to a cone-shaped rock, the same one I sat against when I cradled my dead aacha's head in my arms. My knees buckled. I sat down in the sand, the rock protecting me from the wind. But a soft breeze caressed my cheek. Was that Katya's spirit, here in Akusha? If I fled this place, I'd never feel it again. I got up and ran along the shore to the log Peter and I used to rest on. I sat down again and recalled the night I chanted like I was deacon and he answered as chorus. Peter's spirit was here in Akusha too, I thought, as I hurried back to my warm bed and laid my dream of flight to rest.

The next day, at Evdokie's house, Nellie, Anna, Evdokie, and I sat together working on our different projects. The house had a warm, yeasty smell from sweet bread Evdokie had just baked. Now, she sat on the floor scraping fat from the inside of a sealskin Simon had captured the day before. I was sitting next to her sewing pieces of the gut together for a kamleika. Nellie, at the table, was weaving a mat for the church. And Anna, beside her, was knitting socks for Big Shot. The soft sounds and dear faces in the room made me forget about the uproar in our town until Evdokie mentioned the Old Man's tale about invaders. A gloom fell upon us. No one spoke for many minutes.

Then, Nellie said, "Oh lordy, what's the fuss? What's the fuss? They're leaving us alone."

Nellie's right, I thought. We don't have to stop living because they're here. I don't know what prompted me, but I got up and started to chant and do an Aleut dance my godmother, Matrona, taught me. "Qaganax, qaganax, anging, angitakuqingan."

Nellie and Anna smiled, but Evdokie looked solemn. "I was thinking, after we pass on, who will remember our hand-me-down dances? The young ones don't know them."

"We could teach them," I said, feeling a sudden interest.

"My mama and you are the star dancers, but Mama's joints ache too much to dance," Evdokie said.

"I'll start with the girls in my weaving class," I said.

At evening meal, I let Alicia and Anton in on my plan to start a dance class.

Alicia was enthusiastic. "Ah, Mama, I want to take that class. Agnes and Akinia will, too."

Anton remained silent, but the movement at the corner of his lips, nearly like a smile, told me he was pleased, too. Soon, he left the house. He was gone a lot for the next couple of days, not fishing. I wondered what he was doing, but he didn't explain anything. Then one evening he came in with a gleam in his eyes.

"I've rounded up students for a Russian class and a violin class." For a moment it felt like Peter was here. I forgot about the soldiers camped in our hills and the trucks gutting our paths and berry patches.

But by next day, the military presence again dominated. I realized the promyshlennik were as absorbed in recent events as we were when James Wilson arranged a get-together at the community hall for everyone in town. The meeting was already in progress when Alicia, Anton, and I arrived. We sat on the floor next to Nellie and Cousta. James Wilson and Horace Gump were in folding chairs at the front of the room facing the crowd.

Wilson, his fair hair cropped short like a soldier's, his gray eyes that looked too large for his sockets darting from face to face, was talking about our future as a military town. "Major Sexton, he's the one in charge of the operation, told me he expects additional troops and civilian workers any day."

"How many?" Horace Gump asked.

"He didn't say. But hell, man, the war's getting hotter. Our military are worried about war with the Japanese."

"But we're not at war with the Japanese," Ollie Larsen protested. Ollie owned the herring dock where Nicky worked.

"Not yet, but it's better to be prepared."

Ollie's face reddened. "All that equipment, all those men will wreck our beaches and fishing sites."

"For God's sakes, man, there's a danger of war," Wilson replied, his face flushed, too.

There was a war going on right in this room. I felt like running from it.

But then Innokenty spoke. "It'll be pretty cramped around here. We're a small place."

There was a sharp note in Wilson's voice when he answered. "War is not convenient."

Why didn't Wilson take time to understand Innokenty's meaning? Innokenty was speaking the question on my mind. Our people were used to honoring visitors. But were troops visitors? Were we to welcome them into our homes? Where would they fit, two hundred and maybe two hundred more and maybe two hundred more after that?

Ralph South responded to my unspoken question. "We're preparing to house soldiers and sailors and civilian workers right here in town. Wilson is going to build a hotel on the lot next to the store."

Anton had told me about hotels in Seattle, but I couldn't picture one in Akusha. What use would it serve after the soldiers left?

"I wonder if the military want to keep their men outside the town," Innokenty commented.

"It's better to keep them away from our herring docks," Ollie Larsen added.

"You'll have better business opportunities than salt herring when more troops come. There'll be a boom. You might get rich," Wilson replied.

Ollie Larsen looked like he was going to explode. He turned and left the meeting. I followed him. My stomach was churning from all the arguing.

The following day, a Navy ship—a long, rectangular steel box that looked like a transport to hell—anchored near the dock. We heard it had come for a long stay. A few days later, another gang of men arrived—soldiers and civilian workers. In no time, they were busy putting up quonset huts in the hills in back of the village. It didn't feel like our country anymore.

Victor came over every evening to report the news. His visits turned into regular town meetings. One evening, Victor told us, "Chester Brown, Wilson's assistant, is converting a warehouse near the store into a restaurant." The news that followed was even more startling. "The army plans to build an airstrip at the south end of the island, at Grigori's place."

I started to sputter. "Airplanes here ... on Grigori's land ... the only hand-me-down place in Akusha ... they'll smash the hills where the creeks run water to his barabara ... they'll destroy his boat harbor, steam house, wood shed ... the little village he made for himself." I stopped talking when Anton began gnawing at a loose piece of skin on his bottom lip.

"It's only a rumor, Mama," he said. "Airplanes can't fly in this foggy country."

"It's no damn rumor," Victor said, lighting one cigarette from the end of another. "Just this morning I heard Major Sexton tell Ralph South that the construction crew was ready to start building a runway and hangars."

The Old Man held his head in his hands and groaned.

"Maybe it won't be so bad," Victor said in a sympathetic voice. "Major Sexton said there'd be plenty of construction jobs for the local people, plenty of money to be made."

Stepan was frowning. "I heard those big iron birds make a terrible racket. They'll scare the geese and ducks and fish away."

I smiled at Stepan's words. I noticed Anton and Alicia did, too. I figured everyone but Victor agreed with Stepan. But Nellie surprised me. Her eyes lit up like they did when she caught a big fish.

"I have to wait a month for a letter from Mavra. Those airplanes might bring letters every week, maybe twice a week."

Her words sparked my imagination. I could picture planes flying here from other islands, maybe bringing Sergie and his family for a visit. But moments later, the troubled feeling returned, as I thought about Stepan's warning.

After the visitors left, Stepan and I walked on the beach. There was a full moon lighting a path across the water. The air was still and water splashed softly on the shore. For a moment, I forgot Stepan was by my side. How many times Peter and I hiked on the beach on nights like this; how many times we had sat on a log singing, playing guessing games about the creature that caused ripples in the water. A sudden rush of shame made me push those thoughts aside. Stepan was a fine man, he didn't deserve being erased by a ghost.

Alicia ran up to Stepan and me. "A meeting at the community hall. Better come. It's about an important subject."

"I don't want to hear them fight," I said.

"What's the meeting about?" Stepan asked.

"The Wilsons and Souths and Horace Gump want us to—I can't remember the word. It means we'd be a city like Salem or San Francisco."

"That's goofy. We're a little village. The soldiers will be leaving soon," I said.

Stepan took my arm. "We'd better go."

James Wilson, sitting in the center of a circle of chairs like a chief, had the floor.

"The officers are talking about appropriating this village for an airstrip. They want to build a runway right through this town."

"Do the officers say where the people in this town will live?" Innokenty asked in a shaky voice.

"That's the point," Wilson continued. "We must keep them from taking our land."

"I'm thinking about how we do that," Leonty said.

"We incorporate as a city. Then we have control of the land. The military won't be able to just take it from us."

"You say we can stop the military from building the air field if we incorporate?" Leonty asked.

"No," Wilson replied. "They'll build it no matter what we do. But if we incorporate as a city, they'll have to buy the land from us resident by resident. Why should we let them just take our land if we can get paid for it?"

I wasn't following James Wilson. He was talking as if the land belonged to him and the other whites as well as us Aleuts. When did that happen? I never heard about it. I had to say something. "This land belonged to my mama and her mama before and her mama before that."

"You have to consider, Tatiana, there may be a war," Ralph South said.

Sylvia leaned forward in her chair and with a burst of energy, said to Ralph, "You don't have to come in out of the rain before it's raining."

Ralph looked surprised, like he didn't expect his wife to buck him.

"My dear lady," Wilson intervened, "when storm clouds approach, it's time to put on your rain coat." And then, shifting his eyes to others in the room, he continued. "Friends, there's a good chance we'll be at war with Japan. The Aleutian Islands are a likely invasion point. That's why the military is going to build a landing strip here. That's why they want our land. That's why we should incorporate so we can sell it to them."

"I'm thinking about how we get our land back after the military leaves," Innokenty said.

Ollie Larsen jumped up. "Hot damn. He's right. This is an important question."

Wilson couldn't answer. He was having a coughing fit, so Horace Gump took the floor, cracking his knuckles as he spoke.

"We don't have all the answers. We don't know how long the military will stay here. We don't know what will happen to our town in the meantime. We're all in the dark together. But if we incorporate, we can influence events."

"I wonder what events you're thinking about," Innokenty said.

James Wilson hacked, spit into a handkerchief, and then answered. "For one thing, the city will be in charge of business licenses so we can protect ourselves, we who go into business here. I'm going to build a hotel. Horace is planning to operate a bar and liquor store. And Chester Brown here wants to open a restaurant. We don't want outsiders coming in and getting ahead of us locals."

My anger grew. Chester Brown, Horace Gump, James Wilson—they were outsiders, too. But Wilson was talking as if they lived here always like us Aleuts. Others must have shared my thoughts judging by the long faces around me.

Maybe Horace Gump saw those grim looks, for he suggested benefits that had more appeal. "If we incorporate, the city has the power to tax businesses and raise money for things like electric power and running water and indoor toilets and police and a fire station and a doctor and hospital."

I was surprised at the intensity with which Paulie's teacher, Mr. Tulliver, spoke against incorporation. "After the military leaves, there may be no more businesses to tax. And this little village will be stuck with the responsibility for schools and salaries for teachers and police and firemen, and—"

"Keep in mind that a city council has the power to get government grants," Horace Gump said. "Even if businesses close down, the city can get grants for schools and hospitals and doctors and nurses, things like that."

I didn't know I was going to say something until the words leaped out of my mouth. "We have a chief and a council of elders. They're the suggestors here." Alicia was smiling at me. Did she like her mama to fight like the promyshlennik?

Sylvia, her neck splotched like it gets when she's excited, stood up for me. "President Roosevelt has made a point of promoting Indian self-determination. There's a danger the new council will supersede the Native one."

Ralph gave Sylvia a harsh look. "We have to consider that an incorporated city will give the Aleut people things they never had under their government—a chance to eat in a hotel and have flush toilets and running water in their homes."

Sylvia's face grew redder than her neck. I feared bitter words. I wanted to be someplace else. Others must have felt the same. Our people don't like fighting. One by one, we drifted out of the community hall.

But that didn't end our conversations on the subject. They continued in homes all over town. Many people were stirred up by the thought of toilets and running water. In our family, we had to make six or seven trips a day to Ptarmigan Creek for water. I smiled as I pictured water flowing out of a pipe in my kitchen and toilets inside the house that flush the mess into the ground. It was hard to imagine, but what really caught my interest was the promise of a hospital and resident doctor or nurse. I thought of the time Peter nearly died of a busted appendix and of the many deaths that happened before a doctor or nurse got here. I thought of the rotten teeth in our children's mouths.

Others shared my desire. One night, when we had many visitors, Marie made a strong statement. "If the city council can raise money for a doctor and hospital, I'll vote for incorporation." Nicky and Victor agreed with her.

Stepan didn't. "Maybe a newcomer shouldn't speak. But I want to say, our Aleut councils and church brotherhood have always raised money for what we needed. So why not for a hospital, too?"

"We can't raise enough for something as big as a hospital," Victor replied. "We need taxes for that. And Horace Gump said it's against the law for the brotherhood or Aleut council to collect taxes."

Anton scowled. "If we have a city council, well, who will run it? Only the whites have knowledge about these taxation and legal things. So they'll be the rulers here."

"Maybe it's time we learned about these things," Alicia said.

I wasn't prepared for her comment. Were my children going to fight like the promyshlennik? I wanted to be by myself. My mind was as tangled as a kelp bed. I thought sleep would clear it, but the muddle was there next morning and for many mornings after.

One day, walking along the main path of town with Alicia and Ignaty, I heard rackets in several directions. A layer of snow lay on the ground, but construction was still going on. Looking south, I saw a gang of men widening the dock. Other men were putting siding on Chester Brown's restaurant. But there was a commotion right in the middle of town. It sounded like it came from the church. We hurried in that direction.

The noise was coming from Horace Gump's old house across the path from the church. After he married, Horace moved with his wife, Selena, to the promyshlennik end of town. Horace and a fisherman I'd seen around before were ripping the roof from that old house across from the church.

"Are you thinking of moving back here?" I asked.

"We're converting this place into a saloon and liquor store. There'll be plenty of business now. I thought of calling it 'Fogged Inn.' Clever, huh?"

"First time I ever heard of a marshal running a saloon," I said.

"Oh, I quit the marshal job last month. I want in on the boom."

I was glad Peter wasn't here to see a tavern across the path from the church and a white establishment in the middle of our town. Whites had always lived on the edges. Even the soldiers were camped in the hills.

As we walked on, Alicia tugged at my arm. "It's exciting, the boom. Picture it, Mama—a restaurant, hotel, bar, and there's talk of a real movie theater. And plenty of jobs, too."

I felt like shaking Alicia. "We already have jobs. We fish and hunt and trap and gather plants and take care of our church."

"But sometimes people are hungry. Sometimes they don't have coal or boots in winter."

"Those restaurants and hotels and laws and incorporations will wreck our life. The chief and elders won't be the suggestors anymore." As soon as I spoke those words, my mind felt clear. I was sure Alicia was wrong and we had to defeat that incorporation.

The election was just two weeks away. It was a good thing Alicia and her friends were too young to vote. They favored the new council. So did some of the older people. I wasn't sure how to change their minds. I decided to talk it over with Innokenty.

He was scraping crumbs from a plate into a slop bucket when I opened his door. After he finished, he heated water for chai. We sat quietly together, drinking chai. "Some of our people are going to vote for incorporation," I said after a while.

"I heard that Nicky and Marie and Anesia want the new council," he said.

"So do Victor and Bullshit John and Big Shot and Lupp. Maybe others that I don't know about."

Innokenty didn't say anything else, but later that day, I saw him visit some of the folks I mentioned. Leonty called on others. Ruff, third chief, would have joined our campaign, but he was away helping the military map our country.

Forty-eight people voted against incorporation, but fifty-seven voted for it. Maybe I should have pushed harder. But it wouldn't have mattered. Sylvia was on the committee that counted the votes. She told me that most of the "yes" votes were made by white businessmen and construction workers. Anyone who had lived in our village for three months could vote.

So now I live in a city.

TWENTY-THREE

"Mama, meet Lawrence." Paulie introduced a soldier who'd followed him and Gavril into the house. I nodded a greeting. Paulie was talking excitedly. "We met Lawrence this morning when we were watching him and some other guys build a quonset. Know what a quonset is? Not a small house like ours, but a barracks sleeping twenty men. Magic, Mama, putting that house together in one day. At first there was nothing but stacks of metal sheets. In no time, those guys unpacked the sheets, riveted them together, laid floors, built window frames. Mama, they're building a whole town up in the hills!"

I'm thinking the wind might blow those pieces of tin over," I said to Lawrence.

He cracked his finger joints, then clenched his jaw. "They're tested to stand up in all kinds of weather."

Paulie was still caught up in his adventure. "Lawrence shared his C-rations with us, Mama. Know what C rations are? Like tins of sardines, but filled with all kinds of things—crackers, potatoes, meat. Only thing, I was still hungry when I finished that tin. Are there any alaadix left?" Paulie asked, wandering over to the counter to look.

I brought the bowl of cold fry bread and a jar of salmonberry jelly to the table and motioned Lawrence to join us. Gavril and Paulie ate a couple of pieces of bread, but Lawrence didn't stop until the bowl was empty. He made some humming sounds while he ate, and when he finished, he grinned: "Aleut food's sure good. I'd like to try some other things."

I didn't know what to say about that, but I asked if the boys were getting in the way at the camp.

"We get plenty lonely in this miserable place— oh sorry—but it's so stormy and there's nothing to do. We welcome the kids."

"The soldiers tell jokes, Auntie. They make us laugh," Gavril said.

"And they let us taste their beer, and did they have a laugh when Gavril got dizzy and tripped," Paulie added.

Lawrence squirmed in his chair and began tugging at his ear lobe.

The door opened. It was the Old Man. Shortly after that, Nellie, Evdokie, and Anna came in. Lawrence made a quick getaway, saying he was due back at camp.

Nellie's face was flushed with anger. "No one said anything about a mayor in our town."

"James Wilson and Horace Gump talked about a council, nothing about a mayor," I said.

"Well, I read the city charter at Sylvia's house this morning, and it calls for the election of seven council members, and hear this, the council members choose one of their group to be mayor."

"Ai, a promyshlennik chief in our village."

"When Papa heard," Evdokie said, "he wondered about boycotting the elections. 'Let it be a white man's gang,' he advised."

"I haven't heard of any Aleuts running for that council anyhow," I said.

Alicia, sitting at the table drawing a sketch of Ignaty, spoke in a loud vioce. "I wish Nicky's name was on that candidate list. I wish I was old enough to run for the new council."

"Women don't run councils," the Old Man mumbled.

I tried to picture Mama sitting on that council with James Wilson and Chester Brown and Horace Gump. But Mama didn't like to fight, either. No, Mama would have had nothing to do with the white council. "What do the others say about boycotting the election?" I asked.

"I'd still run if I was older," Alicia repeated.

Anton, who had come in a few minutes earlier, sounded irritated when he spoke to Alicia. "Why would you want to help them turn Akusha into a white town? They'll make this place like Salem, with taverns everywhere you turn."

Alicia rinsed her paint brushes and carried the drawing to the counter. Then, turning to Anton, she said, "You'll be old enough to run in a couple years. I hope you change your mind by then."

Anton began twisting buttons on his shirt. "What good could come of being on that council?"

"We'd have Aleut voices on that council. Aleuts would have a say in the decisions."

"How can we have a say when we don't know anything about those legal matters?"

"We didn't know the English language when we started school," she snapped back.

My head was buzzing. I agreed with both of my children. What a jellyfish I was. I'd better figure out which way to turn. The election was just a week away.

Several days later, while searching the tide pools, Paulie, Gavril, and four soldiers approached me. One of them was Lawrence. I greeted the men with a smile, and pulling some seaweed from the muck, asked if they'd like to try a special Aleut food. Three of them shook their heads.

"Go ahead, try it, it's very good. Didn't you say you wanted to try Aleut foods?" I handed some to Lawrence. He accepted my offer. And then he chewed and chewed and chewed until he gagged and finally, his cheeks red with embarrassment, he spit it out.

I laughed, "I joke. We don't eat that slime."

The soldiers didn't think it funny. They didn't say a word as they walked on past us.

Paulie looked upset. I tussled his hair. "If those soldiers keep coming to town, we'll be overrun. There won't be any room left for us. And Paulie, I fear that the more you hang around them, the more often they'll come into the town."

I never did see Lawrence or those other three again.

Ollie Larsen ran past us on the way to his herring dock. The boys and I followed to see what was going on. Construction workers had torn the platform away, and a machine with a huge rotating arm was pulling the pilings from their moorings.

Tears ran down Ollie's flaming cheeks. "Why this spot? Why this spot? There's a whole beach of sand to put up their gun emplacements."

I felt like weeping, for myself, for Ollie, for Akusha. But a small part of me was also drawn to the magic of this project. Another truck rolled onto the sand, a rotating ball groaning and moaning as it made concrete. We watched them all afternoon, pouring cement, attaching bolts for the base of the guns, and then, at dusk, we saw guns the length of two spears pointing in the air. The magic vanished as fast as I blinked my eyes. Would Japanese airplanes fly over our country? Would they drop bombs? I wanted to flee, to sail far away from Akusha.

The day before the election, Alicia and Anton were still arguing about the new council. Alicia did most of the talking. "Agnes and I have been asking our people to put their names on that slate. No one will, except Victor. Anton, maybe if you talked to them, they'd consider running for council."

"Why would I ask anyone to do something I'm against? Running for that council would be like shoving greased owl shit down my throat. If I talk to people, I'll tell them not to vote."

Nellie, who had come earlier, broke into a hearty laugh. "Never heard that expression before—greased owl shit, greased owl shit. Is that what you learned at higher school?" And then, a serious look on her face, she said, "Innokenty has called the elders to a meeting after lunch."

I sighed, knowing that all this talk about businesses and incorporations hadn't weakened our elders' council. I was in high spirits when Nellie and I set out for the meeting at Innokenty's house. Though it was scheduled for early afternoon, it didn't start until dusk, everyone waiting for Ruff to return from trapping. During the wait, I guessed the subject of the meeting had to do with boycotting the election.

I was wrong. I knew it when the Old Man dragged Paulie and Gavril into the room.

Innokenty began the meeting then. "Thievery and drunkenness are against our ways." Both boys looked at the floor. "I'm wondering why you stole booze from Horace Gump's store." Neither boy answered, but their faces colored. No one else spoke, either.

After a long silence, Paulie finally explained. "We were walking around town when we saw Horace Gump leave his store. He didn't lock the door or anything. We looked in the window. The sun was bright. I could see everything in that store, shelves and shelves with different colored bottles. We went in to look around. I picked up one bottle with green-colored liquid."

"And I took a brown one off another shelf," Gavril said.

"We put the bottles under our parkas and ran off to one of our secret hiding places."

"And we opened the bottles. Mine tasted like piss," Gavril said, "so we drank Paulie's."

"The whole bottle?" Leonty asked.

"I think so," Paulie answered. "I don't remember much about it. Only that Gavril said we'd be late for school. So we got up and went there."

"Mr. Tulliver said you boys staggered into the school room, talking loud and talking nonsense," the

Old Man said. "And then Mr. Tulliver had to interrupt school to take you two drunkards home."

Why hadn't Nellie and I heard about this? Everyone else seemed to know. It happened the day
before, the day Nellie and I spent at Grigori's place.
We checked on that old man every week, bringing
him food and news.

"Sometimes people who steal and get drunk are
sent away from their villages," Innokenty said. His
words were harsh, but his tone was soft. After all,
Paulie was his grandson.

Paulie and Gavril stared harder at the floor.

"Maybe we'll send you away to the army," Leonty
warned. The boys heads fell lower.

"My father told me that an outside man sneaks
into the village in the middle of the night looking
for boys who drink and thieve," Ruff said.

Innokenty rose then and went over to the boys.
"This time we'll forgive you. Next time we might
send you away. You can go now."

The boys ran from the room as if they were being jabbed in the rear by a spear. I laughed all the
way home. I felt sorry for Paulie and Gavril, but I
laughed because my mama and her mama before and
her mama before that would have felt right at home
at that council meeting.

James Wilson was elected mayor by the other six
councilmen—Victor, the only Aleut, Ralph South,

Chester Brown, Horace Gump, Tom Tulliver, and
Ollie Larsen. Alicia and I watched the first meeting
of the new council. The members made a list—
"Goals and Priorities," they called it. The first item
had to do with issuing business licenses. I noticed
that Horace Gump, Chester Brown, and James Wilson, three of the council members, had applied for
licenses. Their list included other activities—con-
sulting a lawyer, asking the military to pay for the
land it used, and asking that the Bureau of Indian
Affairs build a hospital.

But, everyone forgot that list in a hurry.

The next day, December 7, 1941, we were all
sitting around the stove planning costumes for our
Christmas celebration when Victor dashed into the
house, breathless. "Pearl Harbor, bombs dropping,
President Roosevelt on the radio. We've declared war
on Japan. We're really at war."

Twenty-four

It was five months since that dreadful December day. Akusha didn't feel like our village anymore. It was so crowded there was no place to walk, no place to be alone, no room to breathe. Sometimes I'd forget about the military, gather my fishing gear and start out for Rocky Point, only to be immediately reminded by the sight of gutted paths and gun emplacements lining the beach and the horizon cluttered with quonsets, trucks, machines, and troops. So I stayed inside a lot.

One day in early spring, I was sitting by the stove sorting grass when Ignaty tore into the house screaming and clutching my skirt. "Ma, a giant bird in the air!"

Ignaty was talking. In sentences, too. And in Aleut. But I was too frightened by the news to celebrate his accomplishment. I ran outside, Ignaty still hanging onto my skirt. The roar was too loud for my ears. I covered them and stared at a huge cargo plane circling the new airport built at the south end of the island, past Grigori's place. That was the first plane I ever saw. I never understood the idea of airplanes. How could that metal bird balance itself in the air? It didn't flap its wings like a bird.

Days passed. More planes overhead. I never got used to seeing them drop right out of the fog. I never got rid of my fear they'd drop down on our heads. Every time I heard them circling around, I looked for a hiding place.

I heard no planes on this morning when Victor stopped by. We hadn't seen him lately. He'd been working in construction at the new airport. He slid into a chair at the table facing Anton and Paulie who were feasting on smoked salmon. I brought a plateful to Victor and sat down next to him. After eating, Victor turned to Anton and squared his shoulders. "I've just been made assistant foreman of a construction gang."

Anton's face showed no expression.

Victor continued. "We're building hangars and warehouses. We need more workers. Anton, the air force pays a high wage—thirty-five dollars a week. Can you believe that? It's more than twice as much as I earned at the NS store." He paused again, his eyes scanning Anton's face. "Anton, do you want to work with me?"

Anton didn't answer. He kept his eyes fixed on the seal he was carving from a piece of hardwood. Nicky gave Anton one of his carving knives for his

last name day, and ever since, Anton whittles whenever he has a chance.

"I'd like that job," Paulie said.

"You're too young."

"Nearly fourteen."

"You have to be at least sixteen, Paulie. I'm sorry."
Victor turned back to Anton. "It's a great opportu-
nity. How about it?"

"I like what I'm doing. It's important," Anton
replied.

"Important?" Victor asked.

"I'm the only Russian language teacher in town."

"You can do both."

"It takes time to prepare lessons and tutor the
students."

Victor looked puzzled. "You can always teach
Russian but these high paying jobs won't be around
forever."

"What good would it do?"

I was proud of Anton's comment until I heard
Victor's heated response. "What good? What good?
What's the use of Russian classes if the Japs bomb
the shit out of our village?"

I had a sudden urge to get away from this conversation. I got up, wrapped my sweater around my
shoulders, and set out for the beach. It was quiet—
no workers, no machines. The sky was clear and a
light breeze was blowing. I felt calm inside when I

looked out at the shimmering band of sunlight reflected on the water. Then my eyes wandered to Berry Valley, the only place nagoon berries grow. The soldiers were putting a road smack in the middle of the nagoon berry patches. Looking north from the valley, I saw others digging trenches, hiding places if we were bombed. And then my eyes moved to the bay, where four destroyers were standing side by side.

My excursion didn't lift my mood; it made me feel worse. My eyes darted around seeking a place of refuge. I saw smoke coming from Nellie's chimney and headed for her house.

She was sitting cross-legged on the floor bent over her sewing. Bird skins were piled on the floor next to her. The soldiers and sailors loved bird skin parkas; she could sell all she could make. She put her sewing aside, got up and went over to the stove to boil water. I waited on a bench in front of the table. She brought me a sweet cake, store bought, with the chai. I couldn't eat that sticky, squishy pastry. Nellie was so busy making parkas, I guess she didn't have time to bake anymore. A wave of nausea washed through me and I got up to leave. But I had no destination. Nothing seemed the same, no matter where.

For weeks, maybe months, a dream troubled my sleep. I was mist, without weight. I hovered low over the water, but I couldn't see its color or motion. I levitated into the hills, but I couldn't see the ground cover. I floated back to the village, over Innokenty's house, but I couldn't make out its lines. I wanted to land, but I had no weight to bring me down. Innokenty came out of his house. I called to him. "Get a rope, pull me to the ground." But there was no sound to my voice. He didn't see me. He didn't hear me. And suddenly fire fell from the sky and I watched the village below burn to the ground. I always woke trembling from that dream, afraid it would happen.

And then it did. One morning in early June, I was on my way to the shed for coal when blasts of fire—like huge, colored balloons—exploded in the sky. Our anti-aircraft guns were shooting at Japanese planes that were strafing buildings and vessels in the bay. Something nearby shattered. Later I learned that Japanese bullets hit the side of the army supply station. I ran to the children. Their eyes were wide with sleep and terror. We huddled in a corner of the room.

A military policeman rushed into the house. "We're evacuating everyone to the valley. Grab some blankets, food, and water, and get into the truck fast."

The valley was filled with trenches, holes in the ground covered with earth and held firm with heavy timbers, and steel beams. One end of the trench was open so we could watch the doings. I covered my ears to muffle the noise of gunfire, but I kept my eyes open, glued to the sky, watching, watching, my heart pounding so hard I feared it would crack my chest open. Finally, the Japanese planes left. An officer told us we could leave. No one moved. We stayed in that trench until dark.

Next morning, I was sweeping the floor with an eagle wing broom Anton had made when he walked in from the store. One look at his face and my heart pounded.

His lips twitched; his eyes held terror. "Mama, the Japs dropped bombs on Azian Bay. They wiped out the community hall, the school, and the church. And Mama," he stopped for a moment, wiping the mist from his eyes, "And Mama, three deaths. Ruff was over there charting maps for the military. Yes, our third chief Ruff was one of the dead."

An omen—one of our chiefs destroyed when everything else was falling apart. What next?

Minutes later, Nellie came in, panting. "People are leaving this place, yes, leaving this place fast, Tatty."

"Who's leaving?" I asked, holding my breath.

"Sylvia and Ralph, yes, my friend, Sylvia, and Ollie Larsen, too, and Selena Brown, and our teacher in lower class, Miss Stevens."

My feelings were mixed. I wasn't unhappy to hear that promyshlennik were leaving our village. But was it another omen?

Everything was happening so fast it made me dizzy. Victor came in right after Nellie. "The officers are talking about evacuating all our people from these islands."

"Impossible. Sylvia and Ralph are used to living in different places. But we know only these islands."

Lawrence, Paulie's soldier friend, rushed into the house. "I'm carrying a message from our commanding officer. Bombs may fall here any day. Every family is required to build a bomb shelter. Dig them into the hillsides. And hurry."

Finally, the promyshlennik understood the value of our traditional houses.

Anton took charge, like Peter would have done. "Mama, you and Stepan can dig a barabara for our family. Victor and I are going to help some of the others. Little Hunch, the Old Man, Pletanida, Leonty, those old people will all need help." I stared at my son, so pleased with himself when he felt useful.

"Don't worry about Little Hunch and the Old Man," I told him. "Stepan and I will see to them. They'll need food and company. So they'll use our barabara. We'll dig one near their houses."

Speed was on everyone's mind. While Stepan and Paulie dug our barabara, Alicia, Feckla, and I gathered survival equipment.

"Why are you packing Ignaty's toys?" I asked Alicia. "There isn't much space in the shelter. Little Hunch and the Old Man will be staying there, too."

"Mama, Ignaty's so young. Maybe toys will keep his mind off bombs."

"But why your paints, Alicia?"

"Maybe for the same reason."

I continued packing—an oil-burning lamp, seal oil, water, pilot crackers, dried fish, blankets, and a pee pot. Bombs or no, we'd have to leave our shit outside. Then we joined the men at the barabara site. The Old Man and Little Hunch stood around watching them. Stepan and Paulie had finished digging and Stepan was making a sod and grass roof.

We were ready. The next morning the military gave every family a siren—"clackers," we called them—that could be heard all over the village. We were instructed to ring them at the faintest suggestion of a plane, even if it turned out to be a gust of wind. That very day, the sound of clackers drove us into hiding three times. Not a day passed without at least two of those warnings.

When there was time, which wasn't often, I trained the younger children to survive if war came to our town. I took Ignaty and Feckla to the hills to show them the roots and bulbs and greens and berries we eat. And on the beach, I showed them where to dig clams and find mussels and seaweed. Ignaty thought it was a game.

He thought living in the shelter was a game, too. The first few times we went down there, Ignaty laughed as he watched Alicia weave strings into different shapes. "Make a boat," he said to her in English. He spoke in both languages right from the start.

"Make a house. Make a boot." And when his interest waned, he picked up stones and rings and asked Paulie to play qamtidax with him. And sometimes the Old Man would let him play with the chess pieces. But as time passed, the fun wore off. Ignaty started to balk at going inside. "It's too dark," he'd whined. Anton would pick him up and carry him on his shoulders. Ignaty used to love riding high like that, but no more. He fought Anton. He fought anyone who tried to get him into the shelter. We had to drag him in. Even the singing, which he'd always loved, failed to interest him. After a while, Ignaty stopped struggling. Something died inside of him. Active from the moment of birth, Ignaty went limp like a dead bird.

The blackouts in our above-ground house didn't help his mood. The military gave every family black material to make curtains. We all slept close to one another in the kitchen, our clothes by our side, waiting for the sound of the siren.

One night, I lay awake, restless and tense, listening for Stepan and Anton. They'd gone hunting at Bird Island that morning. They said they'd be back in time for vespers. The night was passing. Where were they? Did they run into Japanese soldiers on that island? I listened to every sound. All night.

At dawn, just as we were getting up, Nicky and Little Hunch came in. Their eyes looked to mine for news of the men. I shook my head. Later, when I was frying alaadix, the door opened. It was Stepan and Anton, each carrying an armload of Canada geese. Stepan told us what happened.

"We hunted all day. Then at dusk, we set out for home. Well, we couldn't see a thing. No moonlight. No navigation lights. No lights on the buoys. No lighthouse. No lights in the town. It was blacker than the inside of my boot. We were lost. I decided, no more of this. It was like sailing into a black hole."

"So how did you get home?" Paulie asked.

"We lucked out. We paddled through a channel I recognized. I knew a protected cove lay to the right. We sailed into it, by feel rather than sight, and stayed there until the first light. Then we could see to come home."

Even though we'd lived in the dark hell of war for over a month, I had an urge to celebrate. Stepan and Anton had brought home enough geese for a feast. I had plenty of candles. Everyone was buoyed up at the idea of a candlelit goose feast. "Who should we ask?" I said to no one in particular.

"How about inviting all the men in the quonsets?" Alicia answered, laughing.

"Why so stingy?" Anton replied. "We should ask the sailors on the ships, too."

"You forgot the construction workers," Paulie said, joining the fun.

But I noticed Stepan didn't take part. It was the same during the eating and storytelling after. His body was there, but the rest of him was someplace else. Later, I sat up in bed while he undressed, waiting to learn what was on his mind.

He crawled in beside me, cradled my head in his arms and began talking. "I met my cousin, Sasha, at Bird Island." Sasha had married Nellie's daughter Mavra and they lived in New Harbor. "He wants me to fish with him out of New Harbor. I said I'd have to think it over. I thought about his proposition this way and that all day. Before we parted, I told him I'd go."

I sucked in a great gulp of air.

"There's too much commotion here for fishing," he said. "We're leaving tomorrow, Tatiana."

"Now, when everything here is crazy."

"That's why. So I won't get crazy, too, and be no good to anyone."

Something wilted in my heart, the light and sparkle from Stepan's and Feckla's presence. Feckla? Will he take her? She's just getting used to us. I muttered her name. He didn't say anything, so I did. "Feckla stays with us."

"Yes," he said, and then he turned his back to me and I heard him sniffle.

It was lucky he left when he did. The following day, I heard the roaring, grinding sound of a military truck. It stopped in front of our house. Colonel Sundry, in charge of military operations on the island, walked in. He spoke in haste, as if there wasn't time to waste a breath. "We're evacuating all Aleuts except those in New Harbor and Kooney Pass."

My throat closed up. My voice came out in a whisper. "Where to?"

"Someplace where you'll be safe."

"Where is that place?"

"It hasn't been decided yet, but there's a steamer in the bay waiting to take you away from the Aleutians. Every person is allowed one suitcase, not a single thing more. Hurry, we want you aboard and ready to leave in four hours."

"Wherever we go, we'll need our churchbooks and icons," I said.

The colonel hesitated before responding. "There'll be churches where you're taken."

"Russian Orthodox churches?

"I don't know what kind. Won't any church do?" He was clearly irritated.

I tightened my jaw. This was not an issue we could overlook. If we couldn't live in our Aleut country, at least we could live our Aleut life.

"We need our churchbooks," I repeated.

"All right, but remember, you have four hours," he said as he turned on his heels and left.

There wasn't time for any more discussion. I issued orders to Anton and Alicia. "Get the younger children ready. Pack as many clothes, blankets, and cooking things as you have room for in the two trunks and four clothes boxes. Take clothes for Feckla and me, too. Then go to the store for some lumber and board up the house."

"I'll need my Russian language and music books, and skin for a drum," Anton announced.

"So okay, find room in the boxes. I'm going over to the church to pack books and icons, some to store, some to take with us. I'll meet you on board," I told the children as I got ready to leave the house.

Others were on their way to the church at the same time—Evdokie and Parascovia, Nellie, Anna and Big Shot, Sophie and Bullshit John, Matfay, and Innokenty. The men set out to find boxes for the books and wrapping material for the church valuables. The women lifted icons from the walls and candelabra from shelves. After the men returned, we packed eight icons and seven boxes of books, and the men took them to the ship. Then, the women wrapped the other valuables for storage, tied them with cord, and carried them to the church attic. We covered the whole lot with a large piece of canvas.

Four hours later we were on board, everyone in the village except Victor. The military wanted him for construction work.

TWENTY-FIVE

I leaned over the side of the ship, my face whipped by spray from waves breaking against the hull. Alicia was standing beside me.

"Mama, where are they taking us?"

I didn't have an answer. I reached over and tucked some loose hair back into her braids.

"Will we ever see Akusha again?" she asked.

"I wish we were Canada geese. We'd be heading back right now."

Her fear deepened my despair. I wondered what Akusha would look like when we returned. Would the soldiers wreck everything? Would they steal our valuables?

I thought of Peter's violin. "Alicia, did you bring Papa's fiddle?"

"I'm sorry, Mama. There was no room."

His fiddle had always been there to comfort me in black times. I yearned to play it on this journey of grief.

The weather was as bleak as my mood. A thick fog hung low over a surging, gray sea. Not a single mountain was in sight, nothing but the color of ash wherever my eye lit. I don't know if it was my dark mood or the constant roll of the ship that made me feel like heaving.

If I got sick in the open air, I wondered how the rest were doing below deck—Nicky on his first sea voyage since he was three, Marie in her seventh month of pregnancy, Innokenty with his joint pains. I decided to go below and check on them.

I held tight to the rail going down to the steerage where they packed us—two hundred in one room, no air, our sleeping mats so close they touched. Nicky was splayed out on the floor like a landed crab. Marie was stretched out next to him, lying on her back. Innokenty sat cross-legged near Nicky. He understood Nicky's terror of the sea.

Gloomy as I felt, I laughed as I watched Ignaty bound around the room, Little Peter crawling after him as fast as his stumpy legs could go. How quickly Ignaty forgot the terror of bomb shelters. Here, on the boat, surrounded by every person in the world he knew, he acted as if this was one gigantic name day party for him. He ran over to Vassa, who was taking pilot crackers from a sack. Ignaty knew he'd be given one just by standing near her.

Stuffing it in his mouth and giving some to Little Peter, Ignaty scurried over to the Old Man, who was sitting with Little Hunch and Makary. When the Old Man saw the cracker dangling from Peter's mouth, he grumbled to anyone within hearing. "My stomach growls."

Matfay opened a can of corned beef hash and spooned some in a cup for the Old Man.

"I don't eat vomit."

Little Hunch reached into her sack for a piece of dried fish and handed it to the Old Man. He ate slowly, savoring every bite, maybe not knowing when he'd taste Aleut food again. When he finished the fish, he called over to Innokenty, "Where are they taking us?"

Innokenty shrugged.

Matfay rose from his seat. "I'll go above and see what I can learn." Anton and Simon joined him.

I was asleep when they returned. It was the shuffling of feet and the movement of so many people that woke me. Everyone was gathering around the three men to hear the news.

"The captain has instructions," Matfay was saying. "He's taking us to Bear Cove on Alexander Island. That's in the southeastern part of Alaska. They're housing us at the site of an abandoned salmon cannery."

"I'm trying to remember what's known about that country," I said, looking at Innokenty.

"My grandfather told me the Russians once took many Aleuts over there to hunt sea otters. Some stayed there. We may even run into cousins in that place."

"I wonder if people over there fish and hunt?" Vasili said.

"The Tlingit Indians live in that country," Anton said. "They hunt land animals, animals we don't have at home—deer, wolves, hares, and squirrels. I've seen pictures of those animals."

I was proud of Anton's knowledge.

"Maybe those Tlingits live in barabaras," Vasili said hopefully.

"We're going to forest country where there's plenty of wood for modern houses," Anton explained.

Vasili cast a quick look at Vassa and the two of them walked over to the wall and sat down on the floor, looking forlorn. I went over and sat down beside them, but I didn't say anything. I didn't know what that strange country would hold.

Five days later, we reached our Bear Cove camp—a few run-down buildings on a thin strip of beach at the foot of headlands that were smothered with large trees. Slowly and tentatively, the ship tied up at a rotting dock. Walking from the pier toward the campsite, we passed a cannery, bunkhouse, and three shacks. Not a single human in sight except Mr. Canfield, the Indian Bureau agent from Juneau, there to help us get settled. Ignaty kept staring at him, maybe because his face was so red and flabby, or maybe because he wore a crown of thick white hair. Mr. Canfield walked with us, past the cannery that was decomposing like a corpse. The shacks were in decay, too. Water pipes lying on top of the ground were broken. Outhouses had caved in. The bunkhouse was the only livable place, and at that the floorboards were soft with age and had a musty smell. Mr. Canfield never said a word, but he took notes when we were in the bunkhouse.

"Stinky in here," Ignaty complained.

"It's just a camp. We won't be here long," I said.

"Let's camp up in those trees, he said, pointing to the thick stands of spruce and hemlock covering the inland view as far as we could see.

"We're going to explore there, later," Paulie said, "after we set up camp here."

The bunkhouse was like a warehouse, no individual rooms, just one huge space with a long table and two large stoves at one end. We hung blankets to mark rooms, about ten square feet for a family. Trying to cheer Ignaty, Alicia said, "See, we have a big window; it's not dark in here like it was in the Akusha shelter."

"I want to go home," he answered her. Poor Ignaty, so young to bear this sudden leap into a foreign country.

There wasn't room for everyone in our family to sleep at once, so we took turns: Alicia, Ignaty, Paulie, and the Old Man, first shift starting right after evening meal; Little Hunch, Feckla, and me, second shift starting in the middle of the night and sleeping most of the morning. But no matter what time of day or night we slept, we couldn't get away from the rats. They ran all over the bunkhouse. We chased them and killed them day and night, but still more came.

Maybe it was the rats that started the boil epidemic. The boils attacked everyone—men, women, and children, old and young. Few escaped. Ignaty had them all over his rear end, big red swellings with hard, pus-filled centers. He whimpered at first, and as they hardened and got more painful, he howled. It was the same with the other children. The adults twisted and turned in pain. We tried soaking the boils in creek water. It didn't help. We tried soaking them in hot water. Still, they kept spreading. I asked the teacher, Mr. Ginsburg, to radio Mr. Canfield in Juneau to send a doctor. The Indian Bureau boat, *Pioneer,* called every week. Mr. Canfield didn't waste time. Dr. Albee showed up on the *Pioneer's* next visit. He put poultices over the boils and painted them with tincture of iodine. When that didn't work, he stabbed the swellings to get the pus out of the center. He stayed all week, treating one boil after another. Still, they persisted. That miserable epidemic lasted a month. Maybe the cure came from Dr. Albee's treatments, or maybe the boils healed on their own. It didn't matter—we knew we had to get rid of the rats.

And that wasn't all. Sickness was spreading like a fire gone wild—colds, flu, pneumonia. None of our living places were insulated. Our breath and bones seemed to be turning to ice. Both chiefs, Innokenty and Leonty, were weak and feverish from flu. Pletanida, the oldest person in camp, came down with pneumonia. We were worried about Marie and Akinia, both pregnant and both thin as pipe cleaners.

At least our water was good. Leonty had located a creek a short distance from camp. It was a marvel that Leonty with his sightless eyes saw what none of the rest of us did. At the start of our search for a nearby creek, we divided up into gangs, each armed with whistles as we explored different paths. My group—Alicia, Agnes, Paulie, and Gavril—climbed a headland directly behind the camp. We weren't used to a forest, one tree looking exactly like a hundred others, so it was hard to keep track of our location. We circled back and forth, blowing our whistle every few minutes until we heard an answering signal.

But those answers kept growing weaker, and soon we heard none at all. We tried to retrace our steps, but in that patchwork of animal trails we became completely muddled. At dusk, we talked it over and decided to stay put and wait until someone found us. A couple hours passed. The air became chill. The moon showed bright against a blackening sky. We didn't speak our fear, but it showed in every eye.

How far had we wandered? Were they searching for us? Would they find us before morning? Alicia and Agnes sat huddled together for warmth. Paulie shivered, but didn't complain. I started to cut leafy branches from the trees for covers. I tucked some around Paulie and began to cut more when I heard the sound of yelling. It was Simon and Anton. They led us back to camp, and not once did they tease us about our muddled mission.

Leonty was the star in finding creek water. Evdokie recounted the amazing story. "Papa walked along the beach for a long time. 'Papa,' I said, 'we can't lug water from this great distance. We need to stay closer to camp.' Papa nodded, but kept right on going. What was he thinking? After a while he came to a place where water flowed down a hill into the sea. Then he led us along the bed of that creek until it began to wind back up the hillside. When the creek branched, Papa seemed sure which arm to follow. Finally, we came to a widening of the creek. I could see the camp from that spot. I asked Papa how he knew which leg of the creek would bring us close to camp. 'I listened for the sounds of hammering in the camp.' Papa knew men were repairing the bunkhouse."

So we had good water, but the food was bad. The berry season was nearly over when we first arrived. As soon as we could, Anna, Nellie, Vassa, and I went out to gather what berries were left. Hard as it was for Vassa to climb hills, she stayed with us. For berries, I think Vassa would walk on her nose. And there on the hillside, I heard Nellie yelp, "Lordy, lordy, a sea of blueberries."

We followed the sound of her voice until we stood before a dense growth of blueberry bushes. Vassa cried with joy. Farther on, we found salmonberries. Vassa and I stuffed our stomachs double in size with those berries.

But they didn't go far. Food continued to be a problem. Most of us didn't like the canned meats and fish Mr. Canfield supplied, and we weren't used to eating the forest animals that lived around us. Mr. Canfield had suggested we hunt porcupines because they were simple to catch. They move so slow there's plenty of time to club them to death.

One day, when the berries had fallen from the bushes, I invited Anna and Nellie to hunt porcupine with me. "Lord, no, I'd rather eat sand than porcupine," Nellie complained.

"How about some cow's tongue," I teased her, remembering the lunch Sylvia South once fed us.

"I'll eat the cow's tongue if you eat the hole in its nose," Nellie joked. Anna didn't join in the fun. She was worried about porcupine quills. "One of the dogs came running in the other day with a quill stuck up his nose and it took Matfay and Simon many minutes to get it out. And the dog howled the entire time."

"Mr. Canfield told me to start skinning the animal at the belly where there are no quills," I said. So come on, we'll have a porcupine adventure."

A light snow was falling that day, but it wasn't cold. We hiked a long time before anything happened. Then I heard a melodic hum in a variation of three notes. I turned my eyes in the direction of that sound and soon a dark-colored porcupine waddled toward us, humming the while. We killed six of them that day.

On the way back, we dropped one off at Leonty's cabin. I shivered; it was colder and clammier on the inside than out. Rats and cold, no wonder everyone was sick. Leonty, a blanket around his shoulders, was sitting on the floor playing chess with the Old Man.

When they finished the game, I asked the men, "I wonder why the council doesn't meet." Both men gave me a questioning look. "Maybe to discuss how to get lumber and insulation for our buildings," I went on.

After a long silence, Leonty answered. "We'll meet when Innokenty is better."

I didn't say more, but I was thinking, maybe he wouldn't get better unless we insulated our houses.

After we left, I confided my fears to Nellie.

"What can we do, yes, what can we do?" I considered the question and after a while suggested we talk directly to Mr. Canfield about the problem. He arrived that morning on the *Pioneer* carrying an ax and a saw as long as a skiff. He was going to train some of our men in cutting down trees. There are no trees in our country, just shrubs, so no one had any experience with that activity. Nellie, Evdokie, and I hiked up into the headlands in back of our camp to watch them.

Matfay and Simon, one at each end of a crosscut saw, were bending their bodies back and forth in the rhythm of a dance. Mr. Canfield showed them how to notch the trunk to direct the way the tree fell.

But I guess he didn't want to take any chances. When it came time for the tree to topple, he told us to go back to camp. We didn't. We just moved back a tree length and continued to watch. No one of us ever saw anything like this before. What a racket it made falling.

That tree looked taller on the ground than when it was standing. We all stared at it a long while. Then I walked over to Mr. Canfield. "We need wood and insulation to keep the rats and the cold out of our buildings."

Mr. Canfield smiled. "I've already ordered lumber to build cabanas. It should be here next week." Cabanas are small, two-room temporary houses, but larger than the three cabins the men had fixed up.

My heart felt lighter after that conversation, and my spirits rose higher when I walked into the bunkhouse and saw Anton, sitting on the floor of our living space teaching Russian to four students.

A short time later, Simon came over to Anton. "Grab a shovel. We've found a spot to build a barabara for Vassa and Vasili."

The thought of a barabara for Vassa and Russian language lessons for our children reminded me we could live Aleut wherever we were. We'd be together, nearly everyone in the village. We'd have church services. Maybe we'd build a steambath, too. I started to chant Aleut songs.

TWENTY-SIX

"It's getting to be a habit," I said to Nellie when again she asked me to act as suggestor. We were watching Mr. Canfield climb down the ship's ladder when she prodded me.

"Tell him we need a schoolhouse."

"Okay," I said.

He hoisted his gear and without looking in our direction made a beeline for the school, housed in our bunkhouse. Nellie and I hurried to catch up with him.

"Mr. Canfield," I called in a soft voice.

He dropped his duffel bag and turned toward me.

I told him right out that we needed lumber for a school. When he didn't say anything, I filled him in with details. "Mr. Ginsburg's a fine teacher, but hard as he tries, he can't compete with the commotion—men hammering, women cooking and chattering, small children yelping and interrupting the school lessons. It's no good."

Mr. Canfield made a clucking sound with his tongue against the roof of his mouth. "Not good. I agree. But there's a war on and lumber is in short, very short supply. I'm having enough trouble round-ing up lumber for your cabanas." Mr. Canfield clucked again and after a long sigh, said, "I'll do my best for you folks." Then he went inside to talk to Mr. Ginsburg. It was late afternoon; school was over for the day.

At first people wondered if Mr. Ginsburg was one of us. His dusky-colored skin and black hair and eyes looked like ours. But the texture of his hair didn't—a mass of tight curls. Mr. Ginsburg was our only teacher, so some of us got busy helping him— Alicia with art, Nicky with ivory carving, Parascovia, wise in memories, with stories of our ancestors, and I read to the younger children. Mr. Ginsburg was the first government teacher I ever knew who was interested in passing on the children's inheritance. I figured it was because he valued his own. Sometimes, sitting around the stove with us in the evenings, he told tales about his Polish Jewish ancestors who lived in camps like ours—"ghettos" they were called.

Nellie and I went into the school room, too. Like the teachers in Akusha, Mr. Ginsberg was in charge of the mail and he was sorting it when we walked in. He smiled and handed me a letter from Stepan, the first in many weeks. Stepan didn't know how to read or write, but once in a while Mavra recorded his spoken letters and sent them to me. There was no mail for Nellie so she followed me to my living space, hoping my letter had news of her daughter. Evdokie, also eager for news of home, joined us. I read the letter to them.

"Sasha and I are busier than one-armed house painters. The government needs canned fish for the soldiers and the cannery pushes us to catch more, more, more. But these good times won't keep me here when my family returns to Akusha. I've been asking around, why don't they send you home? There are no Japanese on your island. No one seems to know what's going on around our islands."

I had the same question in my mind. So did Nellie and Evdokie. "When Innokenty heals," Evdokie said, "he should ask Mr. Canfield why we can't go home."

"He's so frail. We may have to wait a long time," Nellie said. And then as an afterthought, she suggested that my words are strong and I should speak for Innokenty.

I didn't want to represent our chief. But I didn't want to wait around either.

I nodded agreement. Then the three of us got to our feet and went out to find Mr. Canfield. He was standing outside the school room door smoking a Lucky Strike.

I said it right off, "We're thinking about when we'll be going home."

"I'm sorry, but you can't go home until the last Jap is driven from the Aleutian Islands."

A flame of anger darted through me. "We're wondering why the government hasn't evacuated the New Harbor people."

"There are no Japs on that island."

"There are no Japs at Akusha, either."

"Mrs. Shemikin, there's a war on. We need those New Harbor canneries operating."

So, we're still in the dark. But Mr. Canfield didn't ignore us altogether. A week later, the *Pioneer* unloaded enough lumber for a one-room schoolhouse and four cabanas. Only four. We needed ten times that many. We didn't gripe, though. The men got busy putting them together. It was a good thing Anton and Simon had learned carpentry when they built Anton's new room. They took charge of construction, even training Paulie and Gavril as helpers. Of course, Leonty watched over the work. The men completed the job in a few days. Then, the brotherhood met to make assignments. Three houses for the older people and the fourth for Marie and Akinia, both pregnant, and their families. Those cabanas were plenty crowded, but they were warm and they smelled fresh and clean compared to the spongy, rotting floors in the bunkhouse.

One day, as Alicia and I were hauling water from the creek, Nicky came racing toward us. "The baby is coming!" We ran back to Marie's cabin with him. Marie was on the bed against the far wall. Anesia bent over her, massaging her stomach. Sweat rolled down Marie's face and neck. And though she made no sounds, the color drained from her face and I feared she'd pass out. Why was she having so much trouble? This was her third child. Was it another up-side-down delivery?

Anesia kept up a steady stream of talk. "Take deep breaths. Now try to rest. Now push down, push down harder."

Nicky was making everyone nervous, pacing in the small space already jammed with people.

"Go out for a while," Anesia told him. And then she turned back to Marie. "It will take only so many pushes, Marie. Remember, each one means fewer left to go."

Hours passed in this way. "Breathe, push down, a little harder, there, now we're getting close."

Marie was wearing out. Then, we saw the baby's bottom. Another breech. Anesia maneuvered the body out of Marie's passage. It was a girl. She was blue. The cord was wrapped around her neck.

So, we had our first funeral at camp. It was held in the bunkhouse. Leonty, who knew the services by heart, offered the memorial. Innokenty wasn't there; he was still too weak to get up. In fact, it seemed he was getting worse. Maybe he was starving. Our dried fish was gone and he had no appetite for hare and squirrel and porcupine.

After the memorial, Nellie and I carried a pot of canned tomato soup to Innokenty. He didn't like food from tins, but I told him to drink it so he'd get his strength back. He sipped maybe a couple spoonfuls, then lay back. I tried to give him more, but he sealed his lips.

Back in our bunk after leaving Innokenty, Nellie, Evdokie, and I discussed Innokenty's weakened state. "I wish this rain blizzard would stop so we could trap some ptarmigan. Innokenty loves boiled ptarmigan," Nellie said.

Evdokie's brow puckered in worry. "The rain may not end for a while. Innokenty needs to eat something now."

We were silent for a while. Then I jumped up, put on knee-high boots and a raincoat and went over to lift some traps out of a storage box. Without saying a word, Nellie and Evdokie joined me. The campground was a sea of mud, but the forest floor was firm. We set a dozen traps that afternoon.

The second funeral took place a week after the first. Pneumonia claimed the old lady, Pletanida. Anesia and Parascovia had taken turns sitting with her, never leaving her alone for a second. Had she starved herself? She, too, refused the strange food in this country. But maybe she was too weak to eat any food. Catching a breath consumed her energy. I sat up with her the night before she died, listening to her wheeze and gulp air and gasp. Then, suddenly, just as the morning sun touched her window, there was total silence.

Without planning it, without even being aware it was happening, we began preparing ourselves for the worst in every situation. Then our fortune shifted. Akinia produced a healthy girl, and popped her out in less than half an hour even though it was her first. She named the baby, Katya, after my aacha. That warmed my insides, realizing that my aacha's tragedy helped Akinia avoid one in her own life.

But by next day, we knew something was very wrong. Little Katya pursed her lips shut every time Akinia tried to nurse her. Anesia said bad food had spoiled Akinia's milk. Marie's breasts had already dried up and no other woman in camp had milk. Parascovia, Evdokie, Agnes, Alicia, and I chewed dried fish and hare livers into a fine pulp and fed them to Little Katya. She spit most of it back. Every day she became more frail, more listless. Sitting with her one night, I imagined my aacha rescuing her. Come close, Katya. Breathe your spirit into Little Katya. At that moment, a breeze touched my cheek. Ah, Katya, I feel you near.

"How is she?" It was Lupp, checking on his baby. I shook my head.

Later that night, Little Katya fell into her final sleep.

Afterward, strolling on the beach with Alicia and Agnes, Alicia questioned me. "Mama, was Anesia right? Did the bad food spoil Akinia's milk?" I took a deep breath and sat down on a log by the water. The girls sat one on either side of me.

"Did it ruin her milk?" Alicia persisted.

"Maybe."

"What are you going to do about it?" she asked.

I didn't answer.

She kept at me, finally saying, "What would your mama do if she was here?" I smiled inside. My daughter was becoming a suggestor.

"If we were home, Little Katya would be alive. Mr. Canfield's due tomorrow. I'll tell him it's a life and death matter. We have to go home."

Next afternoon, watching the *Pioneer* anchor and a man come ashore, Alicia squinted her eyes. "Is that Mr. Canfield?" He had the same large nose and red, flabby cheeks. But this man's hair was black, shiny black, and Mr. Canfield's was white as snow. Alicia started to giggle and turning to Agnes, said, "Our Mr. Canfield paints his hair."

Agnes laughed, too. "Looks like he used shoe blacking."

The girls covered their mouths as Mr. Canfield approached.

"Mr. Canfield, our people can't stay here any longer," I said.

"I wish the Japs would leave the Aleutians so you could go home, Mrs. Shemikin."

"One by one, our people are dying from bad food. They're not used to eating hares and squirrels and muskrats and porcupine. We've had three deaths this month."

"Maybe deer or bear meat would suit them better."

"We heard those animals were around, but no one has seen them."

Mr. Canfield became thoughtful. After a while he said, "I'll send some skiffs so the men can hunt at sea."

My stomach did a flip flop. I realized he was not even considering sending us home soon. He was preparing us for a long stay.

That afternoon, Nellie, Evdokie, and I checked our traps. We caught six ptarmigan and three squirrels. Nellie cooked a big pot of stew and I stuffed and roasted two ptarmigan for Innokenty. He was in bed when I arrived. Anesia told me he hadn't left his bed for two days. I carried the plate of food to his side. He turned away from me. I sat there a long while waiting for him to face me. He never did.

Despair crept into my bones as I looked at Innokenty, thin as a stick, his skin stretched over his face tight as a new drumhead. Innokenty, our chief for thirty-seven years, was walling himself off from me, from everyone. There had to be a way to bring him back. I thought of his stories. I paused, recalling the raven story, the one he told to support Peter's and my marriage. I thought about the dangers that flock of ravens faced from owls that stole their young and of the two young ravens leading their flock to a safe resting place. I must have dozed off, but I woke with an idea. Innokenty's spirit would revive in a familiar place—a Russian Orthodox church with icons and lighted candles and someone offering a service.

I rounded up Nellie and Evdokie and we three again went in search of Mr. Canfield. He was at the dock ready to board the *Pioneer* for its trip back to the mainland. "We need lumber for a church. It's urgent," I said.

"I told you lumber's in short supply, Mrs. Shemikin. I can only requisition it for essential items."

"Our church is our life," I said. Nellie and Evdokie nodded. After saying those words, we remained silent, studying Mr. Canfield for a sign he'd soften. He did.

"I can ask for lumber for more cabanas. I guess you can use it for anything you want."

Mr. Canfield didn't send lumber but sheets of metal for the sides and roof and planking for the floor. While Anton, Simon, and Matfay built the church, Leonty and Nicky made an Orthodox cross for the top. Too bad there would be no dome on this church, but we felt proud seeing our cross in the middle of that dilapidated camp. We then got busy unpacking the icons and candelabra we'd brought from home.

A gang of us went to tell Innokenty the news. I pictured him getting out of bed, dressing and hurrying over to see the church. But he didn't move and his eyes were dull as if he hadn't heard us. Anesia urged him to drink some herb chai. She looped her arm under his neck, lifted his head, and put the cup to his lips. After a few sips, he fell back. His faded eyes were crusted and spit drooled from the corner of his lips.

"We have a church," Leonty said.

Innokenty whispered something. I leaned over to hear.

"I have anguish in my chest and anguish in my heart."

Leonty, who hadn't heard him, kept talking. "We want you to bless our first service."

"You know all the services, you offer them," Innokenty whispered. And then he closed his eyes, as if to say the talking was over.

We stayed with Innokenty many hours. The Old Man joined us. He sat down next to Innokenty, gazing at him as if he wanted to print his face in memory. Innokenty didn't look at him. He kept his eyes shut tight. I returned to the bunkhouse to cook the evening meal. People gathered outside of Innokenty's house looked to me for news. I shook my head. I was trembling. Sorrow was killing our chief.

I went back to Innokenty later that evening. Leonty, the Old Man, Parascovia, and I were by his side. The Old Man's hand shook uncontrollably. He kept clearing his throat. Then, bending down close to Innokenty, the Old Man spoke into his ear. "Council has gathered for a meeting."

Innokenty gave no response, not even a movement that showed he understood. If only Innokenty would fix his eyes on someone or something, on the Old Man's face, hands, on his quilt, on the ceiling. But his eyes were like black holes.

I decided to say something. I put my mouth close to his ear. "Peter would want you to lead the council meeting."

Innokenty made no sound, not even a slight movement.

In a silent, shuffling vigil, visitors came and left all night.

Once I heard someone sob and then run from the house. I looked outside. Children were standing around, silent. This night, no one sent them to bed. Everything felt unreal. I never pictured life without Innokenty. He was chief when I moved to Akusha as a child, chief when I married his grandson, chief through the years Peter and I raised the children, chief when they sent us away from our country. If he died, what would happen to our life when we returned to Akusha?

I went to Innokenty's side again. I reached for his hand. It was cold and as limp as wet seaweed, but he was trying to say something. I couldn't make out his words. I bent over and put my ear next to his lips.

"Tatty, it's time to join Peter."

TWENTY-SEVEN

I t's hard to believe we hunt and gather wood and eat and sleep as we did when Innokenty was alive. It's hard to believe we visit each other and play with the children and laugh and cry as we did before. It's not that he's forgotten, it's just that there's a wall of silence surrounding the subject. Maybe we should break through it. I ran that thought by Evdokie and Nellie one rainy morning in the spring of 1943, four months after his death. We were sitting on the edge of my cot in my family's ten-foot-square living space.

"There's nothing to say," Nellie said.

"There's plenty to say but talking makes it feel worse." Evdokie replied.

"I'm thinking about the vow we made at his memorial service." Both women pinned attentive eyes on me. "We promised to take his spirit into our souls and keep our Aleut life going."

Nellie and Evdokie nodded.

"Then we need to talk to the children about him and pass on his stories."

At that moment, Ignaty and Feckla raced past us. "Give it back, give it back," Ignaty yelled, but she ran on, clutching his drawing in her hand.

"The children are fidgety," Evdokie commented.

"No wonder after being corked up in this small space for days," I said.

In our country, the weather changed several times a day, but here it had been steady rain for two weeks. We kept the younger children indoors all that time.

"We need wood for the stove and something different for the children to do," I said as I got up, put on rain clothes, and started for the door. Nellie and Evdokie got ready to leave, too. They went after wood and I made my way to Little Hunch's cabin, sloshing through mud, at times sinking halfway to my knees.

Little Hunch lived in a cabana with Nicky and Marie. She was squatting on the floor helping Nicky stretch a deerskin. Nicky was one of the first in camp to learn to use a gun and the very first to bring in a deer. The meat was strange, but we ate it. What was more important, Nicky was drunk with excitement; he had skin for drumheads and tusks and bone for carving, more bone than he'd ever had before. I could already see the miniature seals and baidarkas he'd make.

I watched them for a while and then spoke to them about the children. "Two weeks cooped up, the children are restless." Little Hunch didn't say anything in words, but several minutes later she was bent over a storage box pulling out scraps of bright-colored material. It's surprising what people had filled their suitcases with when we were ordered to leave Akusha with four hours' notice. Little Hunch packed material for making quilts and dolls. She handed me an armful of colorful scraps.

Back home, Ignaty squealed when he saw me lay the material out on the table. "Mama's going to make a doll?" he declared. Ignaty called all his caretakers "Mama"—Little Hunch, Evdokie, Anna, me, Alicia. He, along with Feckla, Little Peter, and a couple of other children stood around the table watching Alicia and me cut and partially sew the doll material before we stuffed it with buckwheat. After we finished stitching the doll together, the children's turn came. They picked buttons and stones for eyes, noses, and mouths. I rewove a piece of rope into hair. Then we handed the doll to Feckla.

Meanwhile, Ignaty rounded up some boxes and towels for a playhouse. He laid two boxes side by side for a bench and stacked two for a table, then filled a third with towels for a crib. When he finished, he took the doll from Feckla's hands and laid it in the crib. After that he assigned roles to the other children. "Feckla, you're the mama, Little Peter, you're the papa, Lupia, you're the sister. And I'm the chief."

By mid-afternoon, the children grew weary of the game. Paulie, who had just come in from school, began to play his drum. Nicky had also planned ahead when we left Akusha, filling his suitcase with two sealskins for drumheads. Paulie thumped the drum while Evdokie and I taught the children an Aleut song and dance.

Suddenly, in the middle of a dance, Simon burst into the room, his eyes wide with fear. "I never thought they'd come for us." After catching his breath, he explained. "Uncle Matfay and I were standing at the pier watching men unload the *Pioneer*. Mr. Canfield and another man came up to us. 'This is Mr. Howard Hickey,' Mr. Canfield said. I wondered who this Hickey was. Pretty soon, Mr. Canfield told us. 'Mr. Hickey is from the Selective Service. He's here to register men for the draft.' I never expected the draft to affect us. Matfay didn't, either. 'We're Aleuts evacuated from our islands,' he told Mr. Hickey. 'It doesn't matter. All Americans between the ages of nineteen and thirty-eight are required to register for the draft. It's the law.'"

I wasn't prepared for this. No one from our country had ever gone into the army. I broke out in a cold sweat and I noticed the blood rush to Evdokie's face. But Vassa, who was visiting, had the opposite reaction. She turned pale. She had lost two sons. Lupp, her remaining child, was twenty, the same age as Anton and Simon. I felt like screaming. Not now, not when Anton had finally found his Aleut legs. He'd taken charge of construction and cutting trees and filling woodsheds all over our camp. No, let

Anton stay with his people. I glanced at him. His lips were twitching, so I figured he felt the same about this draft business. Curse Mr. Hickey.

Maybe my worry was in vain because for a couple of weeks after the men registered, nothing happened. Anton and Simon and Lupp never mentioned the army after Mr. Hickey's visit. They were busy building a steambath, our first at the camp. Alicia, Agnes, Nellie, and I searched the beach for rocks for the bath. Like seeing our church, building that steambath made me want to sing.

As soon as it was finished, we sisterhood women decided to meet there. Nellie and I were just leaving for the bath when we saw people carrying mail from the new schoolhouse—only one room but it was off by itself. We walked over to it. Lupp, Anton, and Simon stood by the door of the school, each holding a paper. Draft orders! All three were to leave on the *Pioneer* that day— Simon and Lupp for an army base in Anchorage, and Anton, to Fort Ord in California. I never heard Vassa speak in a loud voice. But after the orders arrived, she stung the air with her words. "Stay here." she ordered Lupp.

"Mama, it's the law. They'll put me in jail if I don't go."

"We'll hide you in the hills. They'll never find you. You're not to go."

"I won't live hidden in the hills," Lupp protested.

Anton tried to comfort Vassa. "I heard they teach many skills in the army. It's a free education, Auntie."

She didn't answer.

Lupp reached over and touched her shoulder. "I'm going to pack my gear, Mama."

Vassa followed him, and I followed Vassa. She watched Lupp until he left the house; then her body crumbled into her chair, like her bones had melted. She stopped speaking after he left.

"She won't even speak to me," Vasili complained a couple weeks later. "I think she's decided not to speak another word until Lupp returns from that war."

I didn't expect a letter from Anton so soon, just two weeks after he boarded the *Pioneer.*

"Mama, they say it never gets cold in this country, that it's summer all year round. The cots in the barracks are hard, the food is awful. But that's nothing compared to my loneliness. And my worry about all of you. Who's in charge of building? Who's cutting trees? Who's filling the wood boxes? I wish you had a phone at that camp.

"I've got my assignment. Radio operator school. I was disappointed at first. I'd wanted language school, but the class was full. Then, after thinking about it, I was glad about radio school. Mama, when I come home to Akusha, our town will have a radio operator. We won't have to go to the store for radio messages.

We can send them and receive them right from our house.

I wanted to be alone, to think about Anton's letter. I hiked on the beach, picturing our reunion after the war. I saw us painting the house, inside and out, setting up Anton's radio equipment in his room, people coming and going to check on their relatives and the fishers and hunters who were away, and Anton contacting the Coast Guard and the *Aurora* and supply ships. I could see our people puff up about Anton the way they did about Peter.

It was getting late. I turned my steps toward the bunkhouse and as I neared, Alicia came running up to me. "Mama, I've been looking all over for you. There's a meeting at the schoolhouse with Mr. Clump from the Alaska Employment Office."

I had been so involved in Anton's letter, I hadn't taken time to ask about the stranger who came in on the *Pioneer* with Mr. Canfield. "The employment office? What does he want with our people, eh?"

"Jobs in Juneau is what I heard."

I felt a sudden chill and wrapped my arms around my shoulders as we made our way to the school house.

Lawrence Clump was sitting on a chair in front of the teacher's desk. He leaned forward, his eyes burning with intensity. "With so many men in the army," he said, "we're short of workers. We need people in the canneries and women to work in offices and shops in Juneau and Ketchikan."

No one said anything.

He went on. "Everyone is making sacrifices for the war. It's your duty to keep things going while the soldiers are over there."

Still no one spoke. He tried to lure our people with windy descriptions of the shops, theaters, and restaurants in the city. I was surprised to hear Alicia interrupt him.

"What language do they speak in the canneries and offices?"

"Why, English of course."

"Will we learn how to run things in those offices and canneries?"

"Well, I'm not sure what you're getting at."

"In our village, we're incorporated; we have a city council; we have to know how to run a city."

Mr. Clump cleared his throat and blew his nose before answering. "Well, you'd learn a lot living and working in Juneau or Ketchikan."

I glanced at Nellie. Her face was the color of a plucked goose.

Are we to lose our young women, too?

Alicia and Agnes were up half the night whispering. I lay awake, too, catching part of their conversation.

"Our elders' council decides things at home? Why do you talk about the city council?" Agnes asked.

"Our elders follow the ways of our ancestors. They don't have answers to these modern questions."

"But you spoke about us learning to run the new council; women don't do that."

"Remember that movie we saw with Katherine Hepburn when she managed a newspaper?"

"Why do you want to manage things?"

"Maybe I inherited it from my mama and my grandmother."

It was clear Alicia was planning to leave. Ai-yee, she was like my heartbeat. Like Katya had been. Ah, Katya, if you were here, you'd help me keep my daughter close.

The next morning, Alicia greeted me with unwelcome words: "Mama, please don't be upset. Agnes and I are going to work in Ketchikan."

"The choir needs you, Alicia."

"Others can take my place."

"Ignaty—you've always been his little mama."

"I'll miss Ignaty in my bones. He's like part of me. He's the main reason I want to stay. But other reasons make me want to go."

"What are these reasons that are so important, eh?"

"Mama, I want to live among whites, work with them, learn their ways. It will help me understand what's going on in our town, in our new council."

"What's going on is the promyshlennik want to take over our life."

"That's why I want to understand their ways, so we can speak for our Aleut life. I want to do that, Mama. I thought you'd want me to."

As she talked, I felt a tearing inside me. "I'm thinking about the time Anton got lost in Salem. He nearly died shivering in a doorway all night. And what if he had been a girl? Would some promy-shlennik have taken advantage, like the sailor who raped Marie?"

"I'm afraid, too, Mama. And maybe you were afraid when you and the other women sat in Mrs. Parker's classroom until she agreed to let us talk Aleut in our homes. And maybe my grandmother was afraid when she sailed in a small open boat from village to village all across the Aleutian Islands. And maybe I'll be afraid if I ever get elected to that new council."

I smiled a little at her brave words, but at the same time a rush of fear went through me like cold air. What harm would come to her? Would she forget our life like Katya did? If only I'd known how to stop Katya from deserting our ways. If only I now knew how to keep Alicia with me.

Alicia and Agnes left for Ketchikan on the next trip of the *Pioneer*. I paced the shore watching for its return, wondering if Alicia had a place to live, a job? Wondering if she was safe. A week passed. It was time for the Pioneer's next trip. The night before the ship was due, I had a bad dream. I was two people.

One me was in the city with Alicia, staying close, watching over her. The second me was waving good-bye to Alicia as she boarded the *Pioneer*. The ship moved out of the harbor. Alicia's face blurred and then it turned into Katya and Katya into Mama, and Mama became Peter, and then Peter faded away like smoke and I screamed. The scream jerked me awake. I looked around. It must have been imaginary; no one else in the room noticed.

There was no letter on the next trip of the *Pioneer,* but one came the following week. I wanted to be alone to read it so I ran into the forest and sat down at the base of a huge spruce tree, rays of sunlight filtering through its branches and lighting the needles on the ground.

"Mama, I found a wonderful job on the Ketchikan newspaper. I'm so glad Papa taught me to do layouts and graphics on our Akusha paper. That's what the *Ketchikan Daily* hired me to do. I earn eighteen dollars every week. I'm sending some money in every letter." She had enclosed a crisp five dollar bill. Her next words were even more surprising.

"Living in the next door room in my boarding house is a woman, name Olga Krenin. She's from Umaka. She's second cousin to Gregory Mensoff, the Islik man you told me about many times. Everyone in Umaka was sent to an island, Kalisook, near Bear Cove, and she and her sister came here to work.

"I asked Olga about your godmother. She is stooped with arthritis, but is otherwise in good health."

Tears sprang to my eyes. Matrona so near. I had to see her. The *Pioneer* must call at Kalisook, too. I'll appeal to Mr. Canfield, explain that this may be my last chance to see my godmother.

I found him at the schoolhouse talking with Mr. Ginsberg. "Come in, Tatiana," Mr. Ginsberg said as soon as he saw me. Then both men looked at me expectantly.

"Mr. Canfield, I was thinking about visiting my godmother at her camp in Kalisook."

He shook his head from side to side.

"It is said to be near here."

He continued to shake his head.

My heart sank. Maybe my words weren't strong enough. Maybe he's thinking of the cost. "I can get money for travel," I said, thinking of Alicia's earnings.

"It's not about money, Mrs. Shemikin. There are no ships available for nonessential travel."

"My godmother is so old she might die any day. Is that essential?"

Mr. Canfield clucked his tongue. "I'm sorry."

Alicia was gone. Anton was gone. Matrona was so close and yet as far as if she were still in Umaka. I walked slowly back to the bunkhouse. Nellie was there waiting for me. I knew by the excited tone in her voice that she had news, too.

"Lord in heaven, this is some letter, yes, some letter," she said, waving the page in the air. "Good news from Sylvia. They're in a city up north—Fairbanks." She sat down on my bed and read the letter to me.

"Ralph found a job managing a Safeway store. And I've got a dream job at the university museum, in charge of organizing the native collection. As soon as the war ends, my boss wants me to travel to remote villages to collect native artifacts. So, you can guess what I asked: 'Can I go to the Aleutians where I have contacts?' He thought for a while. Then he said I should visit Umaka, the most traditional Aleut village, also the most distant, and I should line up a translator. Do you think Tatiana would be interested?"

Her letter kindled a light in my soul. I thought of Matrona. "I'll be with her soon," I whispered to myself.

Twenty-eight

Nineteen forty-three. Summer. Every morning we gathered at the school to listen to the news. Mr. Ginsburg had the only radio in camp. Every morning I prayed for a change. Every morning I left in a black mood. Then, one day in August we learned that our military had chased the last Japanese out of the Aleutians. Ah, I imagined myself already on that boat headed for home.

The next day, Tuesday, when the *Pioneer* was due, a gang of us stood around the dock eagerly awaiting Mr. Canfield. We were sure he'd give us a departure date. But the *Pioneer* never showed up. We were puzzled. The seas were calm. Mr. Ginsburg said the radio reported fair weather. Same next day and the next. On the fourth day, a dense fog fell, but a few of us hung out at the dock anyhow—hoping. I had just decided to start for the bunkhouse when a vague, ghost-like object crept out of the fog. I squinted my eyes. The *Pioneer* hove into view. None of us shouted an announcement, but people began to show up anyhow.

Immediately after coming ashore, Mr. Canfield approached us. We smiled, waiting for the news, but he just nodded a greeting.

"We're ready to leave," Leonty said.

"I'm still waiting for the order to come through."

"Do you expect it soon?"

"I hope so," he said as he walked off in the direction of the school.

If Mr. Canfield had reason to hope, I did, too. In fact, I was so sure we'd receive repatriation orders any day, I hurried home and started packing. Others did the same. Later that day, Nellie, Evdokie, Anna, and I began rounding up paper and boxes for packaging icons and churchbooks. Mr. Ginsburg sent radio messages to our young people in Ketchikan, telling them to hustle home. We wanted everyone ready to leave on a moment's notice.

The following week, the moment we heard the low hum of the *Pioneer*'s whistle, everyone around rushed to the dock. But aside from crew members unloading supplies, no one, not a single soul, came ashore. I craned my neck scanning the deck. The captain was the only person in view.

"We're going aboard," I said to Nellie and Evdokie. They both gave me a questioning look. "We have to find Mr. Canfield." They followed me up the ladder and to the pilot house. No one was there but the captain. "We're looking for our agent, Mr. Canfield."

"He's not here."

"Is he sick?"

"Beats the hell out of me."

"He's supposed to bring us the repatriation order."

"Don't know anything about it."

"We're Aleuts from the village of Akusha," I said. "We've been sitting in this camp for two years. We're ready to go home now that the Japs are gone from our country."

The captain just shook his head from side to side and walked off.

Maybe we'd have felt better if we had an explanation. Then we could decide whether to pack or unpack. Everyone chose to do the latter. There was no use speculating about when the order might arrive. There was nothing to do but get busy and try to pass the time. Nellie went to work on a birdskin parka for Little Peter. Luckily she had found puffins and murres, her parka birds, right here at Bear Cove. Nicky and Paulie started making a deerskin drum. I was knitting a sweater for Feckla. Somehow the days passed until the next trip of the *Pioneer*. This time Mr. Canfield was on board. Leonty waved him over and again asked about the repatriation order. I knew from the clucking sounds Mr. Canfield made that the news was bad. "You see," he began, "the navy has no spare ships, no spare crews. I'm so sorry."

After supper, Leonty called the elders together. There weren't many left—only Bullshit John and the

Old Man, besides himself. They met at Leonty's cabin. Observers crowded into that little room, hardly bigger than a barabara—Nellie, Parascovia, Evdokie, Mr. Ginsburg, and me with Feckla and Little Peter. The children sat on the floor rolling a ball of blue yarn back and forth.

Leonty started the meeting. "We should talk about getting that repatriation order." Bullshit John and the Old Man nodded, but didn't say anything. Minutes passed. Still no one spoke. And no one told stories from the past to guide us. This wasn't like any council meeting I'd ever attended. Little Peter let out a wail. The ball of yarn had completely unraveled all over the floor. I shivered, thinking that our council had unraveled just like Little Peter's yarn. This meeting was a conversation, not a deliberation. Something had to happen. My mouth opened and words came out unbidden. "One time we sent a petition to Mr. Canfield for materials to build a church."

Nellie followed me. "Another time, we sent a petition to the bishop telling him to send a visiting priest to Akusha."

Parascovia added her thought. "Many years ago we petitioned the head of the Baptist mission to stop converting our Aleut children."

Our remarks were met by a long silence, then Leonty, looking defeated, said, "There's no bishop of the army, no place to send a petition."

"Send it to the head of the military," Bullshit John suggested.

"Do you know his name?" Leonty asked.

John shook his head, but Mr. Ginsburg quickly supplied it—"President Roosevelt."

Leonty was pleased. "Tatiana"—he called to me—"Help me write the petition." We went to work right then, Leonty and me joined by Nellie and Evdokie. And we finished it before the moon rose.

"We Aleut people of Akusha have been banished from our village to this Bear Cove camp. Our people in this camp are sick and dying. We despair to go home. There are no Japanese on our island. Please send us home right away."

Every adult at camp signed the petition and we mailed it before the *Pioneer* left the following day. Then we waited. Two weeks. A month. Two months. We feared the petition had gotten lost. We sent another. A couple weeks later, right after Russian New Year's, a wire came. We read it to our people gathered at the school house.

"Sorry you had to remove from your homes. Have referred your petition to General Dunkin, head of the Alaska Command."

Certain that the telegram meant action, our people congregated in the mess hall for a celebration. Little Hunch passed around a platter of pilot crackers spread with peanut butter. Mr. Ginsburg

produced a container of cider he'd been saving for
an occasion. Nicky and Paulie thumped on their
drums. People started to dance and sing. Holding
Feckla and Ignaty with my hands, I whirled around
the room. No one slept much that night. We didn't
need to. Hope restored us.

Our spirits remained high all week, waiting for
the mail call. Nothing from General Dunkin. Not
that week or the next or for many weeks after. I
could bear bad conditions at the camp, but not this
endless waiting. Finally, word came. General Dunkin
said he was sorry but there was no way he could
arrange to return the evacuees at this time.

Leonty called another get-together at his cabana.
I noticed no one referred to it as a council meeting
any more. Mr. Ginsburg was the first to speak. He
was angry, shook his fist at the imaginary authorities
keeping us incarcerated. I suggested we send another
petition. Everyone agreed. "But to whom?" I asked,
looking at Mr. Ginsburg who knew about these
things. He didn't hesitate—"Secretary of War,
Stimson." So okay, Nellie, Evdokie, Leonty, and I finished another petition that evening.

"Our people are sick and dying," we wrote. "We
want to return to our Aleutian village. All the Japs
are gone from our islands. If white businessmen can
live in our village, we can, too. We, the Akusha people
in Bear Cove camp, petition you to end our exile."

A few weeks later, in early spring, Mr. Ginsburg handed me a telegram from the War Department. I carried it to the mess hall. Nellie, who was with me, left to round up the others. The hall filled in a hurry and I read the wire. "The return of the natives to Akusha Island would place an additional burden on our already overtaxed shipping facilities in your area."

Little Hunch seldom cried, but tears splashed down her cheeks.

Seeing her distress, the Old Man sputtered, "They should have thought about their 'overtaxed ships' before they dragged us to this hole in hell."

Leonty tried to calm him. "I'm thinking this war's been going on a long time. I'm thinking the end is near." Leonty's voice cracked, then, and he said no more.

I didn't realize what I was doing until Nellie called attention to it. "Tatty, we may need that wire." I was ripping it into shreds. I wanted to forget it was ever written. I wanted to believe the repatriation order was on its way.

The next afternoon, Nellie and I sat on my bunkhouse cot, moping.

"Ah, Tatty, what's to become of us?" Nellie said. "We've been in this camp nearly two years, yes, two years, living in icy bunkhouses, with sickness and death all around, with anguish in every heart. How much longer?" She paused and drew a deep breath.

"I don't know if I can last another winter here." As she talked fear cramped my stomach. I made myself think of something else.

"C'mon," I said, jumping up. "Let's check our traps, I'm hungry for squirrel." I went to the storage box in the far corner of the room and gathered two clubs, knives, and sacks.

We walked in silence for a while, and then I plunked myself down at the base of a tree to breathe in the fresh smell of bark and leaves. I became fascinated by the intricate patterns on the forest floor, lighted by patches of sun seeping through the leafy branches of the spruce and hemlock. Nellie was looking skyward.

"Tatty, I'm remembering the time we sat by the Akusha shore dreaming about Gavril and Paulie building their own baidarkas."

"Nell, I could levitate when I picture the beach at home."

"What else do you picture?"

"My kitchen table crowded, all the children home, Gavril and Agnes and Little Peter, too, and the Old Man and Little Hunch. A hot fire. Alaadix sizzling to a golden brown in a pan on top of the stove. The Old Man and Stepan playing chess at the table. Ignaty amusing Feckla by standing on his head and making faces. Alicia drawing a picture of Little Peter squatting on the pee pot. And Anton and Paulie setting up radio equipment in Anton's room." I would have said more, but it was time to be on our way. I stood; Nellie did, too, and we headed deeper into the forest where we'd set traps.

I squealed as we approached the first one. "Luck, we've caught a flying squirrel." The animal was barely alive, limp and wimpering. I picked up a club and whacked it on the head. Nellie turned away; she hated that part of the hunt, but later she helped skin the animal.

I started dreaming again as we walked to the next trap. "Nell, I have another vision. After we return, maybe I'll talk to the teachers about classes in Aleut inheritance, classes that teach the children our songs and dances and how to weave with grass."

"We can teach those things at home."

"We can, but many don't. In the classroom, Nell, all the children will learn about their heritage" Nellie didn't say anything, but I was so stirred up by my dream that I kept going. "And maybe Anton can start up a Russian school like we had when we were young. Anton can teach Russian language and carpentry and music. I can teach music, too, and maybe Russian history."

Nellie was looking toward camp. "The *Pioneer*'s in. People are carrying mail from the schoolhouse."

"I'll meet you there after I take the meat to the bunkhouse," I said. We'd caught two flying squirrels, a muskrat, and a hare.

As soon as I opened the bunkhouse door, my heart started to race like a wild thing. That voice in the eating room. I ran in. Alicia, standing by the stove and talking to Evdokie, was holding a bundle in her arms.

"I thought about having the baby here so I could be with Mama." Alicia said excitedly. "But I decided it was safer to have it in the hospital. I thought I'd come back to camp right after the baby was born. But they made me stay in the hospital for fourteen days. Ah, grief, those fourteen days felt like a year."

Alicia saw me and moved toward me, a half smile on her lips. She handed me the baby. I couldn't absorb the meaning. Was this Alicia's baby? She hadn't written about a pregnancy. No one else had mentioned one. Had she married some Ketchikan promyshlennik?

Ignaty came prancing in, saw the baby, and, without any expression of surprise, went to the corner of the room opposite the storage box to build another playhouse. When he finished, he came up to me and announced, "I'll have the baby now." He must have figured a real live doll was better than the ragged ones I made for him.

"Wait until the baby is older. It was just born." I realized I didn't know my grandchild's name. "What do you call the child?"

"Her name is Jane."

I was surprised. Maybe stunned. Jane, like the Jane in the Dick and Jane books we read in government school. That's a promyshlennik name. I never knew anyone in all the Aleutian Islands with the name Jane. I wondered again if Alicia was married to a white man who chose that name.

But she never mentioned a papa and as the days passed I noticed she showed no interest at all in the mail or passengers on the *Pioneer*. So I knew the papa didn't matter, at least not to Alicia.

It did to Mr. Ginsburg, though. On his first visit to see Alicia and Jane, he opened the subject. "Who's the lucky fellow?" His question stirred up memories of the missionaries pressuring Marie after her rape—"Who's the father? Who's the father?" I started to feel mad thinking about promyshlenniks' disgust when children don't have a father. They have the cruel habit of calling those children "illegal," like they're thieves. It was unnatural. Even Sylvia South expressed that prejudice. "I'm pretty liberal about most things," she once said, "but illegitimacy is dead wrong. It's just not fair to burden children with shame."

I remember trying to explain our ways to Sylvia. "We're concerned, too, when a mother is alone. But if there is no papa or brother, others in the community help out."

Sylvia had paused a long while before her next remark. "I guess we give shame instead of aid. What a beautiful world we'd have if all people followed your system." So Sylvia understood after all.

"Where's the father?" Mr. Ginsburg was asking Alicia. She shrugged, but didn't answer.

Little Hunch changed the subject. "Any plans for the baby's baptism?"

"Maybe we should petition Mr. Canfield to send a Russian Orthodox priest to the camp," Nellie suggested.

Alicia opposed that idea. "I want Jane baptized in our Akusha church."

I had the same desire. But when would that be? Would this evacuation never end? A gloom fell over me until I nestled my cheek against Jane's skin, softer than silk.

Leonty was humming when he came in, others right behind him.

"It's here, it's here!" Marie shouted.

"Mr. Canfield showed us the repatriation order," Parascovia grinned.

Alicia started to clap her hands in rhythm with Leonty's singing. "When do we leave?" she asked.

Evdokie read the order. "Navy steamer *Franklin* will restore the Akusha Aleuts to their home. Due to depart Bear Cove on April 25. *Pioneer* will return Ketchikan workers before *Franklin* departure."

It was April 23. I got up and started collecting things to pack.

As the transport ship entered the passage to open sea, I caught my last glimpse of Bear Cove—the rot-

ting dock, tattered bunkhouses and warehouses, broken water pipes and pieces of twisted roofing blown
off in a storm scattered on top of the ground—a
dismal and ugly reminder of two years of misery. I
closed my eyes, trying to shut out the memory. When
I opened them later, I could see only the vast and
dense expanse of evergreens, a shimmering gold light
pouring off them. I wanted to save that memory, the
beauty of the forest and of our departed buried near
it. I paused. Maybe their spirits were on this ship,
traveling back to their country. A soft breeze blew
across my face. I smiled and welcomed them aboard.

TWENTY-NINE

I had dreamed this moment so many times I wasn't
sure it was real. We were actually sailing down
Akusha Bay. A heavy fog lay on the water like a dark
shroud. It didn't matter. I saw the village in my mind's
eye—the houses lining the beach, the boats moored
in front of the houses, Ptarmigan Creek from where
we hauled water, the rolling hills folding into ever
higher peaks, the schoolhouse, the community hall,
and our church and the cemetery where our digni-
taries were buried. The fog began to thin. We passed
Rocky Point where Nellie and I fished for sculpin
and pogy. It had caved in. I searched the beach for
the log where Peter and I rested on the night we
pretended I was the deacon and he was the choir. It
was gone. The shoreline had receded so far I couldn't
see Evdokie's house. It wasn't there. Then, I remembered. Soldiers had hauled sand and gravel from the
beach before we left, wrecking our sea wall. The
beach itself was cluttered with junk—garbage, pieces
of siding, broken windows, parts of military vehicles.
Where would we find clams and mussels and sea

urchins? I scanned the beach from one end to the other. Where were our boats? Not a single baidarka, dory, skiff, or dinghy in sight. I lifted my eyes to the hills, gouged and slashed as if by an angry god. The horizon was marred by hundreds of quonsets, barracks, gun emplacements, and military vehicles.

Chills crept up and down my backbone and into my chest and arms. My legs trembled. We neared the dock. Some crab fishing boats were tied up there. I'd heard crabs had started showing up in the water near Akusha and that large boats from Seattle were coming around to fish them.

As soon as we came ashore, a man approached us, walking stiffly as if his legs were made of fence posts. It was Colonel Smelling, officer in charge of the troops. "Welcome home," he said, without a smile, without even a pause for any more conversation. Immediately he turned, waved his arms toward six military vehicles that were parked on the street, and issued instructions. "Our trucks will take you home. Climb aboard."

The Jeep I was in drove first to the far end of town, so I got a close look at every building. A cold wind blew through me. The school and community hall were in shambles, windows smashed, siding torn away, outhouses gone, lumber stripped away from every house, and the streets gutted by military trucks.

Walking into my decaying house, I saw a huge web with a spider curled tight in the center. I swatted it and broke up the web with my fingers. Inside, I gasped as I looked around. Rain had come in through cracks in the window and holes in the roof, rusting the stove and rotting the floorboards. I walked over to the wall, streaked with waterstains, where Peter's pipe shelf had been.

Peter's fiddle. I rushed into the bedroom and touched the spot on the wall where it had been mounted. My eyes snapped shut. In fierce denial, I reached over to lift the fiddle down. My hand touched the empty rotted rack that once held it. I ran my fingers over the rack, and a rusty nail scraped my hand. Alicia was by my side. "Oh, grief. I dreamed about playing Papa's fiddle." Her voice was choked. "The accordion and guitar, my paints, Nicky's ivory carvings, everything's gone. What happened?"

"Mr. Ginsburg warned me that soldiers ransack and loot wherever they go."

We returned to the other room. Ignaty was pinching his nostrils closed. "Phew, phew, it stinks in here worse than an old, dead seal."

"Mold," Alicia answered.

"Rat shit," I said as I watched rats scurry across the floor. We had rats before the war, but not gangs like this. A picture of Mama chasing them with a sea lion bone came into my mind. That was when we first moved into the house, a short time after we arrived in Akusha. Leonty, Bullshit John, and the Old Man built this house. Seems everyone in town helped get it ready. When we moved in, there was an oil stove, counter, table, chairs, and shelves on the wall. Some of the women made quilts for bed covers. Even Father Paul made a contribution—an icon of the Virgin. What a housewarming we had. For three days and nights, visitors came, bringing gifts of food and dried and salted fish for the winter. Mama couldn't stop looking around the house.

"A palace, a palace," she kept saying. I guess it was, compared to our one-room shack in Umaka. Ah, Mama, I'm glad you're not here to see your palace shattered.

Colonel Smelling came in through the opening where the door used to be. He looked around the house, then pulled a tablet and pencil from his pocket and made notes. "I hadn't realized the extent of the damage down here in town. This place isn't worth rebuilding. We're putting up cabanas for those needing housing. I'm putting your name on the list. In the meantime, you can stay at the barracks. I'll take you there now."

So we were home, but homeless. Only a few houses were fit to live in—Leonty's, Victor's, and Vassa's and Vasili's barabara.

The very next day, soldiers and workers started cobbling together temporary cabanas, like those at the Bear Cove camp. Life at home resembled the camp in other ways, too. It was our land, but we were landless. The military had stolen most of it. It

310 DOROTHY JONES

was our country, but we lived like prisoners. Colonel Smelling restricted us to a small area—2,500 feet long by 400 feet wide. We needed special passes to go beyond the enclosure. Most of us had no need for passes. The berry patches were ruined. Icy Creek was polluted. The codfish were gone.

Crabs were plentiful. But we had no boats. Even if we had, they wouldn't have been large enough for crab fishing.

We ate K rations when we stayed at the barracks. I wondered what we'd eat when we left there. We talked it over at a gathering. Leonty wasn't present. He rarely went out anymore. Before the evacuation, Leonty knew the exact distances between one place and another in the village. But now, all the signs that once guided him had shifted or disappeared. Small wonder that at the age of seventy-five he became confused and stopped going out.

Bullshit John opened the meeting. "We need to get together and clean the creek."

Everyone agreed.

"Without boats we'll have to be satisfied with flounder," Matfay said. "There's still plenty around the dock. And we can get pogy and mackerel in the kelp beds. Only thing, we don't have any line, hooks, or sinkers."

"I wish Stepan was home," John said. "He's a star at kelp fishing."

"He should be back by now," Big Shot remarked, looking at me.

"I asked the storekeeper to send a radio message. I'm waiting to hear," I told him.

"He doesn't seem to be in a hurry to get back here. Tell him to come home now and also to bring us some fishing gear."

My face flushed. Why was Big Shot needling me about Stepan's absence? I was plenty worried already. The storekeeper, Andy McMoon, hadn't been able to raise Stepan on the radio since we returned a week before. But the New Harbor people knew we were back. They could have gotten word to him. I checked with Andy McMoon a couple times a day.

By meeting's end we agreed to ask the New Harbor people to send us fishing gear and also to find out if Colonel Smelling had any in his storehouse. John was named to speak for us.

Our cabana was one of the first to be ready. A couple days before we moved in, Mr. Edison, the Indian Bureau agent, visited our community. He gave every family $100 to get settled, and he asked no questions about how many people ate at our table, like that social worker, Matilda Witherspoon, had done. There was not much left of the furnishings in our old house. All the sharp knives were gone, but there were some eating utensils, cooking pots, dishes, and old clothes. There were no boots, either. We used the Indian Bureau money for flour, sugar, coal, blankets, rain gear, and boots for Paulie. Everyone needed boots, but Paulie first so he could hunt and trap—providing he got a pass, of course. Every time I thought about having to get permission to gather food in our country, my stomach knotted.

Our cabana was near Ptarmigan Creek, but we didn't need the creek water. We had cold running water, linked to the water system the military had put in. Feckla, Ignaty, and Little Peter believed those faucets were magic. They couldn't stop turning them off and on and washing their toys and socks in the sink. They never seemed to tire of playing in that water. Then, one day when Victor was visiting, he told them to stop before they made the well run dry. They kept peeking at those faucets, anyhow, and when someone would wash dishes or clothes in the sink, they'd stand on chairs and watch.

Running water was our only advance. We still used an outhouse and an oil drum stove. One day, while Nicky was making the stove, I asked Alicia and Feckla to go to the store with me. I wanted to price teapots. Our old one had cracked in two. Both girls were eager to join me. They loved looking around the store. Alicia ran first to the shelf holding jars of water colors. Feckla was drawn to the toy counter where a boy was spinning a red, yellow, and green top. "Wanna try it?" he asked, handing her the top.

I wasn't used to cash shopping, so I read the labels on the four teapots on the shelf with care. In the background, I heard the ham radio crackle with static. Feckla ran over to show me she had learned to spin the top. I was watching her when I became aware of a sudden silence. The radio had gone dead. I figured Andy McMoon, the storekeeper, had turned it off. Why was he coming over to me? Andy McMoon was a tall, broad-shouldered man whose face was the color and texture of bread dough. But his skin was bright red when he talked to me. I didn't know he knew my name until he used it. "Mrs. Shemikin?"

I nodded.

"I have word about your husband, Stepan."

Evdokie, Akinia, Aunt Sophie, and a couple other people shopping at the store gathered around.

"Mrs. Shemikin, your husband died this morning. They said he had TB. The Coast Guard cutter was on its way. He died before she arrived."

I felt like someone had slammed my head with a sledgehammer. Lung disease. It killed my papa, it killed my husband, Pletanida, a hundred others in our country. My knees went weak. Keep standing. You have to get yourself home. I thought about Feckla, poor Feckla. She had lost her mother, her village of birth, and now her papa. I glanced at her. Her head drooped like a flower after the first frost. Alicia and I, one on either side, steered her out of the store and toward our cabana.

"What did Mr. McMoon say about Papa?" she whispered.

"Your papa isn't," I answered as I took her hand in mine.

"Oh, oh, oh, oh," she whimpered all the way home. Once inside, Feckla ran to the corner of the room where she hid when she first came to us. And then she started to pull at her hair. She tugged at it until she yanked out a clump. I went over and lifted her hand from her head.

"Not good to hurt yourself," I said, sitting near her. She quieted down. In fact, she sat as still and motionless as a corpse. Finally her head fell onto her chest. She was asleep.

Alicia had taken Ignaty and Little Peter out. I wanted to be off by myself to absorb the news. I covered Feckla and left for the beach. I couldn't think. Soldiers and workers were all around. I returned to our cabana and lay down on my sleeping pad. Somehow, I fell into a deep sleep.

It was late afternoon when I first lay down, but I didn't wake until the next morning. I felt like I'd been cleft in two when Peter died, like I was broken, unfixable. Stepan never seared my soul like Peter had. I didn't feel ravaged by his death, but I felt as weak and limp as a rag doll. Get up and do something, I prodded myself. I didn't stir, not until I glanced at Feckla sitting against the wall, chewing on her hair, and looking as listless as I felt. I got up.

I invited her to walk with me to the warehouse. The soldiers hadn't painted our house, but they offered to give us paint from their warehouse, free. Feckla didn't say anything, but she put on her parka and followed me.

A racket greeted our ears as we left the cabana. I looked around. A bulldozer was crushing our old house. I had crazy thoughts, like rounding up people to shove that machine and the men driving it right into the sea. They were smashing my house. One image after another whirled through my mind— Anton building his room, Nicky carving Peter's pipe stem, Peter playing the fiddle, Alicia sitting at the table drawing a picture of the Old Man bending over the chess board. Mama's spirit lived in that house, and they were grinding it to shreds. My house was as dead as Peter and Stepan.

I forgot about the paint. I wanted to shut myself away from everyone and everything. I returned home, lay down on my sleeping mat, pulled a cover over my head, and stayed there all day.

Next morning, Alicia called to me. "Mama, what color paint shall we get?" I guess she was trying to stir my interest in something.

"I don't care."

"Mama, you always liked bright colors."

"Okay," I said.

"Mama, shall we get blue or green?"

"Either one."

Ignaty decided to settle the matter. "I like the sunshine color of the water buttercups in Ptarmigan Creek." Nicky had taken him to the creek on a bird hunting trip the day before.

I didn't answer him. I didn't care. I closed my eyes and turned my back on both of them. I heard someone come in. It was Vassa. She came over to me. Mute since the day Lupp left for the army, she found her voice the moment the repatriation order arrived. "I thought I'd come over to warm up."

I turned toward her. "Is it cold in your barabara?"

"I bought a bottle of cooking oil at the store. It doesn't burn in our lamp."

I couldn't come up with a solution. We had no seal oil and there were no boats to hunt seals. "Stay with us for awhile," I suggested.

She shook her head and got up and left.

The next day there was a big storm.

"Mama, I need boots," Ignaty said.

Again I tried to fix my mind on the problem. The cash we received from the Bureau was gone. I shivered and huddled under the bed cover. I felt so tired. I just wanted to sleep and forget everyone.

THIRTY

I woke slowly. Something didn't fit. The family was in the other room: I recognized everyone's voice. Yet, I felt a presence next to my bed. I turned my head and caught a glimpse of brown serge slacks and black shoes laced to the ankles. The scent was familiar. I sat up and gazed into the eyes of my oldest child. Aang hlax, I whispered.

"Mama, our house?" Anton said in a low, taut voice.

"They crushed it with a bulldozer."

"Chrissakes. Why?"

"It was falling apart. Vandals ripped doors and windows out and the rain rotted the wood."

Anton stared into space for a long time, maybe trying to get used to the idea. I got up then and slipped into a dress. My movements were slow and unsure. Anton watched, concern showing in his creased brow. "Mama, you're sick."

"Sick with sorrow."

Anton's eyes roamed around the room. "Where's Stepan?"

I told him.

"Chrissakes. Chrissakes. Chrissakes." He cradled his head in his hands. "How is Feckla?"

"Maybe she'll perk up with you home."

We went into the other room, then. Alicia was standing at the stove waiting for water to boil. She sighed with relief to see me up and dressed.

"I haven't had a chance to talk to Anton. He rushed right in to see you," Alicia said as she brought chai, bread, and fried trout to the table.

Anton inhaled his food. Alicia filled the platter three times before he stopped eating. Living on K rations, I understood why he was starved for familiar food. After a while, he leaned back in his chair, let out a belch so loud it rang in my ears, and began talking. "I walked around town this morning. Where is everyone? At fish camp?"

"They can't get to fish camp. All the boats are gone," Alicia explained.

"I didn't see anyone fishing around here, either."

"Those big navy ships fouled the bay. The cod and salmon are gone," I said.

"But where is everyone?"

"A gang of men, Paulie and Gavril, too, went to the Pribilof Islands to harvest fur seals. Akinia, Agnes, and some other women are in New Harbor working at the cannery. Anton, there are no cash jobs in town. Andy McMoon at the store hires only whites, except Victor. The herring docks are gone. The supply station has a full crew of people, mostly soldiers who decided to stay here after their discharge."

"Great snakes! I spent my mustering out pay on radio equipment. I want to set up our own station. I've thought of nothing else for months. But, oh shit, there's no one around to listen to the radio."

I couldn't think of an encouraging word. Alicia looked downcast, too.

"I'm going out to find Simon," Anton said, starting for the door.

Later, he told us about his visit. "Simon and I walked on the beach and he talked fast, in an excited way. He pointed to a lulu of a fishing boat, and said, 'Bill Henderson, Seattle fisherman, owns it outright. And the big news is that he's training me—where to drop the crab pots and how to handle the crabs.' 'What good is training without a boat?' I asked him. Simon looked off in the distance and didn't answer, and I had a creepy feeling he'd leave Akusha and go off crabbing with Henderson. And next, I thought, others will follow." Anton shivered. "This is one rotten homecoming."

Alicia put Jane in his arms, her way of comforting him. Anton was fascinated with his niece. He stared at her a long time. "She has your fat lips," he teased Alicia.

"Poor little baby," Alicia answered, "My fat lips and your flat nose."

Anton laughed as he touched Jane's nose. "It's like a tiny button. Think I'll call her Buttonface."

Maybe Jane didn't like her nickname. She started to bawl right after Anton gave it to her. I picked her up and rocked her, chanting songs I once lulled my own children with. In a few minutes, she was asleep.

Later that evening, after Feckla, Ignaty, and Jane were in bed, Victor dropped in. It was the first time he'd seen Anton. He stood at the door smiling and looking into Anton's eyes. Anton returned the greeting. Victor and he were close from birth, like Katya and me.

He came in and sat down at the table, his eyes still glued to Anton's face. "I had nightmares about you fighting in France," he said. "In one dream, a German with a pointed beard held a gun to your head. In another, you were blasted apart by a bomb—your blood-covered arms and legs flying off in different directions. Mama and I prayed for you every night. Ah, Anton, what a nightmare it must have been for you."

Alicia and I moved closer to Anton. We were as eager as Victor for news, for we had received only two letters from Anton after he landed in France. "I was plenty safe. See, I was stationed at headquarters. My job was to relay messages between headquarters and the front lines. I wasn't in the direct line of fire."

"What about bombs?" Victor asked him.

Anton bit his lip, and I knew he must be remembering some horror.

"First you hear a long, low whistle in the distance. It gets louder, closer, louder, still closer, until you're sure it's going to crash into your face. You run to the shelter for cover."

"Oh, grief," Alicia sighed.

"On the way to the shelter, you look up and see the sky splotched with fireballs. You duck into the shelter, plug your ears, sing, scream, think of home, anything until silence returns. Those bombings are burned into my brain. I can't forget them. I realized that when I was riding a train in France on my way to the port. A kid sitting next to me popped his gum in my ear. I jumped up like someone had just jabbed a poker up my ass. I guess I scared the hell out of that kid as much as he did me."

No one spoke for many minutes. Then, Alicia asked Anton if there were any other Aleuts at his station.

Anton blinked his eyes. "I was their Eskimo. Harold Butcher never let me forget it. He was sort of a headman among the guys in the barracks. He bullied the others into following his lead. Sometimes they called me 'Nanook.' Other times, 'Igloo Sam.' And a couple times when I walked in they just hunched their shoulders down and said in a chorus, 'Brrrrr, brrrrrr.' When officers were around, they'd whisper those words to me. One day, I said, 'Harold, I don't like to be called 'Igloo Sam.' He slapped me on the shoulder and said, 'Lighten up, Nanook. You're as serious as a polar bear trapped on an iceberg.'"

"They look down on Aleuts same as James Wilson," I commented.

"Mama, it was so confusing. Those men changed color from day to night. During the day, they respected my work. They counted on it. But in the evenings sitting around doing nothing, they started griping and teasing and making nasty remarks. That was their way of creating fun. So they rode me. Me and Tommy Briggs. Tommy was white, but he was shorter than you, Mama, and he didn't shave yet."

"Couldn't you have gone off by yourself?" Alicia asked him.

"Hah. Go off where? We lived together in barracks." Anton gnawed his lip again, then turned to Victor. "Horace Gump still run a bar?"

"Yeah."

"Do you go there?"

"Yeah. It's fun. There's a nickelodeon that plays western music and room to dance."

"Who do you dance with?"

"Mostly locals. You'll see. Wanna go?"

Anton jumped up and headed for the door.

I drew in a deep breath, afraid the Oregon devil luring him to drink would take him over. I didn't sleep until I heard him come in. His gait was steady, and so was his voice when he greeted Alicia. I should have faith in my son.

By the time I got up, Anton had already left the house. "Anton left early," I said to Alicia.

"He's buying lumber."

"Lumber?"

"He said he needs to build a table for his radio equipment."

Anton and Simon worked on that table for a couple of days. When it was finished, we gathered around watching Anton unpack boxes of equipment and piece it all together. The first time his radio produced sound, Ignaty ran to the table.

"Show me that trick."

"It's no trick. When you're old enough, I'll teach you how to work it."

"If it's not a trick, it's magic," Ignaty said, bringing a smile to my lips. But Anton was grim, grimmer as the day wore on and no one came to see or use his radio.

But by next morning, he'd recovered, joking and laughing with Alicia while she made alaadix. He bolted his food again, grabbed a wind breaker from a hook on the wall and moved toward the door. "You're in a hurry," I said.

He smiled and nodded. "I'm in a hurry to find students for a Russian class. I noticed repairs on the community hall are finished. I can teach there."

I smiled too, seeing him breathe life into part of my Bear Cove dream.

Strange how close my mood was tied to his. I felt as glum as he looked when he returned home that evening. He was edgy and angry—scowled when Jane cried, bawled Ignaty out for speaking English at home. And he didn't mention anything about a Russian class. So I knew his plan had come to grief.

After that disappointment, Anton's old restlessness returned. In and out, up and down, fiddling with this and that, unable to stay with anything for long. Then, he disappeared for six long days.

Nellie and I searched everywhere. He wasn't with Simon or Victor. People told us that he and Lupp were hiding in an abandoned quonset in the hills, "drinking, yes drinking."

"Where did they get so much booze?"

"I heard Big Shot say they rolled drunken soldiers who passed out on the street."

My knees began to shake and I thought I was going to stumble. I grabbed Nellie's arm to steady myself. "This wasn't what we planned, Peter and I."

"You didn't plan for a war and the ruin of our village, either," Nellie reminded me.

When I'd exhausted places to search, I sat at the window at home watching, waiting. Six days after he disappeared, something happened. My hands were steeped in soapy water cleaning the fish pan when

Alicia dashed in, yelling. "It's over, over, over! The war's over!"

I ran outside with her. So did everyone else in town. Smiles and laughter everywhere. What was wrong with me? I couldn't join in. The war was over but that didn't bring back our boats or chiefs or Stepan or Anton hiding in the hills. We were moving as a body along the main path of town, in the direction of the mission when I spotted a dim figure zigzagging down the hill. I watched for a long time until I recognized my son. He fell down, got up, and staggered past us on the way to our cabana. I followed him. When I walked in, I found him whacking his head against the wall and howling like the wolves near Bear Cove. I made him stop, put my arm around his waist and led him to his bed. Then quickly, I crawled into mine.

Oh Peter, I'm so weary.

THIRTY-ONE

It was September, the time of year that used to make my heart sing with the joy of ripe berries and golden leaves and full creeks. But it was only three months since Stepan died and since Anton lost hope, and my body still felt drained. Lying in bed on this first day of the fall school term, I prodded myself to get up and help Feckla. This was a first for her, too. She'd never been to school. I tried giving myself a lift by recalling my Bear Cove dream—teaching our heritage in the school room. The dream soured as soon as I called it up, realizing that I'd probably run into the same disinterest Anton did when he tried to organize a Russian language class. But another small voice in my head argued with my gloom. It was my mama's voice. "Get busy and do something." I followed her direction.

Feckla was too excited to eat, too excited even to dress herself right. Her hair was tangled. Her undershirt hung below the short sleeves of her blouse. She was wearing a black sock on one foot and a brown one on the other. I fixed her up and she ran out, but a few seconds later, dashed back. She'd forgotten her jacket.

Alicia was heating water in a big pot on the stove for Jane's bath. That was the high point of Ignaty's day, watching streams of water roll over Jane's tiny body. Standing on a chair next to Alicia, he yanked the soap from her hand. "I'll wash her today," he said, like he was the one in charge. He rubbed that soap on her legs, stomach, chest, arms, face, even in her eyes. At that, she started to scream. Alicia took over then, rinsing, drying, and wrapping Jane in a blanket. Then she handed the baby to me. I rocked her and sang, hoping that sweet-smelling child would rouse my interest. She didn't. I tried to absorb my mother's attitude, but my dark mood clung to me like a barnacle to a rock.

Later, I heard children in the street running home for lunch. I started to hustle a meal together—bread and caviar and salmonberries Nellie and I had picked the day before. Anton ambled in, pulling his trousers up with one hand and picking matter from the corners of his eyes with the other. He was at the sink washing up when the door blew open and Feckla came in with two classmates—Minnie and Clara McMoon, the storekeeper's daughters. I fed the children. Alicia, holding Jane on her lap, sat down and filled a plate, too. But Anton paced the floor, casting angry looks at the McMoon girls, the first promyshlennik to attend our school. As soon as the girls left, Anton sputtered: "Great snakes! Soon the whites will take over our whole town." He expressed my fear.

It was heightened later that day when Nellie rushed in, her face flushed. Anton was on the bench whittling and Alicia, sitting next to him, was nursing Jane. Both of them turned their attention to Nellie.

"Three strangers, total strangers came to town last night," Nellie went on.

"The new teachers?" Alicia asked.

"No. Baptist missionaries—Harvey Bottom, the pastor, his wife, Minerva, and J. B. Bloomberry, the pastor's assistant. They came to restore the old Baptist mission, yes, we're going to have a mission and missionaries here again."

"Chrissakes. Chrissakes!" Anton groaned.

"That's a sour note," Alicia scolded him. "We have our church. Maybe the whites want one of their own. Fair is fair."

"Missionaries aren't fair; they don't missionize their own; they go after others. They were after us all the time in Oregon. I told them I was Russian Orthodox. Do you think that stopped them? Not for a minute. I told them I wasn't interested, but they never let up."

"Mama, we had a mission here once. Was it a bad thing?" Alicia asked.

Memories flooded my mind, good and bad. "I'm thinking about Pastor Lowell, the missionary here when I first came. He wrested Katya away from me before we'd even said 'hello.' He yelled at Marie for being pregnant. He lashed out against our church and Father Paul, our Russian priest." Suddenly I stopped talking and broke into a smile.

Alicia looked alarmed. Maybe she thought I'd gone goofy.

I reassured her. "I'm thinking about Christmas at the mission. A high moment in the year. Pastor Lowell invited everyone in town to the celebrations. We were together, like one family, exchanging gifts and food, singing and telling stories in three languages—Pastor Lowell in English, Innokenty and Leonty in Aleut, and Father Paul in Russian."

"But that was one day out of a year," Anton grumbled.

"Is that right, Mama?" Alicia asked.

My eyes grew moist, thinking about the pastor's wife risking her life during the flu epidemic. "Thelma Lowell was a nurse and took charge during the flu epidemic. She put her life on the line visiting the sick. She did other nice things, too—taught us handiwork we didn't know before—embroidering, crocheting."

I paused to find words for a conclusion. "Maybe the mission will help us. Maybe it will be good for our village."

I changed my mind a week later, the day the Baptist church opened its doors. We had just returned from matins at Russian church when Clara McMoon, the storekeeper's oldest child, came by.

"It's time for service," she said to Feckla.

"I'm ready," Feckla answered, lifting her parka from a hook on the wall.

"Where are you going, eh?" I asked her.

"I'm going to church with Clara."

It was one thing to go to a Christmas celebration at the mission, but another to attend their services. Memories scorched my mind. Tanya's death. Pastor Lowell insisting on conducting the memorial service, but refusing to bury her in his cemetery. Katya's conversion. Her marriage to Buddy Thomas. Those missionaries had turned Katya away from our life.

"Stay home," I said in a voice Feckla had never heard me use before. Feckla looked from Clara to me and back again.

Clara shrugged and in a stiff voice said, "I'll see you at school."

Feckla was crying. I didn't have words to comfort her. I shuddered at the thought of Feckla converting. I clenched my fists.

I decided to go over to our Russian church and cut the grass before snow fell. Nellie joined me there. When we finished, she said, "I'm going to the store for flour."

I tagged along, knowing I'd feel better in her company.

Nellie was chatty. "I'm going to make a mossberry pie. That's Mavra's favorite pie. Maybe I can send it to her on a fishing boat. Tatty, I wonder what those men are building in back of the store."

I looked over and saw two men putting up a frame for a house. Nellie and I ambled over to watch. One of them, a husky fellow with a birthmark covering half his cheek, waved a greeting.

"I was thinking about who's going to live here," I said.

"I am," the man with the birthmark said. "Name's Bill Henderson. And this here's Pat Cochran. He fishes crab with me."

I knew Simon went crab fishing with Bill Henderson, but I had the impression Henderson lived in Seattle.

"I heard you have a house in Seattle."

"I did. But there's a boom in crab coming. I want in on the ground floor. So my partner and me, we decided to settle here."

A lump came into my throat. After we were out of earshot, I complained to Nellie. "Crab boom. More Seattle fishermen coming. More white kids in our school. Ah, Nell, where will it end?"

Nellie didn't answer. I glanced sideways at her. Troubled creases lined her forehead. Without a plan, we sauntered down near the water and sat in the sand. I watched the swirling patterns formed by waves breaking on the shore. I stared at the flecks and dots and splash of the water. I wasn't prepared for the words that fell from my mouth.

"I hate the sea."

Nellie looked stunned. "You hate the sea, this sea, our Akusha sea?"

"It swallowed Peter and it swallowed Katya and Alexi and your Kiril, too."

Nellie moved closer, the side of her body touching mine. "That same sea gives us our life, Tatty."

"Life—without boats, without chiefs, with our people scattering here and there for cash jobs, with whites in our school and missionaries converting our young."

Nellie remained silent for a long time. Then she said, "Tatty, at the camp, you showed us all how to keep going. When low spirits fell on Evdokie and Anna and me, we'd talk about you, how you never rested while there were things to do. What was the secret at Bear Cove? How did you keep your spirits from turning black?"

I started to skip stones, listening to them plop as they hit the water while I searched for an answer. After a while, ready to skip another stone, a realization came to me. "At Bear Cove, I stoked my spirit with dreams, dreams of coming home and living our Aleut life. Those dreams are as dead as this stone."

"Then make another dream," Nellie urged me.

I turned the question back to her. "I wonder what dreams fill your heart, Nell?"

A lone tear rolled down Nellie's cheek. "Maybe my dreams are small. But they seem big to me." Nellie paused. "I dream about Mavra coming home for Christmas. Every Christmas."

"That wouldn't be enough to keep me going, Nell. For me, there is no dream beyond passing on our life."

I sat bolt upright. Suddenly, images of Umaka exploded in my brain—Katya and me lying in the lupine fields and rolling down the grassy hill in back of the village, my spirit doll, Matrona touching my face and telling stories about our ancestors, Papa bringing in a sea lion, Mama and Ekaterina making everything we needed from the animal skins and organs. For the first time in many weeks, excitement stirred in me. "Maybe Sylvia will show up here and take me to Umaka as her translator."

Nellie smiled. She recognized the birth of a dream.

Alicia was reading a letter when I returned home. "Something terrible has happened, Mama."

My knees felt weak. I sat on the floor right there in front of the door. No more, no more! I've reached my limit. Alicia was by my side, tears streaming down her face. She clutched the letter in her hand. "Read it," I said. It was from Olga Krenin, the Umaka Olga who lived next door to Alicia in Ketchikan.

"We sailed for home last month on a navy ship, everybody at the rail, singing as we rounded Cape Onagin. Umaka is right around the corner from that bend. But the ship sailed right past the cape, heading south, away from Umaka. No one understood what was happening. We were plenty scared. They settled us, every one of us at Islik. Alicia, Umaka is no more. The army burned it to the ground so the Japanese couldn't use it. They burned our boats and houses. Matrona hasn't spoken a single word since she learned we'd never go home again."

A numbness crept into my bones. I felt nothing—no sorrow, no anger, no hope. Where were my feelings? My mind went blank, too. Was this what death was like? I lay down on my bed, craving sleep, but none came, not for the entire night. In the morning, I tried to get up, but fell back. Alicia parked little Jane in my bed. That baby could outstare a dog. She peered into my eyes without flinching for many minutes. I didn't laugh. I didn't care. I got up, pulled on my bathrobe and carried Jane to her crib in the other room.

Alicia was at the stove. "I'm fixing alaadix, Mama." Her cheer sounded forced. Her face was tight and lined with worry. I coaxed myself to eat some fried bread, but I couldn't swallow. My bones started to ache. I returned to my bed. I pulled the covers over my head, and in the dark, I blotted out everything and everyone—except Peter's face—his half smile and the scar over his lip. He looked so peaceful. I fell asleep.

I awakened to the sound of a muted voice. It was Nellie, leaning over me, so close I could feel her breath on my face. "Trout in the creek, Tatty. And we don't even need a license. Yes, Colonel Smelling lifted the restriction. We can go anywhere we want."

I shook my head and turned my back to her.

I must have dozed. I heard another voice— Evdokie's. She talked to my back. "Tatty, come with us to the hills. We've found some goose eggs."

I didn't turn around.

Others tried to rouse me throughout the day. In the dark, when visitors had left and everyone was in bed, Innokenty's last words came to me—"It's time to join Peter." I talked to Peter, then. Ah, Peter, I want to rest by your side, too.

THIRTY-TWO

I knew I was failing. Just chewing my food or getting from my bed to the outhouse was a trial.
Most of the time, I didn't care. Once in a while, I'd
feel a small spark, more like a dying ember, and I'd
start to dress but my bones would feel like jelly and
I'd return to bed. I was aware of a gang of people
coming and going. Always, someone was by my
side—the children, sisterhood women, Little Hunch,
Vassa, Anesia, and Nellie. Everyone tried to capture
my attention. I couldn't concentrate on their words.
My mind wandered, often to imaginary conversations with Katya or Peter.

"Mama, drink some halibut soup." Alicia was
standing by my bed holding the cup of soup.

I turned aside.

"Mama, please eat something." She was begging me.

I felt a fleeting pang of sorrow for her. Poor Alicia, watching her mama die.

"Mama, what's wrong? Tell me."

"It's time to die."

Alicia burst into tears. But they stopped as suddenly as they started. Urgent words rushed from her mouth. "Mama, remember the stories you told me about your mama walking off from Umaka, sailing across all the Aleutian Islands in small boats with four children."

I didn't answer.

"Remember, Mama, at Bear Cove when you wrote a petition to the president and all those other top dogs."

Alicia was trying so hard to revive me, just as I did when my mama lay dying. I lifted myself up on my elbows. I tried to smile, but my lips wouldn't curl. I turned away from her again.

A little while later, Nellie, Evdokie, Sophie, and Vassa surrounded my bed. Vassa was the first to speak. "Aang, Tatty, I was thinking you should taste this pogy. I just took it out of the smoker."

When I didn't respond, the women started talking among themselves. They were planning a basket sale to earn money to buy candles for the church. In the middle of their conversation, Nellie addressed me. "I've got plenty of grass, Tatty."

Her invitation didn't stir me. I felt so light, as if I was floating on a cloud. Everyone, even their voices, seemed very far away.

Pretty soon, the women began telling stories. Nellie's tale caught my ear. I hadn't thought of the incident for many years. She was telling the women about the time she and Katya and I saved Alexi's life. Anton, Alicia, Paulie, and Feckla, eager to hear the story, crowded around Nellie.

"It was the year we were fourteen—Katya, Tatty, and me. We would have died that day if we had given in, yes we would have died. It was late winter, bitterly cold. We three, along with Alexi, set out for Frosty Lake. Pastor Lowell bought a pair of ice skates for the mission children, first pair in town, and we wanted to try them out. We girls took turns practicing close to the shore, yes, we hugged the shore. But Alexi, like a big shot, sped off across the lake."

"My uncle was brave," Paulie said.

"He was foolish, that's what he was," Nellie replied. "He considered himself a champ even though his ankles bent to the ground, right to the ground. Then suddenly, his skate caught in a hole in the ice. He wrenched it out at a ninety-degree angle. He heard a sharp crack and then pain and nausea knocked him off his feet. 'My ankle broke,' he shrieked."

Alicia had been staring at me. I think she was watching for a sign of recognition in my eyes. When she found it, she directed a question to me. "Mama, what did you do?"

"Listen to the story," I said, nodding in Nellie's direction.

Alicia smiled slightly, glad to hear me speak.

"We lifted Anton onto our sled," Nellie continued, "and then we tied our scarves together to make a rope for pulling the sled across the ice. That part was okay. But after we left the lake we had to trudge through snow that covered all kinds of holes and crevices. I fell into one of those holes. I cried, yes, wept with pain. How was I to go on? Lordy, Katya and Tatty couldn't carry two of us. I stumbled along, trying to navigate by putting most of my weight on my good ankle. That left Alexi to Tatty and Katya. Oh my, it was cold."

Alicia kept glancing at me, maybe wishing I'd take over the story, but she seemed satisfied to see a spark of interest in my eyes.

"Temperatures were below zero," Nellie went on, "and an icy wind blew hard against us. I don't know how Tatty and Katya managed to pull the sled without my help, but they did until we came to a quarter-mile stretch of open water in Icy Creek. Lord sakes, we didn't know what to do. Our teeth chattered, yes, they clacked together, as we talked things over. Alexi's groans were getting louder. 'Let's stay on the snow until we get to the bridge,' Katya suggested. That bridge was a mile from where we stood. "'That'll take an hour with the sled,' Tatty answered. Alexi started to howl.

"'How long will it take to get to the mission if we cross the creek here?' I asked Tatty, and she said it would take half as long as the bridge route. 'We'll freeze to death in that creek,' Katya wailed. I looked to Tatty for a solution. She was a like a chief even when we were children."

Nellie paused and blinked tears from her eyes. "We were stumped when that thick fog rolled in and the wind nearly knocked us over. Tatty had to yell directions to be heard above the roar of the wind. 'We'll take the shortest route. We'll cross the creek. And hurry.'

"Katya and Tatty held the sled above their heads, wading ankle-deep at the start, then knee-deep through the creek. Lordy, Tatty fell into the water waist deep, pulling Katya down with her. A miracle: they managed to hold the sled above water. We were all trembling, not only with cold, but with terror. When Tatty and Katya got up on their knees, their clothes froze; their bodies were encased in ice. If I felt numb, numb from my toes to my head, they must have been stiffer than an iceberg. I knew that was the last stage before freezing to death. 'I can't go any farther,' Katya cried out. I felt the same, like lying down, lying down right there in the water.

"'Don't give in, don't give in,' Tatty kept repeating, her voice weak from the cold. I shed tears, but they froze, yes froze right where they fell. 'Lordy, lordy,' I kept saying. And Tatty answered every time. 'Hold on, we're nearly on the other side.' Katya moaned that she couldn't make it. 'We'll crawl on our knees,' Tatty answered. Katya whimpered again, saying she was going to drop the sled. 'We'll have to carry it on our shoulders,' Tatty told her. I went over, got on my knees, right down on my knees, too, to lend my shoulder. I was so frozen I could feel no pain. Someone at the mission saw us. Soon, a crowd was running toward us. We were lifted into arms and carried into the mission where Thelma Lowell warmed us, gave us hot chai, took care of our cuts and bruises, and made splints for Alexi's and my ankles."

Holding Jane in the air, Alicia said, "Did you hear that story, Jane? Did you hear about your grandmother who didn't give in? Remember that story, Jane. Tell it to your children." And then, Alicia glanced at me, hoping the story had roused me.

"Nellie, I'll have that grass now," I said. I was still weary in my bones and anguished in my heart. But I was up. And I started weaving. My friends sat with me. They didn't say much, but they were content to see me active. After lunch, my body started to sag. I went back to bed.

I woke at dusk. People were bustling around in the kitchen. I felt a spasm of curiosity. What was going on? I heard Paulie's and Gavril's voices. Ah, the Pribilof workers were back.

My door was open. I could see Alicia spreading papers over the top of the table. That meant they brought lusta back with them. I knew the Pribilof people fermented a lot of seal flippers during the seal harvest. I hadn't eaten lusta since Alexi brought in two seals, shortly before the last trip of the *Azian Bay Native*. Maybe they brought some seal meat, too. For a moment, I felt desire for my food.

But my interest faded fast. All those people talking, telling tales, and laughing made me tired. And I kept thinking about Anton.

He'd been gone all day. Surely he knew that Paulie and Gavril were back. I dozed off. On waking, I heard Simon talking to Anton. I wanted to hear the news. I dressed and went into the other room.

"Yesterday, out crabbing with Bill Henderson, we had a talk. See, I got my mustering out pay this week. Twelve hundred dollars. So I asked Henderson how much his boat cost, thinking maybe I could buy a crab boat. 'Twenty-two thousand,' he answered. I laughed then at my foolish dream. Henderson was thoughtful. After a while, he asked me if I'd like to buy an interest in his operation. 'Turn your money over to me and I'll give you a share of the profits,' he said. All day I mulled over his proposition. Then I said, 'No, I want a boat that everyone can use.' Henderson cocked his head and looked at me for a long time. He never said another word about a partnership. Back on shore, I gave the money to the community fund."

I smiled for the first time in many days, proud of Simon for sticking with our people. I glanced at Anton. He sat very still as if he were holding his breath. A blue vein throbbed on his temple. And then, through clenched teeth, he said, "I want to do something for the community, too. But I don't have anything to give." His head dropped to his chest and my heart dropped to my toes. Anton was lost like a feather tossing in a stormy sea. Drowsiness washed over me. I went back to bed.

I was sleeping when I felt something tugging at my covers. It was Jane. She wanted me to take her in my arms. When I didn't respond, she crept back to the other room. I never saw a child crawl the way she did, scooting around the room on her rear end, one leg tucked under it. A few minutes later, she came back to my bed. She lifted her arms to be picked up. I turned away. She began to whimper. I got up, dressed, and carried her into the kitchen. Alicia brought the pee pot to my chair. I put it under Jane and blew in her ear, but no pee. Okay, it was too soon. I put her down and picked up my weaving.

A while later, Alicia and Anton started to argue about a subject familiar before the evacuation. "The council election is in six weeks," Alicia said. "I know your feelings about the council, but Anton, we need Aleuts on it. Victor is the only Aleut on the slate."

"Alicia, don't you understand, I've had my fill of being looked down on—in Salem, in Seattle, in the army. I came home to be an Aleut. I don't want to talk about this damn council anymore. I'm going out."

After he left, Alicia turned to me. "Mama, I don't get it. Why won't Anton even consider running for the council? He's been to higher school. He knows about those legal things."

"What good can that council do for our town, eh? Can it make things run smooth like Innokenty and the elders did? Can it suggest solutions that we want, that we like?"

"The council can tax the store and supply station and all those crab boats tying up at our dock."

"And what will they do with those taxes? Make more businesses? Make more saloons? Make a drinking town out of Akusha?"

"James Wilson and Andy McMoon say they'd use the money for sewers and indoor toilets and hot water. And also to hire a doctor and build a hospital and maybe even a high school. Think of that, Mama. A hospital and high school right here in Akusha."

I fell silent then, thinking about how different Anton's life would be if he had gone to higher school at home, and what a difference a hospital would make if children got sick. But my thoughts turned bleak. "More taxes, more businesses, more whites. It won't be Akusha anymore."

She touched my shoulder and peered into my eyes. "Mama, I don't live in the Akusha of your childhood; I live in the one we have now."

I stopped talking then. I needed time to think about her words. I always figured Alicia felt just as I did about our life. That's how it was with Katya and me. But then I realized that Katya lived in a different world, too, after she moved into the mission. That's what wrecked her. I didn't want Alicia's world to ruin her.

Anton didn't return until late in the evening. Every few minutes, I found myself listening for his step. I was worried that he and Lupp were drinking again. I was storing my weaving when he came in. He was in a lively mood. After throwing Jane in the air a couple of times, he said, "I have news. This morning, I went to the pier to watch the soldiers leave, hundreds of them. They're leaving faster than they came. Bill Henderson was standing on the deck of his boat watching, too. He called over to me, 'I hear you're the radio operator in town.' I nodded. 'Well, the radio on my boat is dead. Will you fix it?' I told him I'd never studied radio repair, but I knew something about radios, so I'd give it a try. I worked on that radio all afternoon. Couldn't pinpoint the problem. Henderson kept checking my progress. Finally, I said, 'I'm sorry but I don't know enough to fix your radio.' 'Too bad,' he said, 'there'd be plenty of work for an electronics specialist on the crab boats around here.' Then he told me to wait a minute. He ran into the pilot house and came back with a newspaper. He showed me an advertisement for a free six-month course in electronics and radio repair at a

Seattle college. He said he'd heard it was good training. I felt like I'd found my wings, Mama."

"You're going to that school, eh?"

"You bet. Then I'll have something to give, too."

My heart felt lighter. Maybe this time the wind
would blow him in the right direction.

Next morning, walking in the hills behind the
military post, I noticed the sweet smell of wet grass,
the sunlit willow leaves, and yellow buttercups growing wild in the path. I realized I'd been living in a
misty mindless blur for a very long while. I bent
over, sniffed the buttercups, then picked a bunch for
Jane before heading home.

Thirty-three

I was on my way to a sisterhood meeting at Evdokie's house one November afternoon when a light fluffy snow started to fall. Jane, nestled in my backpack, was fascinated by the white flakes. She chuckled as she grabbed for them and fussed when I took her indoors—that is, until she saw Feckla, her little mama. Feckla, who had been playing a stone game with Anna's daughter, jumped up when we arrived and stretched her arms toward Jane. I handed her the baby and joined the other sisterhood women, sitting around the table sipping chai.

The room was silent except for Leonty's soft snore; he was asleep in a rocker near the table. I gazed at his age-lined face, recalling the many times I had watched him play his drum, chant, and leap in the air in old-time Aleut dances. *Ah, Leonty, there's no one to replace you.* Nellie was the first to speak: "There's too much sickness in our town."

"I heard that Vassa has pains in her chest. Who else ails?" Parascovia asked.

"Marie's bleeding," Nellie talking again. "It's been going on for days. It won't stop, won't stop at all. Is she to lose this baby, too?"

"If only the new council had raised enough taxes to hire a doctor," I said.

Leonty was muttering something I couldn't make out. I went to his side.

"We don't need promyshlennik and taxes."

A long silence followed his remark.

Alicia's words came to my mind. "Maybe the young people don't think about life the way we do, Leonty."

Leonty didn't answer but Evdokie was clearly upset. "Our young people have the same ancestors we do. They grew up seeing our dances, picking berries in our hills, fishing in our creeks, speaking in our tongue, attending our church. Just yesterday, Agnes asked me when a priest is coming."

I nodded as Evdokie spoke, realizing she'd furnished an answer to Alicia's statement about living in a different world. Agnes, same age as Alicia, surely didn't share her belief. She was more interested in a Russian Orthodox priest than this city council business. "I'm thinking about Agnes's question," I said.

Evdokie leaned forward in her seat.

"I'm thinking we should petition the bishop in New York to send a priest to live permanently in our town, like Father Paul." I glanced at Leonty. He was sleeping again.

"Ah, Tatty, I like your dream. Yes, I like it," Nellie said.

Her interest encouraged me. "Maybe we can ask the bishop to support an Aleut in seminary training. I feel like singing when I picture an Aleut priest here."

"We should talk this over with the elders," Evdokie said. A moment later, she slapped her hand over her mouth, remembering that there was no elders' council anymore. She puckered her forehead, deep in thought before suggesting we talk to others about the petition.

Everyone agreed and we decided to start the next day.

I woke next morning feeling lighthearted, thinking about our petition. I dressed fast and went into the other room to get things going. Alicia, rocking Jane, didn't greet me. She looked tired, strained, as if she hadn't slept all night.

"Mama, Jane's having trouble breathing."

I bent down and put my lips to Jane's ear. "Ai, she's as hot as burning embers. I'm going after Anesia." I trembled all the way to Anesia's house. Jane had never been sick before. But babies always get sick with one thing or another, I told myself. I met Anesia coming out of Vassa's barabara. As soon as I told her about Jane, she hurried home with me.

"How long has this child been feverish?" she asked, a note of alarm in her voice as she felt Jane's forehead.

"Since the middle of the night," Alicia said.

Anesia began removing Jane's clothes to examine her body. Jane lay limp, making no sound except her wheezing and coughing.

"Shh, shh," Anesia kept saying as she checked Jane's skin, throat, and neck for rashes. She put her head next to Jane's chest. "I hear rattles. That's not good." She handed me some markasha roots to brew while she wiped Jane's face and body with a cool rag. Feckla stood by with a pan of cold water to refresh the rag.

After a few sips of herbal water, Jane fell asleep. Maybe the worst was over. Maybe the illness would end as suddenly as it began. But, after a few minutes, Jane was crying and wheezing louder than before. Feckla ran to the sink for more cold water. I heated more water. I was scared. "I wish Nellie was here," I said to Anesia.

"I passed her rushing to the airport this morning. The *Northern Bird* was on the landing field." Before I had time to think about who Nellie was meeting, Paulie rushed in, looking distressed. He was staying with Nicky and Marie, so sometimes news came to him late.

"Mama, I heard Anesia was here. Are you sick?" At that moment, Jane started a steady wail, interrupted by the labored sucking in of air as she tried to fill her lungs.

"Oh grief, oh grief," Alicia moaned as she walked around the room, holding Jane tight against her chest.

"What's wrong with her?" Paulie asked Anesia.

"I wish I knew. I can't get her temperature down. I wish we had some aspirin."

"The school dispensary has some," Paulie said as he rushed out.

Alicia put Jane back in the crib. She was quiet. Maybe this time she'd rest.

I heard Nellie's voice on the porch stairs. Someone else's, too.

It sounded familiar. Nellie walked in with Sylvia South. She hadn't told me she expected Sylvia. Later, I learned that she didn't know about Sylvia's arrival until she went to the airfield, hoping to see Mavra come off the plane.

"Tatiana, I heard you were sick. I'm so pleased to see that everything is okie-dokie. I've been looking forward to having you work with me. You see, the museum sent me here to record Aleut history, legends, and songs."

Something stirred in me. I closed my eyes. A picture of dead, deserted Umaka flashed before me.

Sylvia was still talking. Maybe she guessed my thoughts. "I know we can't go to Umaka like I'd planned. But you can still tell me legends and sing songs. I've got a tape recorder. Let's set up a date and time."

"Alicia's baby is sick."

"Oh, I'm so sorry," she said as she walked over to the crib and looked at Jane. "What a darling baby. But she's red with fever. Is there a doctor or nurse here?"

Could it be that Sylvia had forgotten we didn't have doctors and nurses in our town? Paulie returned with a container of aspirin. Jane was awake again. She wasn't crying, but her wheezing was worse. Anesia crushed a half aspirin in her fingers and put it in Jane's mouth. Jane spit it out. Then, Anesia shoved it down her throat with her fingers. Jane gagged for a moment and then calmed down and dozed off.

"I'm staying with James Wilson. I hope you'll come see me there as soon as the baby's better. I can't wait to record your Aleut stories," Sylvia said, as she got up to leave.

I laughed to myself. *I'll tell her the story of Sylvia South scorning Vassa's and Vasili's barabara. That was our history, too.*

Ignaty came into the house. He wasn't used to seeing Jane in bed at this time of day. He went to her crib.

"She's sick, let her sleep," Alicia told him.

Ignaty stood there a very long time, whispering Jane's name over and over again.

Many visitors came that evening. They didn't ask questions, but I think they were relieved to see Jane resting, even though she kept gasping between coughs while she slept. That night I slipped in and out of sleep, startled awake by my pounding heart. Jane dozed on and off, but she never cooled down or breathed easily. Toward morning, Alicia came to my bed. "Mama, Jane is getting worse. Her neck is swollen and she can't catch her breath."

"Did you give her another aspirin?"

"Twice. It doesn't seem to help. Mama, I'm scared."

"I'll get Anesia," I said, unable to think of anything else to do. All the way over there, a pain stabbed my chest. By the time Anesia and I returned, Jane was gulping air so fast it made her vomit. Evdokie, Nellie, and Anton stood by, looking scared.

"We have to do something. We have to do something," Anton kept saying.

Alicia fell down on the floor. Her legs wouldn't hold her.

"Chrissakes. Chrissakes," Anton said.

I helped Alicia up. Her lips and hands were trembling. Anesia was whacking Jane on the back. Janes's breath gurgled out.

Anton sat down at his radio and started turning dials. "I'm going to raise a doctor at the Indian Health Service in Anchorage. Damn, damn, I can't get through."

Anesia gave Jane more aspirin. Praise heaven, she breathed easier. Anesia got ready to leave then.

"I'm going to check on Vassa and Marie. I'll be back soon."

The rest of us went to bed, exhausted. But I couldn't sleep. I lay there listening to Jane breathe in great sucks of air. I was afraid she was going to suffocate. I ran to her. Alicia, tears rolling down her cheeks, was rocking her in her arms. Feckla stood by, holding a blanket to wrap Jane in.

Anesia returned early the next morning. Anton was still turning dials on his radio. Finally he succeeded in reaching a doctor named Belcher. "I'm calling from Akusha, a village in the Aleutian Islands. We have a baby here with a red hot temperature and a big swollen neck and she's fighting for every breath. We've given her aspirin and wiped her with cool rags. We don't know anything else to do."

"How long has she been like this?"

"Nearly two days, but she's getting worse. She's choking on her breath."

"Do you have a clinic in your town?"

"No."

"A nurse or medic of any kind?"

"We have a healer."

"Let me talk to the healer." And then to Anesia, he said, "Are you trained?"

"I've been called healer all my life."

"Where did you learn to heal?"

"A shaman trained my grandmother. She passed her knowledge on to me."

"Have you ever done a tracheotomy?"

"That word isn't in our language."

"You must open her windpipe. Otherwise she'll die."

"I have no instructions."

"You'll need a sharp, narrow-bladed knife."

Paulie ran to the box holding utensils and pulled out two sharp, thin-bladed knives.

"We have some," Anesia answered.

"Sterilize them."

"Boil them in water?" Anesia asked.

"Yes. Do you have any tincture of merthiolate?"

"I'll run down to the dispensary and check," Anton said. He must have grown wings. He was back in a few minutes, carrying tincture of merthiolate and a sack full of sterile bandages. Dr. Belcher was waiting on the other end of the line.

"We have tincture of merthiolate," Anesia said.

"Soak the knives in a container of hot water mixed with merthiolate. Then wash the area you're going to cut with merthiolate."

"I'm thinking about where to cut."

"In the hollow of her neck, right below the Adam's apple. Make a vertical cut, then turn the knife ever so slightly to make an opening. You'll need a narrow tube, no thicker than your finger, to insert in the hole you make."

"Can I use a straw?"

"No, no, no. Definitely not. It won't hold."

Simon, who had followed Anton in from the dispensary, talked to the doctor. "Will a piece of tubing for a hose to a boat engine do?"

"Splendid, splendid," Dr. Belcher answered.

Simon ran to the pier. Dr. Belcher was still talking when he returned.

"Cut the tube into a three-inch length before putting it in the hole. Then tie some strips of cloth, flannel if you have it, to the tube and secure it around the baby's neck. That will keep the tube in place. We should get her into the hospital as soon as possible. Does Akusha have plane service?"

"Yes. The *Northern Bird*. But she flies in only once a week. And she was here yesterday."

"Okay, healer, you're on your own. I'll stand by if you need me."

Alicia fainted. I pulled her to a sitting position and pushed her head between her legs. After she came to, I sat on the floor holding her between my legs, her head against my chest. She trembled, her legs, her shoulders, her head, her arms. I rocked her back and forth. Suddenly, we heard a great gush of air. Jane's windpipe was open.

"She can breathe, now," I reassured Alicia.

Alicia was able to stand then. We sat up all night, maybe twenty people, watching over Jane. She wheezed and gasped and gurgled all through the night, but she was able to get air in her lungs.

By morning, she was choking again. Her incision was red and swollen with infection. I fed her makarsha-root chai while Anton raised Dr. Belcher on the radio.

"The baby's incision is infected. Gunk is oozing out of it."

"Is there any sulfa in town?"

"Damn it. I don't think so. Wait a minute. Maybe the military left some."

"See if you can find some. I'll stand by."

Paulie jumped up and ran to the dispensary. He returned with a container of sulfadiazine. We fed her sulfa every two hours throughout that day. The infection got worse. We sent visitors outside so they wouldn't use up the air in the room. I looked out the window. I think the whole town was standing in the yard. Sylvia South, too.

My head fell onto my chest. I must have slept. I woke to a terrifying silence. I walked into the kitchen. Alicia was sitting on the floor, breathing, but as white and stiff as the corpse of her daughter lying in her lap.

THIRTY-FOUR

Alicia fell into a stupor. Her eyes were open but lifeless; her body as listless as a sack of cotton. It's the way I'd felt for many days now. But Alicia was hardly past childhood. I had to find a way to stir my blood so I could get hers going. For a start, I went over and cradled her in my arms, chanting Aleut songs, some from my childhood, some from hers. Feckla, who had been crouching in a corner of the room, came over and sat on the other side of Alicia. Poor little Feckla, losing Jane just two months after her papa died.

We three sat huddled together on the floor near the stove that whole day after Jane died and most of the next day, too.

On the third day, we got ready for the funeral service. It seemed like people mourned a baby's death more than any other. We were greeted with a chorus of sighs, moans, groans, and sobs when we walked into the church. People were swaying from side to side. Few eyes were dry—except Alicia's. She stood as stiff and silent as a stone, her eyes looking off in the distance.

It was the same thing at the burial ground, the same when we returned home. I didn't know how to rouse her.

As the days passed, visitors came more often, all trying to light a spark in Alicia. "I brought you a fine new drawing pad," Nicky said, watching for a sign of pleasure.

No response. No expression.

"Vassa has recovered. She's sitting at her sewing machine again," Vasili said.

She remained motionless.

Ignaty invited her to play a ring and stone game she'd taught him years before.

Still no reaction.

Agnes came over every day, patiently waiting for Alicia to show a sign of interest. But as the weeks passed, Agnes ran out of patience and snapped at Alicia. "I want to shake you, yes, shake you. Will that help?"

Agnes's sharp tone startled Alicia. Her nostrils began to twitch and a mist formed in her eyes. Shocked at her mean words, Agnes put her arms around Alicia and in a soft voice, said, "Tell me what will bring a light to your eyes." Alicia looked straight ahead and said nothing.

How could Agnes expect to do what Alicia's own mother couldn't? I had begun to despair. Walking on the beach with Nellie one afternoon, I moaned about my helplessness.

"Maybe forget Alicia for a while, yes, forget about her, think about what you can do to bring a smile to your lips."

"Nell, how can I smile when my child's spirit is dying?"

"Do you think your gloomy face helps her?"

Nellie's comment felt like a blow. "Ah, Nell, I see. My long face only makes it worse for her. But still, I can't imagine what there is to smile about."

"What did you smile about in Bear Cove?"

"Those dreams are dead."

"I seem to remember you telling me a dream here in Akusha before Jane got sick."

"Ah, yes, Nell, we thought of having our own Russian Orthodox priest, one who would live here permanently. We talked about writing a petition."

"I'll help write it."

I felt a flicker of interest. "Let's talk it over with Evdokie."

Evdokie and her mama, Parascovia, shared our enthusiasm about the petition. Leonty didn't comment, but he smiled with his eyes.

"Let's start, now, yes, now," Nellie suggested. Evdokie brought a tablet to the table, waiting to write down our words.

I began. "We, the Aleut people of Akusha village, petition the bishop."

I paused then, and Evdokie took over: "... petition the bishop to assign a priest to our town, to live here and to serve the other Aleutian villages."

"Tell him we're afraid the Baptist mission here will convert our children," Leonty said.

We added that and finished the petition before dark.

"Want to circulate it after supper?" Nellie asked me.

"Wait a minute. I'm picturing something else— pass the word around that people should sign at my place where Alicia can see them."

"Lordy, maybe that will brighten her eyes."

It seemed like everyone was in town. Nearly all over the age of eighteen came by to sign the petition. I kept glancing at Alicia. Her eyes were dull. Agnes carried the petition over to her. Alicia shook her head. Agnes brought it back to the table. Nicky was the next signer. He was alone. Marie was too weak from bleeding to come over. If only we had a doctor in our town. Why were we making a petition for a priest? Maybe a doctor was more important. But who would we petition for a doctor? There was no bishop for doctors.

I lay in bed thinking about that subject for most of the night. Alicia's words of just a few weeks before rang in my brain. "The new council could raise money for a doctor and hospital. Just think, Mama, a hospital right here in Akusha." Jane would be alive if we had a doctor here. But what kind of a life would

Jane have living in a town run by whites? I knew Alicia's answer. "Mama, I don't live in the same world you grew up in." And then a realization came, that Jane's world would be even more different. Something settled down in me. I pictured Peter's face, like I often do when I'm waiting for sleep. Suddenly, my heart flopped over. His scent was near. I curled up, feeling warm, as if his arms were around me, and fell asleep.

That smile Nellie wanted was on my face when I woke next morning, thinking about the petition ready to go out on the next flight of the *Northern Bird*. But moments later, thinking of Alicia's grief, my smile died. I didn't know what to do. I wanted to be alone to think things over. I got dressed and went to the beach, to the place where Icy Creek meets the sea. A strong wind was blowing. I watched three ravens playing in the updraft, rolling over as they soared. After a while, they flew off. I watched them until they were out of sight. I thought about Innokenty's raven story, about those two young ravens flying off in a different direction to find a new, safer resting place for their flock. Where is that resting place for our flock?

Suddenly, I knew what to do. I set out for James Wilson's house.

It was five days before the city council election. I had heard that James Wilson was making the ballots on his mimeograph machine. It was the first time I'd ever knocked on his door. He stepped back when he saw me, as if I were the devil. Before he could say anything, I blurted out my reason for calling. "I want my name on the candidate list."

He cleared his throat a couple of times, then invited me in.

I followed him through his sitting room to a long eating table. Sylvia South was sitting at the table, a typing machine in front of her. She had told me she was staying with the Wilsons, but I had forgotten.

"You came at the right time, Tatiana. Sylvia has just started typing the ballot. Tatiana wants her name on it," he said.

Sylvia looked astonished. "I like the idea of whites and natives running this town together. But Tatiana, you've always stood for tradition." She paused for a moment, then said, "But don't get me wrong. I think it's wonderful that you've decided to run. You're brave. And being a woman, too."

James Wilson put on his jacket. "I have to get to the office. I'll pick up the ballots when I come home for lunch."

I started to leave with him when Sylvia called to me. "Tatiana, is this a good time to work on my project?"

I wasn't thinking about Sylvia's museum collection when I called on James Wilson. I didn't know what I wanted to do about it. But Sylvia had a talent for convincing.

"I thought you'd like the idea of preserving your Aleut songs and legends. And if we tape record them, they'll never get lost.

"Yes, I'd like to sing and spin old yarns on your recording machine. But I don't know how to dance on it." I laughed.

Sylvia didn't join in. In fact, she looked very serious. "Funny you should mention that. I've applied for a grant to make a movie of native dances in Alaska. If I get the money, I want you to come to Fairbanks to demonstrate them."

I scolded myself for teasing Sylvia when she was doing something to help our people. It was something I wanted, too. I liked the idea of a permanent record. "Okay, I'll help you. But later. Right now I want to talk to my people about the election."

"Can we set up a time for afterward?"

"I'll come by," I said, as I moved toward the door.

I went directly to Nellie's. She was just coming out her house, on her way to see Leonty. Many people visited him every day, maybe wanting to sear the image of our last chief into their brains. He was dozing in his chair when Nellie and I came in. Parascovia was on the floor matching patches of material for a quilt. Evdokie and Akinia were cutting up trout they'd caught through a hole in the creek ice. Evdokie brought chai and a plate of raw trout to the table. Everyone gathered around.

"I have a surprise," I said.

Nellie wagged her finger at me. "Tatty, I love surprises. But only one kind, yes, only one kind—good surprises." There was curiosity in everyone's eyes. "I'm running for the city council."

"I almost can't believe your words," Evdokie gasped. "You boycotted the last council election."

"I'm thinking that Jane would be alive if a doctor was here. Maybe he could have saved Stepan, too. I'm thinking Peter would have died from a busted appendix if the Coast Guard doctor hadn't been nearby. I'm thinking of the children's rotting teeth and Marie's upside-down deliveries. I'm thinking she could bleed to death without a doctor and hospital."

"Tatty, you were heated up about the whites taking over our town with their council," Evdokie reminded me.

My cheeks flamed. "We don't have to sit around and let them take over everything. We want some of the same things they do—a doctor, hospital, new school, hot water, indoor toilets. If we're on that council, we get to say something about these matters. Maybe we can even vote for having Aleut teachers in the school.

Evdokie's eyes flashed with interest. "The way we helped Mr. Ginsburg out."

I nodded. "Maybe even have an Aleut for head teacher. Why not?"

Nellie started to laugh. "I like your surprise, Tatty. But you and Victor are the only Aleut candidates.

Two against five promyshlennik. What chance of our voice being heard?"

"I'm thinking of talking to others about putting their names on the election list."

"Maybe John and Big Shot, yes, they both love to talk." Nellie said. She got up to leave then and I knew she was going to discuss the subject with them.

The dam broke when I told Alicia the news. Her heart, closed tight for so long, opened and tears flooded down her cheeks. She took deep breaths. "Mama, you say you're going to run for city council?"

"Ai, and maybe John and Big Shot will, too. And Victor. Maybe half the voices on that council will be Aleut." Alicia was crying and laughing at the same time. I wanted to keep this moment alive, so I expanded my dream. "Maybe soon we'll have Aleut teachers in our school, too."

"Mama, what will they teach?"

"Maybe I'll write a book."

About the Author

As a professor of sociology at the University of Alaska, Dorothy Jones wrote extensively about Aleut culture, Alaska Natives, and Alaska women. She was also a psychotherapist in private practice in Anchorage. After retiring from the university, Dorothy turned her attention to fiction. *Tatiana,* inspired by her work in the Aleutians, is her first novel.

Dorothy Jones lived with her husband, Bob ("Sea Otter") Jones in Alaska for thirty-five years. Widowed in 1998, she moved to the Pacific Northwest to be near her children, grandaughter, and great-grandchildren.

About the Artist

Cover artist Sara Tabbert grew up in Fairbanks, Alaska. She divides her time between her downtown art studio and teaching printing at the University of Alaska. Sara spends summers in Camp Denali in Alaska's Denali National Park working as a baker and guide.

List of Characters

Some names appear twice; for example, Leonty Sherebin is listed as husband of Parascovia and elder's council.

Akusha Villagers

Tatiana Pushkin (daughter of Anastasia Popoff) and husband, Peter Pushkin, nephew of chief Innokenty

Paulie (son)

Alicia (daughter)

Jane (Alicia's daughter) Anton (son

Nadia(adopted daughter) marries Mathew Domasoff from village of Azian Bay

Ignaty (son)

Tatiana's second husband: Stepan Shemikin from Kooney Pass

Feckla (Stepan's daughter)

Tatiana's Brothers:

Nicky marries Marie

Little Peter (son of Nicky and Marie)

Victor (son of Marie)

Alexi married to Tessa Swenson from New Harbor

Sergie (living in Azian Bay)

Sophie Ilianof (Tatiana's aunt) and husband, Bullshit John

Michael (son) married to Christina

Nellie and Cousta

Mavra (daughter) married to Sasha in New Harbor

Gavril (son)

Agnes (daughter)

Kiril (late son)

Anna (Nellie's sister) and husband Big Shot

Lupia (daughter)

Parascovia and Leonty (second chief) Sherebin

Matfay (son)

Evdokie (daughter), sisterhood president

Akinia (daughter)

Katya marries Buddy Thomas, fisherman

Dmitri (son)

Vassa and Vasili Boroff, immigrants from the village of Bolisof

Lupp (son) marries Akinia Sherebin

Anesia Sorokin, traditional healer

Ilarion (son) married to Natalia

Little Hunch (village elder)

Mr. Herendin or the Old Man (village elder)

Pletanida (village elder)

Grigori (village elder)

Tanya, late resident of the Baptist mission orphanage

Makary, former resident of Baptist mission orphanage

Harvey Bottom, Baptist pastor and wife, Minerva

J. B. Bloomberry, pastor's assistant

Elder's Council in Akusha

Innokenty Pushkin(Peter's father), first chief

Leonty Sherebin, second chief

Ruff, third chief

Cousta

The Old Man

Akusha Villagers: Outsiders

Sylvia and Ralph South(store manager) from Chicago

Miss Parker, teacher

Miss Coombs, teacher

Mr. Tulliver, teacher

Miss Long, former teacher

Horace Gump, U.S. marshall, and wife, Serena

James Wilson, manager of the supply station

Chester Brown, assistant manager of supply station

Buddy Thomas, fisherman, marries Katya

Clarence Collier, former boss of supply station

Pastor Lowell, former resident, Baptist missionary and wife, Thelma

Father Paul, former resident, Russian Orthodox priest

Ollie Larsen, owner of the herring dock

Andy McMoon, storekeeper

Minnie and Clara (daughters)

Bill Henderson, crab fisherman

Pat Cochran, crab fisherman

Villagers from Umaka, Where Tatiana Was Born

Matrona (godmother)

Efgenia (Katya's mother)

Gregory Mensoff from the village of Islik

Igor (son)

Ekaterina (Gregory's aunt)

Ivan and Philip, uncles of Anastasia Popoff

Other

Father Emil Burdofsky, priest based in New Harbor

Zack Swenson, Alexi Popoff's father-in-law from New Harbor

Fred Swenson (son)

Tessa (daughter) married to Alexi

Gregory Mensoff from the village of Islik

Simeon Azimof from the village of Islik

Miss Witherspoon, government social worker

Chief Theophon of Kooney Pass

Dr. Gold (doctor on Coast Guard cutter)

Mr. Steele (principal at Indian school in Oregon)

Tiasook (Anton's roomate at Indian school in oregon)

Constantine Churginoff (late student at Indian school from village of Azian Bay

Akuke Domasoff from Azian Bay, captain of the *Azian Bay Native*

    Marina (wife)

    Agapin (mother)

    Little Akuke (son)

    Mathew (son) marries Nadia

Bill Soporinsky and Radion Kozaken, late sea hunters from Bolisof

Swede, New Harbor fisherman

Lawrence, soldier stationed in Akusha

Colonel Sundry, in charge of military operations on Akusha

Others at Bear Cove Camp

Mr. Canfield, Indian Bureau agent

Mr. Ginsburg, teacher

Dr. Albee, physician

Lawrence Clump, Alaska employment office representative

Glossary, Aleut and Russian Words

aacha	special bond
aang	greetings or hello
alaadix	fry bread
anax	mother
asxinux	daughter
baidarkas	skin boats
barabaras	semi-underground sod houses
chai	tea
hlax	son
kamleika	rain gear
kvas	home brew
lusta	fermented seal flipper
mukluks	skin boots
perok	rice and fish pie
promyshlennik	Caucasian
qamtidax	Aleut game
qawax	sea lion

Other Titles by Vanessapress

Vanessapress is the only press specializing in Alaska women writers. It is a community-based non-profit organization, dedicated since 1984 to publishing the voices and dreams of Alaskan women. Vanessapress provides an outlet for women wishing to write about the Alaska experience from a woman's point of view. Vanessapress publishes works that reveal the courage, humor, humanity, and insights of women living the Alaskan challenge.

To order these titles, use the order form on the next page.

O Rugged Land of Gold is an amazing and moving story of woman stranded alone and pregnant in the Alaska wilderness. Her husband fails to return from a trip, leaving her to give birth and survive a winter at their cabin, alone. Her story, and its happy ending, is hard to put down. 233 pages; $12.95.

Growing Up Stubborn at Gold Creek is Melody Erickson's second book about her childhood on a homestead in the Alaska bush in the 1960s. She and her family hunt and trap and face the heartbreak of a fire that leaves them homeless. "Melody Erickson serves up a hearty helping of both the savory and sad, garnishing the life of a young girl growing up on an Alaskan railbelt homestead" —Jay Hammond, former governor of Alaska. 212 pages; $9.95.